A CHUBBY PONE NOVEL

A FEW CASUALTIES SO WHAT

WILSON JACKSON

The Reading Glass Books
1-888-420-3050
www. readingglassbooks. com
fulfillment@readingglassbooks. com

Dedication

Sharon Elizabeth Jackson

Acknowledgement

To my parents Alfair and Aneita who gave me the creativity and desire it takes to be a writer.

Table of Contents

Author's Note

Chubby Pone is a soft science-fiction, crime noir mystery/ thriller novel series set in the year 2080. A former hit-man turned troubleshooter for Brooke (Red) Brigand of the Brigand band crime family. She is a lawyer and takes over for her late father, a kingpin who sent Chubby out on mob hits.

Brooke, a legit lawyer, has an arrangement with Pone for him to work for her on criminal cases and solve problems to protect the city (Metro City), a fictional Charlotte, North Carolina. Chubby's first adventure carries over with one of his friends getting help from Mercury Slim.

Black Medusa is an extension introducing Mercury in a short story.

The Great Meteor

The Great Meteor, as the science nerds call it, changed everything. Though it missed the Earth by ten football fields, the effect was everlasting.

Nothing happened in particular to change or transform people into mutants—devastating or catastrophic.

There was no zombie apocalypse, all the electricity was still intact, and alien races didn't inhabit the Earth. What happened when the great meteor missed the Earth, the glow from the flaming fire ball released an enormous golden light and left everyone immobilized.

Instead of earthquakes and other natural disasters, a rip in the time fabric caused a chronology change and a culture shock that even the science nerds had a hard time trying to explain. Half of the population got bored with all the scientific chitchat, so the politicians asked the science nerds to simplify things.

Therefore, with the group feeling insulted, they said time stood still, which wasn't a bad thing, but not a good thing. The intense light from the meteor put the century on hold. Nobody knew how long; seconds, minutes, days, weeks, months, and years were hard to calculate, but the decade came to a stop. To make people feel better, the science nerds called it a rebirth and predicted better things to come; they wanted the world to believe.

Some people assumed the bright light lasted for a second, a minute, or an hour. According to the science nerds, everyone was in suspended animation. Several years passed. After the assumption, a minor panic…well, a big panic swept around the globe because if that had been the case, then they should have aged. A legion of people not science nerds used this advantage to voice their own opinion, and that brought in religion. Enter the religious minds to put in their two cents. The great meteor came to aid God in cleansing the Earth. Instead of a great flood or the promise of fire the next time, only a bright flash of light came from a meteor to give the world a new start.

All the religious leaders played their part in convincing their flocks that no one needed to die to cleanse the planet of sinners, but just a purification and numerous people rejoiced with that assumption since no one wants to die and those that do are well, crazy. Most people didn't understand what it meant being suspended in time. That's when the science nerds took their case to the politicians. Science versus Religion made its way to Capitol Hill. Politicians gave the science nerds center stage again, but told them to explain to the world disrespecting no religion.

Science nerds said the great meteor would bring a major change to the world. The first thing they had to explain how light affects the mind. When light enters the mind, it freezes you. Because it's so intense, you lose your train of thought and paralyzes you until your eyes can adjust, like a flash from a camera. Gobs of people bought into it because after all nobody wants to grow old except maybe children.

2080 was now the year, the Great Meteor arrived in 2050, computers reprogrammed, and for some, life continued on as usual, except for civilization. Presidents, kings and queens, or what title other leaders in their country held still had their place to give people a sense of stability, but all agreed to have a council to make world decisions.

The capital cities of each country would still be intact, but each would have a head of council representative. Another change that took place were cities, such as New York became New New York, New Chicago, and a few others cities joined the new phase since things were now different. Around the world, prohibition gangsters abounded.

A significant change developed in the auto industry, cars from the 50s to the present now had the same advanced engine make-up manufactured with state-of-the-art technology under the hood. A result of gang violence, the police had become more like mediators because of the thirties style of gang activity.

When there were shootouts, all citizens along with the police headed for safety until the bloodshed ended. The drive-by's provoked more hits than a baseball game and none more violent than Metro City (Charlotte, NC).

Metro City changed its name from a popular up-and-coming city in the south.

They didn't want the New added, so they altered it altogether, and ran by a crime family called the Brigand Band. J. Paul Brigand and his family had control of the bigger part of Retro, which was the North and South, and despite having influence in the East and West part of the city, he gave those parts to the Prohibitions and the Hip-Hoppers. The Hip-Hoppers represented the present patrolling the streets in their 1970s to modern sedans, music, attire and lead by a man called G. They were rivals to the Prohibitions. An Irish-Italian family lead the Probonos, and the head honcho known as Macone. Both answered to Brigand until he died and now they answer to his children. Metro City, a city within a city, but still abide by the rules of the great council like the other cities in the United States. But once again, the Great Meteor changed everything.

Welcome to Gangland.

One

Twelve a.m. Saturday and the Friday night movie crowd escaped the theater filling the cold night air with teen spirit. The vibrant I'm-going-to-be-young-forever attitude made their way to their respected vehicles. Cars from the past to the present littered the theater parking lot. Sixteen to eighteen-year-old earning the trust of their parents to go out and have a good time came to an end. Well, at least some of the teen kings and queens, over the giggling and I'm-in-love eye contact came your typical teen business of going to a late-night party and hitting the drive-through for a bite to eat.

A sparse crowd decided enough excitement for one night and agreed to head for home. Two teens, both seventeen, made their way to a bright red Nissan Juke. This couple shared a stare from their fellow adolescence. A bi-racial couple now the norm-like homosexuals out in the open.

These two youths, black and white, both the elder children of two of the most prominent crime families in Metro City. Reginald Grant, Reggie, by his family and friends, the oldest of G's four children. Six-foot-four five star shooting guard headed out of state to attend college in the north on a basketball scholarship. A chilly night, he donned a red hoodie, loose-fitting baggy blue jeans revealed his boxers and untied white Nike.

His companion the oldest of four belonging to Macone. Helen Macone, Irish-Italian destined for the Ivy League on an academic scholarship, though her dancer legs could have gotten her an arts scholarship to any university of her choice. Her gray conservative attire from head down to feet and blonde hair worn in a librarian bun. Reggie opened the door for Helen. She strolled inside the car and he hustled to the driver's side escaping the cold. Neither family clueless about the forbidden romance.

Reggie and Helen gazed into each other's eyes, flashed their pearly whites, leaned in, and locked lips. Reggie turned the ignition. The future of two youths proved life is short.

Spaghetti Warehouse at 100 North Park Avenue beside the city monorail tracks. It looked like its namesake: a big block shaped building stained glass windows and brick armor faded 100 percent red hue. On the inside the decor screamed pure restaurant patrolling waiters, waitresses, and a Maître d'. Pictures, paintings, and movie posters of movie stars decorated the walls. A bill of fare listing Italian cuisine: Lasagna, Fettuccine Alfredo, and, Spaghetti and meat balls. Popular eatery attracting standing-room-only crowd every night, which was why it surprised citizens when it went defunct.

Proprietors turned a five-star bistro into the hottest nightclub in Metro city. Nadine was the club's name. They took advantage of its space dividing the factory in sections keeping the brasserie ambiance, but not the original cuisine except for four types of pizza; sausage, bacon, pepperoni, cheese and hamburgers; single and double with or without cheese on the card. Your choice to dance and drink or eat, dance, and drink.

Tables in the front part of the club for lounging, smoking, listening to piano, saxophone a small stage built for one singer the owner herself. Stools for sitting as long as the bar. The club name, Nadine, honored the middle name of the late Sheila Green, who had raised them as her own. Claire's circle called her Song Bird, her stage name because of her hypnotic siren voice. She graced the stage from time to time, but booked most of the acts for her club.

Her close friends called her Birdie.

She made a profit gambling. Nadine housed a mini casino joint down in the basement. It wasn't Las Vegas though it cost you a thousand to enter the hole of poker chips and slot machines. The basement sealed off, but enough room for two Black Jack tables and five small round tables for poker players. It came equipped with two muscular bouncers standing on opposite sides of the elevator dressed in black muscle shirts, slacks, and loafers.

Two eye-candy hour-glass figure waitresses clad in sleeveless black body-hugging mini-dresses, hose, and heels moved among the tables serving drinks. A mid-sized bar with a stocky bartender serve drinks. The club closed upstairs and only four patrons remained playing poker.

All four cold-blooded killers; what club Nadine catered to, but every killer left their bad attitudes at the door and weapons in their vehicles. One of her club benefactors and dearest friend, Chubby Pone.

Pone, sat at the table holding a winning hand. He loved stepping out into the night clad in black and white Doc Marten's wingtips with rubber soles, black slacks, a crisp white shirt, black vest laced with twelve small Ninja throwing knives, and a black bowler enhanced his chiseled clean-cut baby face. His counterparts: Sonny, a past-his-prime almost-senior-citizen, average height and a saggy pudgy body, he proclaimed himself as the world's oldest teenager.

He wore a brown fedora, pink shirt, tan slacks, and brown loafers. Stick looked like a walking skeleton with skin as pale as ivory. He wore a gray suit, black shirt with a loose fitting thin gray tie, and black pointed roach-killer shoes good for killing roaches who tried to hide in a corner joked his buddies. The last of the four poker players, Big Ben Donovan. All six-nine and three-hundred pounds of what he said soul-brother muscle. Black as coal, bald head as smooth as a baby's bottom and pet word shit ending with a D sound at the end. He wore a green polo shirt, black slacks and penny loafers.

The game was nearing the end as it came down to Pone and Big Ben. "What's that you drinking?" asked Big Ben in his baritone voice.

"Malta Goya." A beverage that wasn't a beer, wine, ale, or even soda. A carbonated malt drink that appealed to Pone. He discovered the drink when he ate at a Venezuelan diner.

"Shit'd…that some kind of new beer?"

Pone held up the brown long-neck-shaped bottle examining the label.

"Non-alcoholic malt beverage also made with hops." He took a sip. "Sweet…not bitter," said Pone.

Ben frowned and shook his head. "Give me a classic beer anytime."

"Keeps me alert on my way home." Pone dealt with car chases on his way home including unwanted gun-play.

"How come you the only one I see drinking that shit?" asked Ben.

"You ain't sweet on the owner," said Stick.

The room got quiet; Pone gave Stick a stare down. Stick crossed the line and knew it. He put his foot in his mouth and, like a snake, his long lanky body coiled.

"When you boys going to finish this damn game?" asked Sonny in his raspy voice. "It's late and I need to get home."

"Shit'd…been past your bedtime, old-timer," said Ben.

Sonny took a deep breath and raised an eyebrow. He and Stick already folded and stuck around for the conversation. Stick finished off his Vodka Martini and pulled the Olive off the tooth pick with his teeth while Sonny clutched his Gibson after being called an old timer.

"Sonny, finish your dink. That damn onion making my eyes water," said Pone.

He never understood the drink, a dash of dry Vermouth and two ounces of Gin with a slice of onion. Got to be an old man's drink, thought Pone. "Ben, it's late…let's finish this."

Five-thousand dollars on the table. Pone studied the large man. He could tell Ben craved one of his signature stogies; smoking not allowed in the casino.. Each man took one last card from the deck. Ben nodded with approval.

"What you got, big man?" asked Pone.

Ben laid out three Queens and two Jacks. A full house. He leaned back and his chair creaked struggling to support his weight. He toasted then downed his beer.

Pone glanced at his cards, the cards on the table and then at Ben who displayed a confident smirk on his face.

"Well, nothing like a good woman if you got three and two of them brought their sons along," said Pone.

Ben started to giggle until Pone laid down his hand. Three Kings and two deuces known as a full house Kings high. Ben stared at Pone. He knew his com padre had two nick names: leave him alone Pone and lucky eight. Pone a pool shark as well.

Ben sighed. "Shit'd."

He shook his head watching Pone collect his winnings.

The rest of the observers breathed a sigh of relief because they wanted to go home. Pone and Ben rode the elevator together.

"Mind if I holler at you if you got the time?" asked Ben. Pone and Ben took a seat at the bar.

The temporary bartender a Sicilian name Antonio. He supervised the restaurant and the reason they served Italian cuisine on the menu, and Birdie's boyfriend. Birdie used her expertise handling music entertainment and left comestibles in Antonio's hands. He knew the connection between Pone and Birdie and didn't like it; he accepted the bond between the two because he loved Birdie.

He told Pone and Ben he'd be in his office; to let him know when they finished their conversation.

Ben nursed his Moose head. "So he cool with you and Birdie?"

"If he can't keep her, it won't be because of me," said Pone.

Ben cleared his throat then took another swallow of his Moose head. Pone sipped his Goya. "You remember Al McGee?" asked Ben.

"Your sometime partner," replied Pone.

"He's gone missing."

Partners far and few considering your partner could become your enemy if hired to kill you. Pone didn't believe in having one for possible back stabbing.

He preferred to work alone for in the killing business who better to trust than yourself. He knew some jobs called for two men or women who made a living in the business too. If he needed support, Pone knew his poker buddies wouldn't hesitate to assist him.

"What do you mean missing?" asked Pone.

Assassins and hit man alike once a job finished tend to lie low waiting out the murder investigation. Disappearing at least three months till things quieted down. Pone didn't know much about McGee except what he heard from Ben. Ben carried the man, did the heavy lifting when they did a job together.

Not good since it took a cold-blooded person to do what they did for a living. Pone considered McGee a tick, leach draining blood off another man's work. Pone detected a strong friendship between Ben and McGee so he kept his personal feeling about the bloke to himself. Pone wanted to tell Ben maybe McGee took a solo job and fucked up.

"Gone…disappeared…vanished." Pone exhaled. "You know for what we do, sometimes we have to go incognito."

Ben shook his head. "Naw man, not Al…he don't need to . He don't screw up."

"Nobody's perfect, Ben," said Pone. "Some of us have no business to be in the business."

"Al's always careful."

Pone studied the giant. He saw the concern as well as heard it in Ben's words. He also knew about Ben and Al's partnership before he mentioned it.

Pone took a large gulp of his Goya. "Okay it's getting late so spill it."

Ben nodded. "Al got a woman, Ruby and a couple of kids."

Pone frowned. "When you say woman…"

"Shit'd…he ain't, but we need loving too."

Pone never understood why men in his profession got married or why women in the business did the same. It made problems when enemies found out about the ball and chain. Cold-blooded assassins took out the spouse and kids no matter how pristine. The life of a killer already complicated to involve others. The inculpable clueless what their love interest did for a living and those who knew showed an ignorant blind-eye to the easy lifestyle and money. Naive thinking led to tragedy, thought Pone.

Pone took another sip of his Goya. "You met this Ruby?"

"Yeah," sighed Ben in his deep base voice. "She called me a week ago worried because she hadn't heard from Al. The longest he'd gone without contacting her is two days…that ain't like him. He loves his family."

"Did he go on a job?"

"We did things together. The only time he went anywhere by himself was to bars and clubs."

"Any club in particular?"

"The Viper Lounge."

"Bad booze and cheapass women…owned by a woman named Black Medusa."

"So you know the place."

Pone nodded. "So why me?"

"Shit'd, you know the cops don't give a shit about us and you ain't a killer-for-hire no more… I can pay you."

A zip sound went off in Pone's pocket.

He checked the text message and shook his head. "You know I'm busy?"

"I know you still work for the Brigand family."

Red Brigand to be exact, the youngest of the Brigand Band brood who everyone considered Pone's guardian angel. The reason he still breathed. After the death of J. Paul he left the family business to his offspring. Problem. Pone wanted to ease his way out of the killing business; Red's siblings would have none of it unless Pone left the game escorted by death. J. Paul's older children the twins, not Tweedle Dee and Tweedle Dum; in fact all four Brigands college-educated. The lookalikes Linda and Susan, Sue for short and ten minutes younger, had inherited their father's girth and features, but their mother Mary's petite size. Both sported portly five-two bodies, round faces, wrapped around auburn hair and hazel eyes. Though not ugly, but plain Jane with little help from make-up. Beggars cannot be choosers, thought Pone.

In other words if they found male callers then they better not play hard to get and they didn't, husbands similar, but a couple inches taller. Stanley belonged to Linda. Cue ball bald, a saggy gut on its way to meet with his balls. When he sat down his belly joined him and when he walked people joked his belly and balls sounded like bongos bouncing off each other. An exaggeration, but funny. Sue's man Murray a mop top Moe Stooge style hair on is head and a waist line with more spare tires than the Michelin Man. Put Stanley and Murray together and you'd wonder who would play Larry for a three stooges reunion. They gave J. Paul grand-kids:

Linda and Stanley the proud parents of two girls. Sue and Murray two boys.

J. Paul's younger kids: Paul J. and Brooke (Red) acquired his height, but their mother's pretty features and slender body. Paul J. named opposite of his father. Six-four tennis player body, blue eyes, golden hair, bronze skin, chiseled face, and a deep cleft chin.

He married a trophy wife, Angel a former super-model. A brunette with big brown eyes, oval shape face, olive skin and hour glass figure. Three children came from the marriage: a girl fist followed by two boys which made J Paul happy to have the family name carried on. Skepticism on Paul J rumored he preferred a man's touch from time to time. J Paul knew sugar flowed in his son's veins, but glad Paul J. respected him enough to marry a woman and have children. Angel knew you got old in the modeling business fast and no fool how the industry worked.

A thirty-year-old model got put out to pasture making room for teen queens and twenty somethings. Word of mouth she made sure Paul J. carried plenty of Trojans. Red convinced her father she wanted to work outside the family business and became a lawyer though she knew she'd always have a link to the mobster life.

Sometimes when two people meet a man and woman who are both young it could mean sparks.

No sparks between Red and Pone; a connection allowed them both to feel as comfortable as drinking a glass of water on a hot summer day. Pone told her why a college educated man became a hired killer. Revenge a cruel monster reared its ugly head. Pone, her father's top man since Wisdom's skills decayed. Pone's mentor did everything except hanging him upside down from the tallest building to convince him not to go into a life of crime. Pone knew in order to get revenge on the man who took Sheila Green from them he needed to become a killer to get a killer. He did and Brigand replaced Wisdom with his new knight. He told Red his ordeal and from that moment a special friendship developed between the two. She convinced her family Pone would be under her thumb and work for her as a troubleshooter; no longer a killer-for-hire. The family agreed, but made it clear they'd keep a close eye on him.

"I work for Red… I can't make any promises, ."

He handed Ben a card. Ben never seen any of Pone's business cards before. "Troubleshooter…shit'd," said Ben shaking his head. He nodded then took off.

Pone dropped in on Antonio who he called Tony. Tony sat in his office drinking shots of Jim Beam. Pone felt sorry for the fellow. Antonio treated Birdie good and loved her.

A mystery to Pone why she didn't settle down with him. Pone saw her as a sister; some said they would make a good couple. He and birdie grew up together along with her baby sister Jade. Raised in a group home ran by Sheila Green. It made Pone and Wisdom proud when Birdie used Sheila's middle name Nadine for her club's moniker.

Pone thought the reason she made Tony her manager because she loved the buck too and wanted to keep him a part of the club. Pone hoped Antonio held no grudge to why he and Birdie didn't jump the broom. Pone wondered if Birdie pined for his `amor. He hoped she didn't and if she did then he would encourage her follow her heart and make a life with Antonio. A good guy and he deserved better. Antonio loved her enough to tolerate the brother sister act Pone and Birdie displayed. Birdie sat on Pone's lap, a huggedfrom behind, and kiss on the cheek. Pone didn't encourage or stopped her. Pone let Antonio and Birdie dabble in their own world. Because he led a complicated life.

"About to take off." Pone looked at the half empty bottle of booze and the glazed eye Italian. "You okay?"

"She won't marry me." Tony took another shot of the hard whiskey. "Look at you, baby hair, porcelain skin…no stubble. Mister Hollywood handsome. Ladies pet, men's regret." He shook his head. "Every girl wants you and every guy wants to be you. A real mack daddy, daddy mack."

"Don't forget, I don't have eye-lashes. No thanks to Alopecia," said Pone. Pone hated watching people wallow in self-pity.

Commit to one woman, Pone shook his head. Too many women to be owned by one, thought Pone. "But you have eyebrows and hair on your head."

"A miracle," Pone sighed. "My business is done. You can close shop."

"Good night, Chub," toasted Tony.

2 a.m. Pone inhaled the cold night air to relieve his stress. The great meteor made the planet colder and Autumn and Winter lasted longer than Spring and Summer.

Metro city not the deep south, but not the north either. Pone loved the cold, it cleared his head. He embraced the chill on his face peering at the night sky. A few stars out and the moon winked at him. One of his ladies waited for in the big parking lot. A steel body, big, red, and strong. He climbed inside getting comfortable on her black interior. Pone loved everything about Lucille his Chevy Avalanche. He leaned back and thought, he called me Chub. Antonio drowned his jealousy in a bottle of rot gut. Antonio heard Birdie call him Chub. Pone bit his lower lip Antonio still couldn't grasp he and Birdie raised up together and the hugs and kisses she gave all innocent.

She accepted Pone when he lost his hair to Alopecia. All the kids would call him baldy sitting behind his seat in class whispering in his ear until he retaliated and took blame for disturbing the class. On his Twelfth birthday a miracle or puberty.

He grew hair, soft baby hair, but all the same it covered his head and the teasing stopped. A porcelain face. No five o'clock shadow or razor stubble.

Blondish brown hair and no eye-lashes. Pone smiled because even if bald, Birdie and Jade showed love . Pone turned the ignition, time for the get together with Red his guardian angel. The reason he walked among the living. On his way to see Red, Pone thought about his poker buddies. Chuckling to himself, thinking how many assassins can a killer call a friend. The first to come to mind the old timer Sonny.

His hair facial and head made him look like the famous actor Redd Foxx. His tools and talent for killing, a 357 magnum and explosives. Sonny no longer strong enough to pull the trigger of a gun. He never mentioned his age; Pone figured Sonny at least twenty years over sixty. Wisdom told Pone anything needed to be blown up then no one could get the job done like Sonny. Now the decaying man lived out his years with men half his age playing poker. Pone smiled thinking how Sonny tried to keep up the conversation, but out of touch with today's world. Pone thought of him as a walking library and encyclopedia of knowledge. Sonny helpful when it came to explaining and simplify things like explosives.

Sonny never said what branch of the military he served or if he enlisted at all, or how he obtained his skills; asking him for his wisdom made him feel useful.

Pone collected comic books from the past to the present. He even stocked up DVD's of Japanese Anime. Stick looked like a live Anime character. Maybe radioactive meteor fragments affected his mother while he incubated inside her, thought Pone. Stick possessed yellow eyes, black pupils, a chalky complexion, raven spiked hair like porcupine quills, and custom made jagged teeth.

If they live in a comic book, then Stick would fit right in as a mutant; not an X-man, but a Morlock. A mutant resembling nothing human living down in the sewers. Stick wore a suit. Corporate appearance and crime syndicate his business.

Swore you'd never catch him as a blue collar worker or a 7-Eleven clerk. No Stick came from Japanese Anime born to be a killer-for-hire. Stick dropped out of high school. The military didn't accept drop outs. Air Force, Navy, and Marines won't let you in with a GED.

You can enlist in the Army with a GED, but Stick didn't have either; he did have a mentor who took him under his wing. The man saw and realized Stick would have a hard time making a living. The kind soul unknown. Stick wasn't accepted among his white peers, but comfortable around black people and called himself an albino which Pone, Ben, and Sonny paid heed. Stick loved black women and they adored him and not because he made a lot of loot doing what he did for a living. The ladies called him a silver-tongued devil.

Stick, a contortionist. His gun a German Ruger military handgun. His specialty up close and personal. A garrote cord and switchblade. Stick wrapped his body around the victim like a constricting snake controlling all movement.

He looked his fatality in the eye like a constricting snake watching its doomed prey while strangling and slitting their throat.

He even had a Joker like smile. Pone got chills thinking about his freakish friend.

NBA size Big Ben Donovan not quick, agile, not even close to being a Fred Astaire. The big ox and Pone met over a poker game, both men stuck around long after the game ended to talk about life. Pone knew what Ben did to make a buck and Ben knew Pone's reputation and his exploits with the Brigand Band. The two gunmen felt at ease with each other and formed a friendship.

Pone cringed thinking about the poor soul who had a contract on his life and Ben assigned to be the Grim Reaper. Ben's choice of weapons two shot-gun pistols. His talent earned him Bone Crusher Ben. His mighty mitts snapped necks like a twig.

Pone's thoughts got interrupted by what sounded like hard rain. Except it came from the driver's side and not the roof-top of his red chariot. He glanced in his side-mirror and saw a cream color Crown Victoria. A once popular police car of the MPD. Now they cruise around in SUV s and different models. But as usual, the Po Po's or the Heat as the Hip-Hoppers and Prohibitions called coppers no-where in sight, a protocol. Let the gangsters eliminate each other to clean up their own mess. Quiet streets meant no possible casualties, thought Pone.

A good thing. Drive by's not Pone's first rodeo. The name of the game, take him out and build your resume`. Pone dealt with both Probonos and Hip-Hoppers.

The Crown Victoria found itself side by side with Lucille heading down North Tryon. During the day, cars and patrons made it the most frantic street in the city.

The falling star forced all cities to adopt a curfew since gangster life came back in full effect. Lucille sprayed with more bullets.

Pone glanced long enough to observe his would be assassins. Hip hop wannabes between early and mid-twenties believing a life of crime a great career move.

Whoever hired the fledglings didn't outfit them with upscale weapons.

An assault rifle popular back in the nineteen sixties used by the Air Force and Army. M1911 used 8mm ammo.

Pone drove a truck for height advantage in battle. In Medieval times, the man on a horse believed to have the edge over a man on foot unless the man on foot killed the horse.

Pone invested a lot of money to make Lucille's body impregnable. A shooter would have to concentrate his bullets on one spot to penetrate her.

The delinquents got a curve-ball after several ricochets; the words fuck and shit came from their mouths. Lucille's armor bullet-proof. Pone didn't have time to keep dancing; already late for a conclave with Red. He spotted East Seventh street between two large brick buildings. A two-way street. Lucille made a screeching sharp turn lifting off the pavement, Pone heard wheels squeal and saw the Crown Vic in his rear view mirror, but now on the wrong side of the road. A menu of death waited for the punks: bullets, a head on collision with another car, and reckless driving.

Pone realized no matter where he turned the fools followed . He glanced in the rear view and they continued firing shots. He shook his head thinking that's why kids should stay in school. Pone turned Lucille on North College a three lane one-way street out bound, and on the 500 block stood Tryon House Apartments.

A low rent studio tenement for young people and older adults with humbling jobs. Pone's concern now traveling in a residential area meant they might run into civilians.

The complex four blocks up. Pone tired of the hot pursuit. On Seventh before turning onto North College he set up Sally. A model T1927A-1 Tommy Gun. Preferred weapon of the Prohibitions. Fixed with a detachable butt; he left it on to steady his aim. He liked the fifty rounds in the magazine.

Pone considered the Tommy-Gun gangster cool.

The Crown Victoria and Lucille ran side by side. Pone used his apex leverage on his executioners.

He set Sally to a single shot; take out the driver like cutting off the head of a snake. For almost every plan there's always a glitch, up ahead two homeless people, a woman pulling a suit case and ahead of her a boy age seven or eight.

Great, thought Pone. A mother and son, small family. Hits seldom happened this time of the morning though it still being dark. The juveniles fired non-stop. The woman knew the drill; she hit the bricks, but the child didn't; he played statue. Despite the situation Pone took the shot he wanted, he heard a fuck my leg and the car turned off to the side, but not until they got up on the child and the fool in the back seat kept firing. Pone looked in his rear view mirror and saw a child in a fetal position; the mother ran toward the child, gathering him in her arms screaming to the heavens.

The Crown Vic headed up the wrong side on a one-way street, lucky for them early morning. Pone stayed the course, an appointment to keep. His mind on the delinquents. Shooting into civilians not done. That's the Cardinal rule of the profession. A lesson Pone would teach.

Two

"What the hell is keeping him?" asked Crowe. The deputy mayor. A strong thin five-six physique. His bald pointy-head surrounded by thick curly brown hair making his head look like an egg in a nest.

"Relax Harvey, he'll be here," said Red.

"He better be…this is important."

"You didn't want to meet at the state house."

"How the hell would it look for a killer to meet with a city official at the state house?"

"He is not meeting the mayor. He is meeting you."

Red sighed. "He is not a killer, he is… "

"Pone still kills," said Crowe.

"Only bad people that deserves it."

"Yeah, right?"

"He has helped you Mister ex-D.A. And he still doesn't know he helped you and by the way you have killed too."

Crowe pointed and frowned. "I used to put bad guys away. Not a bullet in them and the judge and jury laid out the sentence."

Red smiled. "Lethal injection, the electric chair… those are the bullets you use.

As I recalled you're the one who sets the table. The judge and jury swallow what you feed them."

"Why are you so protective of this guy?"

That has always been the number one question on the minds of her family. They hoped it wasn't anything intimate. Red, the only one of J. Paul's children not married and not in a rush.

Red enjoyed the bachelorette life going home to peace and quiet. An independent woman she owned a law firm, her own wealth, her family's capital and knew her way around the kitchen. Red, like most women had needs.

She found Pone attractive and wondered what it would feel like wrapped in his strong arms, cheek to cheek with his stubble free face and taste those smooth lips.

For every Rose, there's a thorn. The Brigand Band.

Red's siblings seemed happy with their married lives. They had children and during the holidays, Thanksgiving dinner the men carved the turkey alternating every year after J. Paul died; everyone enjoyed sitting around the Christmas tree dressed in pajamas near the fire-place opening presents. Champagne for the adults and cream sodas for the kids celebrated the new year. The family didn't hide their concern with her relationship with a former hatchet man. Pone now worked for Red as a troubleshooter.

Red loved her father; she hated the life of organized crime matriarchs.

She got into law trying to cleanse the family name of all the blood on their hands and give the public a different perspective; sins of the father.

When word got around Pone wanted out, it wasn't Mary that got upset, but Linda was furious. She saw hired killers as just cockroaches who should count their blessing just for not being stepped on. She embraced her inherited wealth more than the other children despite the spilled blood.

Of all the children she was the one with her father's ruthlessness for protecting the family wealth. Some of the Brigand family members felt a little guilt about how they got their fortune, but not Linda. She implicated Pone would leak important information to their enemies and for that possibility she wanted his head on the chopping block.

Red came to the rescue of Pone and convinced her family he would not leave the brood; he would only answer to her. Linda agreed with the terms except Pone must always live in Metro City, any-where else, then all bets were off. Pone agreed since he had family in Metro; he would no longer be a killer-for-hire.

Red checked her text. "He's in the lobby."

Pone entered the lobby of the Ritz building. He always stopped to stare at the ceiling of the building given to Red by her father as a gift for passing the bar. The ceiling wasn't the Sistine Chapel. God wasn't creating life or anything; the periodic display from the past to the present of powerful men and women looked impressive and sophisticated. The ceiling above showed club carrying cavemen standing over a burning branch caused by a lightning bolt: Roman politicians delivering speeches, colonial revolutionary war, wild west cowboys and Indians, the Wright brothers at Kitty Hawk, and to the present of men and women dressed in suits, ties, business skirts and high heels standing in front of corporate buildings.

The artist of the composition unknown, but Michelangelo couldn't have done a better job himself. The marble lobby colored sand; a secure desk with two guards decked in blue sports jackets, white shirts, red ties, gray pants, and black loafers. Both in their thirties about six-foot tall and military style haircuts. They knew Pone and nodded as he entered the lobby elevators. He got off on the sixteenth floor where he met Benedict Arnold of the legal system, Lars Lambert, who Pone called Lard the third shift janitor.

Pone called the frail man another name, a professional ass wiper. Lars Lambert once a prominent lawyer who worked for a crime family known as the Webb. They were a big family; the problem was they wanted to overthrow the Brigand Band. Lambert worked for the Brigands and the Webb family under the table. He felt slighted by the Brigands and allowed greed to cloud his better judgment. Because of Lambert, the Webb family got every layout of everything old man

Brigand owned and associated with, but a big obstacle the Webb were unaware of was Brigand connections with the World Council. They formed a special task force comprising the Army, Air Force, Navy, and Marines. That special force called the Combine.

Every member of the Combine blood-thirsty, cold-bloodied men trained to discard their own mother. Pone once thought about enlisting in the Marines to join the Combine; a 9 p.m. curfew and 5 a.m. wake-up call not for him.

He heard some of Wisdom's veteran friends say, (don't believe the military commercials when they say be all you can be. The phrase calling a soldier a dog of the military meant you belonged to Uncle Sam and did as he said). Pone decided he didn't need military discipline. Serve your country not for him. Some of his school chums went into the service and it gave them the opportunity to pursue jobs in the law enforcement field. The pros and cons of life.

Some of his peers ended up being low rent security guards living minimum wage lives. The Combine proved a valuable asset for the Brigand Band.

Two brothers, nephews, and cousins part of the Combine helped J. Paul send a message to anyone who had thoughts of defying him. G. and Macone took notice. J. Paul wanted none of his personnel involved, so he asked the Combine to make a swift act of the Webb family. Lars Lambert, the only existence of the Webb crime family not even a blood relative. Why he still lived? Lambert played a double edge sword against the crime families and got cut. Pone got wind of his betrayal and informed J. Paul. J. Paul appreciated Pone's loyalty and asked him what should be the fate of the little worm. The choices: a bullet to the back of the head, slit throat, decapitation, bind each limb to four SUV's and have them go in every direction.

Pone suggested a more humbling fate instead; to never practice law again, never leave the city and spend his life working a humbling job.

Lambert tried the fast food chain, but too recognizable. The only discrete alternative a third-shift janitor. His wife left him and took the kids to live with her sister in Idaho.

"How's life treating you?" asked Pone.

"Piss off," responded Lambert.

"You'd know a lot about that wouldn't you?"

"Fuck you."

Pone smiled. "Now is that any way talk to the man who saved your life?"

An angry sigh deflated Lambert's body. "I have work to do."

Pone nodded. "Yeah you do, and before I leave, I'm sure you'll be wiping the seat my ass was on, professional ass wiper."

Pone continued his journey passing a few prestigious office doors and small secretarial cubicles along the way. He arrived at the imposing mahogany double doors at the end of the hallway. Even Red's personal secretary had an impressive cubicle that stood out from the rest of the lawyer amanuensis's. He opened the door he knew not latched down.

"About time!" said Crowe. He threw up his hands like a wide-receiver saying I'm open. Harvey Crowe used to be a feared district attorney. He had a reputation of putting away criminals.

He never lost a case, a man of pure facts when he went after the criminal element. Crowe's vicious manner toward evildoers became legendary among his fellow attorneys. His tenacity impressed the Mayor enough he made Crowe his deputy mayor to help him wage war on crime. Gossip around the penal system prisoners saying Crowe's name in their sleep.

Pone heard the rumor. He chalked it up as hatred for the man.

Pone abhor Crowe; he knew Crowe shared his animosity. Pone closed the door behind him.

He made his way into the grand, luxurious office. A painting of tress and wildlife decorated the wall. A black leather sofa on the left wall sitting on a pattern throw rug, flanked by two grand brown oak book-shelves featuring law books, hard-back novels, and Encyclopedia Britannica which became obsolete when they created the PC. Near her enormous bronze oak desk was a stained display table with a Star Trek three dimensional chess set given to her by Pone. Both Trekkie fans of the original series. A few plants scattered around the room in an organized fashion to add aura.

The floor smooth charcoal color. Two plush antic chairs in front of her desk with small round brown tables made to hold beverages. Red stood behind her desk, and Crowe stood next to the plush chair on the left. Pone sat in the chair on the right.

Crowe parked it in the left chair.

Red took a seat, rested her elbows on her desk, then placed her chin on her clasped hands. Pone glared. "You need to call the exterminator." He looked at Crowe. "This building already has a rat. No need for a roach."

Crowe cleared his throat. "Thought you handled pest control?"

"Don't tempt me," said Pone.

Crowe grinned. "Really? Here and now?" He sniffed the air. "Bleach."

"You requested a discrete conclave, Harvey," said Red watching the two men like an observing marriage counselor.

Crowe turned pale looking at Red as if he'd seen a ghost.

Red winked at Pone. "You two…" She glanced at Crowe. "Need to be civil."

"Why am I here?" asked Pone.

"Two teens died a little after midnight," said Red.

Pone shrugged. "Driving home drunk after a party. Texting while driving. Sad but it happens."

"Try a car bomb," intervened Crowe.

Pone frowned "Who were these teens?"

Red rose from her desk gliding to the front to perch herself on top. Pone always admired the natural six-foot woman. No freckles on her face despite being a natural redhead.

She sported a librarian bun, hypnotic blue eyes, a sleeveless emerald dress hemmed just above the knee that gloved he hour-glass figure. She showed enough cleavage and thigh to tease. Crossing her firm legs clad in black panty-hose and black pumps added definition to her magnificent presence.

"Helen Macone and Reginald Grant," said Red. Pone nodded. "A job for the MPD."

Crowe broke his trance on Red. "Your job. You know these people...how they think and act. This is above the police."

"I've killed these people, and they still want to kill me," remarked Pone. Crowe shifted his body toward Pone.

"The city, mayor...we need you.

We're afraid that this might escalate into a gang war."

Pone shrugged. "You think one was trying to take out the others kid and fate played a cruel trick?"

"Both Helen and Reginald were in the same car," said Red.

"So they were dating?" questioned Pone.

"Afraid so," replied Crowe.

"What's that supposed to mean?" asked Pone. "Because one is white and the other black?"

Crowe snorted. "Heard you had a sense of humor. Guess in your line of work death is like lint on your shoulder."

Pone twirled his bowler. "Death doesn't discriminate. Natural causes, incurable diseases, tragic accidents, crime and self-defense. We're all going to die." The derby spiraled down on his lap. "How we depart is a mystery."

"Heard you're a college graduate too," said Crowe.

"Took a philosophy class instead of religion," remarked Pone. "You can add that to your file."

Crowe squirmed like a worm on a hook.

Pone smiled. "Fish ain't biting and I'm hungry,"

Crowe frowned. "What does that even mean?"

Pone shrugged. "I don't like fish. A song lyric. Thought it sounded cool."

"You think we want to use you for bait?" asked Crowe.

Red exhaled. "We don't want another Black Halloween."

Pone stretched and twisted his neck. The bloodiest gang war in the history of Metro City. Prohibitions and Hip-Hoppers lost a lot of men. Vehicles pulled up on both sides of the street wedging in unsuspecting patrons dying in the cross-fire. It ended without a true victor. It took years before the city recovered. A lie because nobody won. If it was a fight for control of Metro then both parties failed because they served under Paul J. The Brigand Band rule Metro and Prohibitions and Hip-Hoppers answer to them. A cryptic truce between the gangs orchestrated by Paul J. Macone and G in their own way continue to try and undermine the other till they can find a way to dethrone the Brigands.

"Harvey and I concluded Macone and G wouldn't be cruel enough to go after the others offspring," said Red.

Crowe held up a finger. "One will blame the other."

"Give it to Bolden," said Pone. "He's a one man MPD by himself."

Red shook her head. "Too bull-headed. Not enough finesse."

Pone nodded. "End up dead in a week."

"Okay…" said Crowe. "If the ancients didn't off the other one's kid and did his own by accident then who would do this?"

"Oh I don't know…pulling the trigger themselves, ordering deaths for over twenty…forty years," remarked Pone. "Decades of enemies."

"That's why we need you," said Crowe. "Before things get worse."

"Worse…right?" remarked Pone. "Somebody put two crime lord kids in the bone yard?"

"You can stop a possible gang war?" said Red.

Pone pursed his lips. "Well, it's nice to be appreciated in a good way, but…"

"I promised the mayor you'd handle this, and remember, you work for me," said Red with an raised brow.

Pone glanced at Crowe, the ex-DA sat back crossing his miniature legs as if he won a court case.

Pone felt like a black knight on a chess board getting captured by the white queen. "Both killed in the same car?" Pone snorted. "Damn…they were dating."

"Thought we made that clear," remarked Crowe rolling his eyes. "And I don't believe the parents knew about it," said Red.

"Somebody on the outside did this," said Crowe.

"You think," said Pone.

Crowe pointed his finger. "Now look…"

"We need to have a conference with the Prohibitions and Hip-Hoppers," said Red.

Pone glanced at Crowe. "Beautiful minds think alike. I'll make calls and set up a junction between us and the lieutenants."

"Where will this meeting take place?" asked Crowe.

"The state house," remarked Pone.

Crowe almost had a seizure. Eyes wide, mouth trembled, and he stuttered. "A-A-Are you crazy? How do you think it would look?"

Pone shrugged. "Like a politician not afraid to get his hands dirty."

Crowe shook his head. "Criminal element in the statehouse… I can't have murderers, racketeers parading in and out like a boys club soiling an establishment of justice."

"Bravo," applauded Pone. "Use that for your campaign and you'll have my vote."

"If it was only that simple," said Crowe.

Pone knew the deputy mayor didn't take over if anything happened to the mayor like the vice-president would if the President got impeached or assassinated.

Pone laughed. "Pull your heart out of your ass. The convocation will take place at Nadine."

Crowe adjusted his tie. "Yeah…a lawless sanctuary… right… because that's where all… "

"The cool people hang out," said Pone.

"Why would anybody want to kill two kids?" Crowe shook his head. "You think a conspiracy against the bigwigs?"

"A lot of toes get stepped on, and nobody has enough manners to say excuse me," said Red.

"You make a lot of enemies in organized crime. Red, how are your nephews and nieces?" asked Pone.

"Under lock and key," said Red. "So you're on board?"

"Oh, I make you real proud, massah," remarked Pone. Crowed looked bewildered and Red straightened up.

Pone smirked. "You're the boss. Besides nothing irks me more than mobsters using kids to make a point. But I need concessions."

Crowe frowned. "What are you talking…"

"The file you have on me," Pone glared at Crowe. "When this is done…"

"It will be in my hands," said Red. "Right Harvey?"

Crowe loosened his tie. "What's important here is the children."

Pone leaned forward. "I expect business as usual with the Probonos and Hoppers, but you're the deputy mayor. No longer the District Attorney. Why would you keep a file on me?"

"Yeah Harvey, why would you?" questioned Red.

"You should have no problem obtaining it," Crowe eyeballed Red. "You and the new DA are already connected."

"Jealous are we?" asked Pone. Red gave Pone a disgusted look.

"Whatever," said Crowe. "Heard you're a gambler."

"Always keep an ace up my sleeve," remarked Pone.

Crowe snorted. "Queen of hearts."

"That's not all," said Pone.

"Name it," said Red.

"Contact the families for a parlay so I can do my job. I'll confirm the get together with the lieutenants."

"What if this doesn't work?" ask Crowe.

"Then we call in the combine," said Pone. "What? You thought I was going to tell you keep that file on me?"

Red and Crowe turned a different shade of white. A long eerie silence broke by Pone's laughter. "Take it easy, you two should play poker with me. I'd win lot of money."

"A bluff…" said Red hitting her forehead as if she would've had a V8. Pone studied Crowe.

"Spill it, Pone…what's on your mind?' asked Crowe."

"Let's get one thing clear, I work for Red," said Pone.

Crowe pursed his lips. "You a detective…right?"

"No detective, no private-eye, and no killer-for-hire," responded Pone.

"Bravo Miss Brigand," said Crowe with a scrutinized look. "You can teach an old dog new tricks."

Pone rose glaring at Crowe.

"You better go Harvey," said Red. "Remember, you wanted to be discreet." Pone stared the politician out of the plush office.

"Does he have my number?" asked Pone.

"How long have you known me?" smiled Red. Ever so the lady she eased off her desk gliding over to Pone face to face. Before Pone could blink, Red slapped him twice and pointed her finger.

Pone known Red for a long time and knew he pissed her off with the slave remark. His guardian angel the ultimate professional, so he knew he crossed the line.

Pone shrugged. "You need a sense of humor." Red's glare bored into him.

Pone nodded. He remembered Red smacking one of her nephews for referring to a black man using the N word.

"Won't happen again, boss."

"Don't bring that attitude to…"

"They still don't think I'm all in?" asked Pone. "You know I hate it the way your sisters look at me sitting at the dinner table."

"For me," said Red.

Pone shook his head. He figured agreeing to be Red's errand boy would keep her family in the loop. Pone knew Red didn't see him that way, but her family took their jabs at him to amuse themselves. The insults nonverbal, but the look on their faces:

Linda sneaking in an icy glare, Sue at times gave a smile and casual wink her husband Murray too busy to notice stuffing his face, Paul J. sitting next to Murray playing the good son and wife Angel picking over her food eating like a bird. Not this year, thought Pone. Time to level the playing field.

"I'm bringing a guest or two," said Pone.

"Wisdom? Birdie?" questioned Red.

Pone snorted. "He'd love talking about the good old days with your mother, but you and I both know those days weren't that good." Pone twirled his bowler. "Do you want Birdie to kick your sister's ass?"

"It would be a first… I'll tell mother to set extra plates."

"You know what let it be a surprise. I want to see the look on sister's face."

"Sue does not give you a hard time."

"Dinners are boring," said Pone. "Me, you, your mother, brother, sisters and their spouses. Children tucked away safe in their beds away from a killer." The children one day if not already will realized they're born into a family of sin. "No fun."

Red nodded. The dinners a mockery. Pone didn't need to be present. Her sisters wanted amusement and Pone played court jester. Lind hated Pone because he wanted to leave the family. Sue her twin but flirted with him wishing for a fantasy. Yes he should bring a guest.

Red got moon-eye snapping her fingers pointing at Pone. "Nobody from your circle."

Pone laughed. "Not because of table manners. Though I'd love for Linda to meet Stick."

Red glared at Pone. "Hearing you say his name makes my skin crawl."

"He has that effect on people." Pone smiled. He told Red about the company he keeps letting her know he might need their help depending on the assignment she gave him. Red frowned. "A human serpent? Ewe."

"Sonny would connect with your mother and fall asleep at the dinner table."

"My mother's not that old."

"She's over sixty."

Red nodded. "Yeah, but you said Sonny…"

"Okay. Okay." Pone held up his hand. Sonny looked at least eighty and not many his age around anymore. He'd be out of place and Linda would make sure of it. Pone wouldn't let her torture him. "The nieces and nephews would enjoy Ben before bedtime." Red rolled her eyes. "Yeah, right."

I won't invite Ben, thought Pone. They'd get on his nerves and he'd snap their necks. No Ben wouldn't hurt children.

"Trust me, you will approve," said Pone.

"Why the mystery?" asked Red.

"I deserve to have fun too."

Red looked Pone straight in the eye. "What's with you? Never known you not to be punctual."

"Ran into some gun-play."

"What?" Red escorted Pone over to the sofa. Many including her family believe she and Pone have a more intimate than a business relationship. She kept the wondering minds and her beloved family in the dark.

"I'd rather have coffee than bullets any morning."

Red shook her head. "Not that it's ever a good time for a drive-by…but this early in the morning…"

"They knew."

"What do you mean, Pony?"

Pone felt like a teenager when Red called him Pony. "I wasn't supposed to make it to our huddle."

"This was tight. You, me, and Harvey."

"Right…they were setting for me."

"Are you sure?"

Pone gave a look. "Played this game a long time." Red shook her head. "Strange?"

"The kind of world we live in."

Red studied Pone. "Did you get a look at your hatchet men?"

Pone chuckled. "Hatchet boys. Late teens to early mid-twenties. Hip-Hoppers."

"My God!" Red shook her head. "Desperate."

"There are two kinds of desperate, low rent hoods still trying to make it big and punk kids waiting to live in the fast lane. Somebody tried to get kids to do what a lot of men couldn't."

Red squeezed his knee. "At least you're safe." She looked him over. "No worse for wear."

"Not quite."

"What's wrong, Pony?"

"A mother and son…homeless…somebody didn't teach those boys the code.

You don't fire into civilians." He swallowed hard. "Drive-by shooting is an exception because it's planned."

"Sounds to me this was planned," said Red.

Pone nodded. "Those boys weren't schooled on the rules."

"Pony, it's not your fault."

"I'll set up the moot with the lieutenants of the families." Pone gazed into Red's sapphire eyes. "I need you to do me a favor."

"Anything."

"Call the hospital ask about the boy. Let me know if miracles still exist."

Roland White sat in the white Chevy S-10 out in the middle of nowhere on his burner cell.

"Hey you said you wanted the best, well I can't do that with what you're paying me."

"You got kids to do a man's job."

"Ain't no man putting his ass on the line to take out Chubby Pone. You have to break the bank for that."

"You better find somebody other than kids or your black ass going to end up back in the pen."

"Hold up, man. I'll get the job done, but if you want the best then you have to put up more cheddar."

"I pull the strings. You and your boy are my puppets. You trying to squeeze me, huh?"

More like a dummy with your hand up my ass, thought White.

"Look, we came through for you blowing up them kids. We didn't fail you then and we ain't going to fuck you now. But even you should know Pone ain't no joke. He's dodged bullets for years."

"I don't give a shit how good he is, he needs to be dead. I'll go back to the hoosegow and swap your sorry asses for somebody that can do the job."

"Calm down. We need more loot."

"All right, I'll get you more money. Fail me again and you won't be homesick for long."

"Hey, you said so yourself people can't know we out and so I got to dig deep to find someone to handle your task while staying on the down low."

"You ever play baseball, Roland?"

"Yeah."

"You only get three strikes." The voice hung up.

White sighed. I ain't going back inside, he thought. He looked at the dark morning sky. He took it for granted until the sound of clang which still rang in his ears. The caged bird's song never so true until you go inside. Having coffee alone felt good.

Prison made a grown man feel like a child. They told you when to go to bed, get up, to eat, go outside, and to come inside.

Twenty-four seven nonstop supervision; you lived among rapists and killers. Two years in the army was enough control for him. They had rules as well: when to go to bed when to wake up; it sure as hell wasn't prison. You shared quarters with others; you didn't live behind bars.

White surprised his family by joining the army. They considered him a shit ass. Plain and simple a no good-for-nothing bum. He'd showed them he could break the cycle of being a dirt farmer out in Rock Hill. He used those two years to learn a trade that helped him to get in good with the Hip-Hoppers. He knew how to make bombs and blow things up and made good money doing it. No more being told to go to bed and when to eat. Good times don't last and end too soon.

He shook his head trying to figure how things went wrong so fast.

His incarceration surprised him. White smelled a set up. He thought it would be a good idea to try freelancing without the Hip-Hoppers knowledge, he became a bomb maker for hire sub Rosa. White intended to work independent. The Hip-Hoppers called it Bronco (You broke away from the crew).

White sat pondering perhaps he made a mistake and maybe the reason he ended up in prison. He got a call from a man whom he did not give his name; offered a lot of money to blow up a building so the owner could collect the insurance policy, the building supposed to have been unoccupied. He blew up the building and some people were inside became casualties; that made him a murderer, on technicality; when the Hip-Hoppers found out about his outside business they dropped him like a bad habit. White prosecuted and before he knew it behind bars. Once inside, you lose your membership with the Hip-Hoppers. White got out, he had to stay under the radar because the judge sentenced him for at least five to ten years and got out in three which confused him since he murdered a few people in the bombing. According to his attorney the DA's office overlooked evidence.

White held the smoking gun. His attorney never told him what missing clue got him out; he did not care. No square barred up box with a toilet next to his bed.

Freedom caressed like a cool breeze on a scorching summer day. Whatever fell through the cracks reduced his condemnation.

White had more confusion jammed into his head being thrown into a cell with an outcast from the Prohibition gang. A man named James Krasko became his new partner in crime when released the same time. He never bothered to ask Krasko how he ended up in the hoosegow because he was glad to be out of prison. White thought more about his situation when he found out Krasko had bomb making skills. The first job they completed together taking out two kids from their former employers. He and Krasko knew getting out of the pen early label you a snitch and a guaranteed death sentence.

Murdering the children of two of the city's crime families gave them a place in the bone yard. So it benefited Krasko and him to lie low. Only he, Krasko, and the man pulling the strings knew what they did because he ordered them too, which made him an accomplice.

White didn't care to know the name of the puppet master because for now he'd just enjoy his freedom.

"I ain't going back inside," he whispered sipping his coffee.

Three

9 a.m., Pone yawned, stretched, and shook his head as he rolled off his king sized bed. He arrived at his fortress of solitude around four-thirty and Mister Sandman wasn't doing his job. He didn't want to get hooked on sleeping pills; in fact he tried to keep his body from being dependent on any medicine.

Pone knew he needed supplements to combat old age.

He made a beeline to the fridge and took out his half-empty can of Chock Full Of Nuts.

A cool name for coffee, he thought. The company explained why the coffee carried the name because they used to peddled nuts in the 1920s and added coffee in the 1930s. Now only coffee and they like their name so much they kept it.

Two scoops in a filter, tap water, and let the black Proctor Silex do the rest. French roast flavored brew became a morning ritual. He sat at his mid rectangular butcher board table with coffee teasing his nostrils. He leaned on the table musing. The Great Meteor created a world of confusion; people scratched their heads trying to comprehend what the science nerds and religious leaders told them. The nerds won.

A rip in the time fabric caused the past to merge with the present, bringing prohibition back from the dead and breathing new life into the future. A forthcoming most people thought they would travel in air cars like the Jet-sons.

Instead no ray guns, beam me up Scotty, or anything science fiction. Cars fueled by gas, electricity; and rolled on tires. The only advance in technology, electric cars.

The owners bitched when non EV models parked in their space; EV cars only and active charging.

People died of natural causes, disease, bullets sharp blades, and animal attacks. The difference in society, the Prohibition era came back.

Gangster style language from the 1940s and a dress code: suits, fedoras, conservative dresses for women, and the Tommy-gun which Pone used himself. They even brought back the classic cars from the fifties, sixties, and up. All built with, state-of-the-art engines used in modern vehicles of the present. People chose between Prohibitions and Hip-Hoppers. Hip-Hoppers the modern gangsters and rivaled the Probonos. Gang wars and drive by shootings became too real. The hoppers didn't use Tommy-guns; AK-47 their choice of weapon, and they drove vehicles from the seventies to separate themselves from their rivals. The dress code for the Hip-Hoppers saggy, baggy clothes dropping off their asses showing fruit-of-the-loom underwear. Pone preen like a Probono; he preferred their choice of weapon and the dapper look over the unkempt attire of the Hip-Hoppers. He killed members on both sides and they considered him an enemy. Now Red ordered him to play peacekeeper because a heartless fool took out two kids with a bright future.

Damn life was cruel, thought Pone. He wasn't a father and never thought of becoming one; he couldn't imagine what a parent goes through when losing a child.

Overtime, he believed you stop crying, but around home, a reminder brought pain to the heart. Pone didn't care for the Probonos or the Hip-Hoppers; the kids didn't deserve to pay for the sins of their fathers. The person who caused such a tragedy wanted to hit home. He thought the MPD should handle the job; a song lyric came to mind, what are you good for nothing.

The police not considered keystone cops, but the joke around town, when you say hide the women and children you might find the MPD with them.

An exaggerated expression used often. The police handled basic crimes: bank robbery, mugging and helping the fire department. A good leader in Captain Bolden, a throw-back to the ball busting days when coppers waged war on crime at all cost. He got little support from Mayor Winslow whom made rare public appearances and who could blame him? Organized crime ruled once again, and those who stood against the mob ended up dead. Politicians in the back pocket of mobsters, not Winslow.

Several citizens didn't look forward to going to the polls because they tired of electing a bonehead with colorful dialogue not delivering on his promise. The current mayor safe for now.

The police stayed in the background hoping the gangs would cancel each other out. Pone didn't want good police officers putting their lives in danger, they had families, and most of them green for dealing with organized crime.

Red made the right move getting him involved. He dealt with both gangs, and his background gave him an upper hand. The city's Troubleshooter, and he'd stop a potential war to save innocents who would end up in the cross-fire.

Mayor Winslow worried the two crime families blamed one another and a gang war on the horizon. Civilian triage a concern not categorized as friendly fire.

Why would they use kids to make a point, thought Pone?

He would take the case for the kids because they deserved justice.

It was time to get to work, call his contacts on the East and West side of Metro to set up the caucus. A not so last supper at Nadine, he thought.

Pone not in the mood for talking. Thank God for texting. The smell of coffee captured his attention. Add fat free French vanilla and the java good to go. The Pinball ring tone of his cell in his ear on the bookcase. He picked that sound because of the woman who raised him. Sheila Green introduced him to the pinball machine. She said it was the rave before Nintendo, PlayStation, and X-box.

He checked the screen of his cell. Red. She must have news about the boy.

"What's the deal?" asked Pone.

"And a good morning to you too, kind sir."

Pone sipped his coffee. "That depends on the news," Red exhaled.

"The kid was DOA."

"Damn!"

"It's not your fault."

"His death won't be in vain."

"What are you going to do, Pony?"

Pone needed to hear Red call him Pony. It brought comfort. "What I do well."

"You be careful."

"I've reached out to my contacts, their prompt in responding. You and the deputy mayor clear your calendar, the meeting will be at Nadine."

"Bye, Pony."

Four

Pone wasn't a vampire, but day light his Kryptonite. While others basked in the sunlight, he shunned it. Darkness his friend; it would be awhile for the heavenly shades of night-fall, so he would make use of the sunlight traveling to the west-side of town.

Wilkerson Boulevard was a grave-yard of failed hole in the wall businesses. Pawn shops, thrift stores, and health department independent grocery stores. All not lost though, gentleman clubs, Burger King, Church's fried chicken to compete with a recent built Popeye's fried chicken. Pone had no intention of clogging his arteries with grease and red meat. On the outskirts of all this a hole in the wall auto shop.

The shop that gave Lucille her body. Owned by a man named Otis Blue. An MIT brain for car engines. Otis liked Pone because he never questioned his background or how he got the things to do what he did. Pone met Otis through Wisdom and he knew Otis worked on Hip-Hoppers automobiles.

Pone slowed when he saw Otis auto and body repair. He pulled up in front of the pale white smudged mid-sized building. Surrounded by a collage of vehicles, repaired to beyond repair. Cars good for spare parts. Pone zigzagged through the labyrinth till he got to the garage door opening like it expected him. Lucille eased inside the motor oil gasoline fumed establishment. Pone greeted Otis, a five-foot-eleven pale yellow splinter physique man. Loved to smile despite missing teeth making a Jock-O-Lantern handsome. Black hair the color of motor oil slicked to his scalp under a faded blue ball cap.

His grease stained tan jump-suit wore him instead of him wearing it.

The man worked on his third wife, Peggy. She matched him in height, burnt tan complexion, and all her teeth. She donned long dark dresses looking like a nun; Otis boasted she knew what to in bed which made Pone frown. Long black silver stranded hair; she sported in a tight bun like a librarian that suited her high cheekbone long face and beak-like nose supported her eye-glasses. Both in their mid-fifties. Peggy didn't like Pone, she sucked her teeth, shook her head, and turn up her nose. She stood in the side door-way then strolled back inside her hole. Pone acknowledge Otis with a hand-shake and half-hug.

"She hates me," said Pone.

Otis flashed a toothless grin. "No man, she doesn't trust you." Pone nodded. "Is everything ready?"

Otis pointed to a tarp near the far end wall. "Who you plan on taking out?"

"I got into a drive by."

Otis ran over to Lucille. "Is she scratched…dented… window cracked?"

"You are a credit to your profession."

Otis studied Pone. "Who you going to kill?"

"You judging me?"

Otis leaned on Lucille. "If you want people who ain't got no business to judge then go to the laundries."

"What do you mean?"

"My dryer put me down and for two months, I was among the common folks. Riffraff, ragamuffin, down-trodden, and damn if I know skid row young and old is what you find at the laundries. I went in that place casual dress wearing my Nike, cargo shorts, and a loose fitting white polo shirt." Pone nodded. "Okay?"

"I was sitting at a table watching my clothes dry and reading a book near this couple. They had a little boy… any-way, the man asked the woman if she had spoken to her dad. Her whole body exhaled and she forced out a hadn't gotten around to it yet, which meant they needed money."

Pone shrugged. "Okay?"

"Their clothes dried and they went to another table to fold them. A bald headed neanderthal called me a teenager, and the bitch had the nerve to say I know right with her trifling ass man in agreement. I got my clothes and walked out with a few judging eyes…one guy bald and silver beard dressed in some brown short jump-suit had his judging eyes on me. After that, I took my hard earned cash and bought me a dryer."

"Was Peggy too busy to take care of the laundry?" asked Pone.

Otis exhaled. "I'm whipped. Damn I love that woman."

Pone smiled and shook his head. Despite Otis features: dental work, and dealing with the public every day proved him human.

"You worked on a late model white Crown Victoria?" asked Pone.

From the east and west side of Metro City, people knew if they wanted their jalopy to run like a new you took it to Otis. He took off his cap and scratched his head. "Yeah. Some boys with a lot of cash wanted their car souped up…no Pone, no. They boys."

"They became men when they tried to take me out."

"But they didn't, you can let them go."

"You know they will try to make a name." Pone shook his head. "Not off of me."

"No man," Otis held up his hands as if being robbed. "Young fools who want to dash for cash. All that damn rock did was bring back the nineteen thirties style ofliving. Where's the zombie apocalypse when you need it?"

"Otis… ?"

"Okay maybe not the zombie shit, but call the blue jeans or something."

"Cops don't like me and you know the gangster's credo."

"Yeah, no second chances. But they boys. Pone…"

"An eight-year-old homeless boy died because of that drive by."

Otis slid down ending up on Lucille's bumper. "Guess this happens when your mama don't raise right. Check out the old King and Queen club on Brevard off of West Trade."

"No longer in business."

"Makes a nice hide-out for wannabe thugs."

"You think Lu…"

Otis jumped up like his ass was on fire. "No! I don't care for his way of living, but he doesn't fuck with boys."

"Relax…take it easy. You got what I need to go stealth?"

Otis motioned toward two small tarps. Pone strode over, lifted the covers and found two 2008 diminutive black vehicles. A Toyota Yaris and a Crossfire. Pone liked the Crossfire but knew he needed to go under the radar, so he chose the Yaris.

Pone looked at Lucille. "Leaving her in your care."

"It ain't the first time."

"I'll take the Yaris, but keep the Crossfire for something later."

11:30 p.m. Pone got closer to his destination. In his head he heard the slow, sad sound of a Saxophone. To make matters worse, the night joined by rain.

A downpour putting a damper on any plans for a good night out on the town. Pone planned to dampen his assailants evening; he had retribution on his mind.

The atmosphere dark and gloomy to his liking; decked out in black from his water proof bowler hat to his Doc Martens. Sally accompanied him in the front seat and two gas cans in the back seat.

The rain came down faster, hard, and furious and so would tears from the women who spawned the demons. Before he reached his terminus ad quem. Sitting high inside Lucille made him feel like a king on his throne. Pone enjoyed the Yaris. Compact, easy to turn, good on gas, and the look of boring to keep a low profile.

He liked the Crossfire; the roadster would come in handy down the road. He told Otis to keep it on ice. He approached Brevard. Things on the west side nothing like its cousin the east. The north and south of Metro immaculate, and the east close. The west-side, ghetto, projects, and slums; the black side of town with a sprinkle of Hispanics and whites considered trash.

Once Pone got on Brevard, he moved at a snail's pace studying the abandoned building until he spotted the now defunct King and Queen club. It sat across from the forsaken transit. A new transit built on the south side because too much youth gang activity concerned patrons who depended on public transportation.

The Greyhound station though remained on West Trade street.

Pone gave memory lane a rest and concentrate on the task at hand. He dimmed the lights and used what little streetlight to continue his journey. Despite the deluge he heard loud gangster rap music booming profanity and disrespectful lyrics about women.

He shook his head. The days of Run DMC, Sugar Hill Gang, Curtis Blow, and Grand Master Flash ancient. The rain didn't let up; Pone eased the Yaris into the old transit. The storm his ally; no sentry on duty.

The youths argued who would stand guard, and they all rebutted. Pone figured the dim light and music powered by a portable generator within the ruin.

Pone got out of the Yaris with Sally in hand and made his way to the door of the hideout. The music came from the back of the club. A simple nudge and the door opened. The mistakes of youth thinking they will be young and live forever. Not true for those living the gangster life.

The door eased back shut, the club small, but enough space for two restrooms and an office on the side walls. Girls giggling, guys laughing, and music booming. A party.

Under a small door light joined the laughter and giggles. Pone made his way past a few tables and a square bar. Pone stood up to the door.

Bottles clanked, the cackle louder, and the names of Ray-Ray, and Pookie from female voices.

Pone took a deep breath. He already detached Sally's butt to get could get a better grip on her. The sound of the sax gone. Only the cloudburst on the rooftop in his ears. He studied the door; it opened inward. The generator tube kept the door cracked; a lowered shoulder force opened the door, and a little breeze blew white powder off a coffee table. All eight froze when they saw the Grim Reaper enter their little club-house. Pone scanned the office. All looked late teens and mid-twenties. High metabolism bodies to eat anything and not gain a pound.

Oh to be young again. In front of a small square beige desk an even smaller round sunburn table supported a cocaine habit. On a footstool sat a bandaged thigh young thug with a look of being spaced out. The affliction needed attention, but because of their lifestyle the hospital reported gun shout wounds to the police.

He had his hoochie on her knees looking as confused as he did.

Behind the desk, a guy looking like the leader of the misfits sat with his girl straddled on his lap. The right side of the desk enough room for two small khaki colored chairs supporting the other two thugs and their honeys resting on their privates.

Gun-shot wound drove the Crown Vic. He used the coke to ease the pain. He wore a white tank T-shirt, baggy black jeans hanging on his knees exposing gray boxer briefs. Bald and a gold tooth in his grinders. His petite shorty sported a cheap yarn looking weave, big ass lips, the body of a first grader, and bug eyes wide with fear. The gal behind the desk pretty and developed.

Hair cut short with one bang hanging over her left eye. Her man looked to use her as a shield. He wore a red hoodie. The two gangsters on the right had red and black T-shirts, baggy black jeans, and white sneakers. Close haircut for one and the other a tall rectangle high top fade. Their girls, twin sisters wearing red and blue body-hugging dresses showing youthful curves. Stiletto pumps, and shoulder length weaves. All the gals wore cloth leaving nothing to the imagination. Shame on the parents for letting them sneak out in such attire. The twins pulled down their dresses as if they had something to hide. Pone relieved they stopped pulling in fear they'd pull the dresses off revealing their assets. The guns all Glock and on the desk.

Only the desk jockey in arms-length to reach them; his girl would have to dismount for him to do so.

"You girls want to live, then you better get your asses out of here!" said Pone.

An emergency exit door stood on the left wall. The girls wanted to live.

One twin slipped. Pone heard the other say, "You better get yo ass up 'cause that fool means business."

Pone thought a fool he maybe, but not like these fools about to meet their maker. Coming after a seasoned pro and killing a child.

"As for you sons of bitches…say your prayers," said Pone.

Sally sang. Coke head got it first, his melon exploded. Thanks to the cocaine, he didn't feel a thing. Hoodie got it next rising behind the desk and making a play for his gun. His body jerked like a puppet with incontinent strings. He went down with a thud. Baldy made his move toward the guns and Sally slammed him against the wall. He slid down it leaving a crimson smear. The last gangster wannabe stood glued to the wall frozen with fear. He looked like the youngest of the foursome. Mouth opened revealing buck-teeth, eyes welling up, he shook his head as if to say please don't; a rule in the killing profession, take no prisoner. You let any-one live and like a ghost they could come back to haunt you. Pone adjusted Sally for a single head shot.

Bucky slumped to the floor. Sally's mouth smoking hot after her performance, no standing ovations.

Pone emptied the gas cans and grabbed a lighter on the desk near the guns. Flicked the lighter and tossed it among the gasoline soaked bodies.

Pone made his way back to the Yaris. The building rumbled when the generator exploded. Pone looked around; alone in the violent rain. It would be a while before the authorities arrive as violence on the west side an afterthought.

Pone conscience came into play, he had allowed a man a second chance; so far it didn't come back to haunt him and because an innocent life connected to his adversary became a fatality; the man sobbed.

Pone decided enough pain for one night and let the man live.

Tonight would differ from any other because for the first time Pone took young lives and he didn't like it. A price to pay for living a gangsters' life and it cost them.

Five

"Here you go, sweetie," said Lorna.

She handed Pone a cup of coffee. He took a long sip and the ambrosia with the right amount of French vanilla cream met his approval. 10 a.m. and Pone conversed on the east side with his contact Lorna. He didn't get much sleep after his business on Brevard. Not because he felt guilty, oscitancy refused to be a friend.

"Is that better sweetie?" asked Lorna.

"Just what the doctor ordered," said Pone.

Lorna called him sweetie ever since she found out he took care of the man who murdered her dear friend Sheila Green. Lorna didn't approve of his lifestyle; she said even angels kill. She thought so much of Pone, she bought a small ranch house on the outskirts of the east side because of dealings with the prohibitions.

A comfortable ranch house nice with a white picket fence and a small garage housing a 1950 Chevy Bell-air she no longer drove. A retired accountant; Lorna did income tax and notary work on the side. She once handled Macone's books and her nephew Martin Boysenberry worked as his lieutenant.

Pone got cozy on the antique furniture; a matching white sofa and recliner with flower patterns, varnished oak coffee table, and stands for her pink oval shaped lamps all encased in a sunflower-colored room. "How are your investments, sweetie?"

Pone sipped his coffee. "They're fine... I get a dividend from Forward Air." Pone took advice from Lorna on investments despite having little time to keep track of them.

"You look tired," she said.

"No rest for the weary," He sighed. "Did you do what I ask?"

"Sweetie, as soon as you told me about those poor children and trying to keep those families from going to war I hopped on it." She nodded and flashed her pearly whites.

Lorna and Sheila were college roommates and stayed close ever since, they attended church every Sunday together and afterwards always had tea-time to talk about those days until her death. "He wants to get who did this awful thing," said Lorna.

Pone took a long sip of coffee. "I'm assign to the case and to keep peace between the Probonos and Hip-Hoppers."

Lorna shook her head. "Where do they come up with these names? Probonos and Hip-Hoppers."

"Just an identity for the two crime families," said Pone.

Lorna rocked back on the sofa and nodded. "Right… right," She pursed her lips. "Now is that slang because I still can't get around that?"

"Yes and no," responded Pone.

"Sheila would be so proud of you," smiled Lorna. "A detective?"

Pone rubbed his forehead. "I'm not a detective."

"Private-eye?"

"Troubleshooter."

"What's the difference?"

"My job is to stop trouble before it begins or gets worse."

"Two dead children…" remarked Lorna.

"To make sure things don't get worse." Pone snorted. He told Lorna about his job; he guessed fading memory a sign of old age.

"Don't do that," said Lorna.

"What?"

"I'm old, but I know why you're hated on the east and west side of this city. I'm glad you're more legit now."

"I meant no disrespect." Pone finished his coffee. "So, you did what I ask?"

"Marty will be at your junction."

They held hands as if to say a prayer. She pulled Pone toward her.

"Oh, sweetie," She gave him a hug and kiss on the cheek. "Shelia would be so proud." She studied Pone's face. "Is something bothering you sweetie?"

"How are you at dinner parties?"

"Oh sweetie," She batted her eyes. "I'm sure you could get some…"

"It's an annual dinner at the Brigands."

Elbows and knees cracked. Lorna made it to her feet gazing in Pone's eyes. Looking into them made her wish for younger days. Brown and blue retinas; clear iris; not cloudy, yellow, or red. Beautiful eyes and a beautiful man more than half her age. Wisdom told her about Pone's arrangement with the Brigands and she didn't like it. She found retirement boring and hated sitting around the house watching game shows. Lorna never explained why she worked with Macone handling his financial books, but stayed out of his personal business. Her nephew engaged the crime game. Not what she wanted for her sister's son, but he an adult made a bad decision she thought. Selling his soul. Lorna knew the rules of being a mobster.

Macone may not be the devil, but like any crime boss she knew crossing him would be cement shoes and swimming with the fishes. She'd hoped he'd take her path to make a lot of money as a bookkeeper and avoid the treacherous world of organized crime.

No such luck. A grown man now making his own decision without her approval. Lorna did the same for Marty's affairs as she did Macone's ; see no evil, hear no evil, and speak no evil. "Casual or formal?" she asked.

Pone sat in the Yaris and inhaled. He looked to the heavens. As he eased out of the drive-way, he thought about Shelia Green. He disagreed with Lorna. She would not be proud of him because he was not proud.

Six

Pone made it back to the heart of the city; he needed to make one more stop before heading home. City traffic greeted him. While stuck in the jam, he studied the citizens.

The good, the bad, and the ugly; those who looked of doing well and those catching hell. Homeless people decorated the transit leaning against walls and sleeping on benches. The gridlock made progress;

Pone let down the window to allow cool air to calm the heat in the car.

He regretted it after he inhaled a strong stench of urine and feces. The window flew back up; he turned off the heater. Pone shook his head and wondered with all the money city made with four professional sports franchises, parades, minority festivals, and events, you would think they could set up Porta Jon's for the homeless.

But the world does not revolve around people caring for one another unless something is given back. The congestion moved at a snail pace, and Pone's attention turned to the working class. Blue and white collar, hard hats, and suits you take your pick of description of who you wanted to talk about.

Pone smiled thinking if they played a pickup game of basketball, who would be shirts and skins? Like democrats and republicans arguing who's the better party. Pone credited the republicans for picking an elephant A stronger mascot then a donkey. Pone favored neither party and stayed independent. Electorates voted for the good, bad, ugly, tall, short, fat, skinny, rich, and poor would serve as a start of a topic for any conversation. Politicians proved their worth once they got in office.

Ignorance of society talking about other citizens.

A multitude who did the jargon believed immune to the same treatment. The populace wrong because everybody gets talk about. Pone raised an eyebrow speculating fact.

Traffic picked up and Pone cruised onto 500 West Fifth where he found his target. Five-eight and two-hundred and fifteen pounds of muscle. The man Pone considered a father figure, the love of Sheila Green's life he blamed himself for her death; Wisdom Jones.

A former cold-bloodied killer now working as a retired parking enforcement agent. Pone put the Yaris in violation parking in a taxi zone. A parking wasteland the taxis never used. Parking sometimes limited and the city made money off violators. Posted banners made it clear spaces for taxis. Square white signs on poles and yellow stickers on meters reading taxis only; Patrons parked anyway. Five cars in violation including the Yaris.

A middle-aged couple walked by eyeballing Wisdom as he made his way down the line. No confrontations like the staged parking war shows. He made it to the Yaris.

Gave it a stern look and inhaled. Pone got out of the car.

Wisdom laughed. "Boy. Lucille at the junk-yard?"

"I'll mention that to Otis."

"So she is at the junkyard." Wisdom studied the Yaris and frowned. "You had a job?"

"No, old man, just needed to be discreet."

Wisdom put his citation phone in its holder like a gunslinger putting his gun in a holster. He looked at Pone. "Here for advice."

"Too late for that don't you think?" remarked Pone.

"You wouldn't listen anyway," Wisdom exhaled. "That early morning drive-by incident I read about in the paper, it involved you?"

Pone peered toward the sky.

Wisdom nodded. "Wished you'd come to me before you did what you done."

"Wouldn't change anything old man." Pone snorted. "Had to be done."

"Did it?" questioned Wisdom.

"They would've tried again," said Pone staring in Wisdom's eyes. "You know how the game's played."

"Too well," replied Wisdom. "Any idea who put them up to it?"

"Hoping you heard something."

Wisdom smiled. "So…you didn't come to me for advice, but information."

"If you got it," said Pone.

Wisdom swallowed hard. "Like you said out of the game. Not my decision, but out just the same. You know how our world works: you get answers from bars, the homeless, shoe shiners…"

Pone laughed. Shoe shining a forgotten trade. He knew a barber shop inside a corporate building on South Tryon and an old man who shined shoes for the suits waiting to get their hair cut.

"I know right. Not many of them around anymore?" Wisdom folded his arms. "Surprised Otis didn't spill."

"Tried to talk me out it," said Pone.

"Good man and on top of things," muttered Wisdom. "Just wound up too tight with that crew. Don't rattle his cage. Handy when you need wheels."

"Tell me about it," said Pone.

"Don't do bars, I prefer drinking alone. Give a dollar or spare change to the homeless when I can and you the only one I talk to that's still in the game." Because we're family, thought Pone.

"And you stop calling me old man and that's not going to happen, huh?"

"You can cross your fingers," remarked Pone.

Wisdom shook his head. "Got to sneak in a joke don't you?"

Pone shrugged. "A reflex."

Wisdom knew when Pone called him old man meant he'd done something bad.

Wisdom raised Pone, Birdie, and Jade, and despite all the other kids in home Sheila Green took care of, for some reason the three of them got his attention. Pone never asked Wisdom why out of all the children at the orphanage he felt dedicated to them. Even when they found out what he did for a living no questions asked, they accepted it.

When Sheila took a bullet meant for Wisdom, things went south between him and the girls; Pone knew how much Sheila loved Wisdom and realized love can be blind; Sheila made her choice being with Wisdom even though she knew he lived a dangerous life.

She became a victim.

Birdie and Jade still spoke to Wisdom, but the daughter and father tone disappeared. He didn't fault them because he shouldered responsibility for Sheila's death. Wisdom took on several jobs afterwards almost causing him his own life.

A sloppy killer does more harm than good to himself and J. Paul respected him enough to retired his stud an unappreciative life of a parking enforcer which some people disrespect calling them meter maids.

Wisdom took the humbling job because he could no longer focus after the death of the love of his life, and he had his fill of killing.

"Yaris is a good small car," said Wisdom. Parking enforcement drove a white Toyota Yaris; unlike the wild west cowboys wearing white hats which meant good and black hats bad, the public saw the little white cars with parking enforcement etched on the hood and side door as public enemy number one. "You know the old saying, don't let your eyes get too big for your stomach," said Wisdom.

"Only if you've gone for seconds and can't clean your plate."

"I heard what's going down this weekend."

"The get together Sunday at Nadine."

"Sunday is sacred, but why Nadine?" asked Wisdom. "It's like a church for gangsters."

"This ain't no time for jokes, boy."

"You see me laughing? The truth old man."

Wisdom shook his head. "Don't know why that girl cater to lowlife and thugs."

Wisdom referred to Birdie as that girl out of anger and thought she could do better for herself. He called Jade baby girl and her eyes sparkled.

Wisdom wanted none of them to be near the gangster life and yet Birdie college educated and all housing cold-bloodied killers every night. He didn't mind her naming the club to honor Shelia using her middle name; he compared being around killers everyday like playing Russian roulette.

"Hey, you know I'm kind of in the same profession."

"And I hate it."

Pone studied Wisdom. He couldn't put a finger on it, but something didn't seem right though for a fifty-eight-year-old he still had an athletic built. Wisdom exercised, watched what he ate, and drank a lot of water.

A flat stomach, and firm physique even the young ladies admired. Wisdom rubbed the small of his back. Pone asked what was wrong when a voice from a passing car shouted, "GET A REAL JOB YOU OLD ASS HOLE!"

Wisdom responded back. "Tell that to your mama!"

Pone nodded and smiled. He leaned on the Yaris. "She's a grown woman and the way her men pat you down makes you feel probed. No need for a Prostate exam."

"I promised Shelia I'd keep you kids away from that type of life."

Wisdom eyes welled up. "I failed, and that's why she's dead."

"You need to stop blaming yourself."

Wisdom snorted. "How's baby girl?"

Wisdom saying baby girl lighten the mood since he knew Jade liked it when he called her that.

"About to graduate with honors and attend grad school," said Pone adverting Wisdom's eyes.

"What do you mean?" asked Wisdom. Reflexes dead; he knew when someone tried to keep answers from him.

"She wants to be a singer like big sister."

"Oh hell no and not in that club."

"Jade's a grown woman."

Wisdom took a deep breath and stared for a moment. The few years he's worked as a parking enforcer took its toll, the daily verbal abuse weighed on him like a ton of bricks on his shoulders standing in quicksand sinking lower and lower each day. Jade getting her degree and staying away from the gangster life gave him hope. And now hearing she wanted to follow her sister's foot-steps in the club drained him.

"Are you at least trying to discourage her?"

Pone shrugged. "Sure I'll have a few words with Jade, but she might listen to you if you spoke to her."

"Only after you talk to her first."

"Consider it done."

Wisdom shook his head. "You and Claire got degrees and they're collecting dust."

"She's putting her business degree to use," said Pone.

"No degrees for killing people," remarked Wisdom.

"Well, doctors, maybe not on purpose and judges putting people on death row."

"Don't be a smart ass, boy." Wisdom pursed his lips. "Troubleshooter..."

"Better than being a hired killer."

"Red's an angel. It's them damn siblings I'm concerned about."

"My connection to Red gives me immunity."

"A prisoner just like me."

"What are you talking about, old man? You're retired and working for the city."

"Shit. Dealing with these crazy ass people crying over a twenty-five dollar citations.

Too dumb to know it got nothing to do with their driver's license or car insurance. Telling you about your background and if they knew mine they'd shit in their pants. Got the nerve to tell you how much money you make that you got a GED…shit."

Pone felt Wisdom's frustration, the gangster life nothing glamorous.

To retire from the profession meant dying or being under the thumb. Wisdom chose the thumb of the Brigand Band. J. Paul dead and gone, but merciful for not killing past their prime killers; he gave them an option. Death or a job where they could keep an eye on you and that meant working for the city. Many tried to leave Metro, but failed in the process. Wisdom a killer; you make a living killing people does not mean you want to die.

A moment of silence between the two men, Pone thought of Wisdom's wisdom, no pun intended, he thought to himself.

Wisdom left the Army as a corporal. He told Pone not to go into the military unless he had to because all that crap about being all you can be is they want you to be nothing but a dog of the military. Pone once heard a homeless man bragging about his days in the Marine Corps. The military like college offered you an opportunity, but no guaranteed success. The military gave Wisdom the talent and skill to kill; he passed it on to Pone. Wisdom hated himself for it.

"Was the world a better place?" asked Pone.

"I ain't going to lie, before that damn rock passed by, the world was still violent, and people were doing what they always do."

Wisdom pursed his lips. "Combination of the past and present has made life interesting."

Pone shrugged. "Good thing we have the science nerds to simplify things."

Wisdom stretched. "Time to get back to pissing people off." He paused. "Look it's been awhile, but how about coming over for dinner tonight and talk? I'll make your favorites."

Wisdom a talented cook, he learned because an old girlfriend before he met Sheila wanted to hang out with her sisters instead of cooking him dinner.

She told him he was a grown man. Wisdom took it to heart and taught himself to be a wizard in the kitchen. He cooked so well he kicked his old girlfriend to the curb.

He'd joke that if a man can cook and clean, then a woman had better watch out.

Wisdom's specialties were Shepherd's pie and goulash Pone's favorites when he was a kid. "You trying to top the Brigands?" questioned Pone.

Wisdom grunted shaking his head. "Forgot about that shit. Why is it so important for you attend those damn dinners?"

"A man has to eat," said Pone.

"I never had to do that shit."

"You never threatened to leave the family." Wisdom frowned. "They make fun of you?"

"I can take care of myself."

"We on or what"

Pone nodded. "Between the usual time of eight and nine o'clock. Better get home and try counting steam," Pone studied Wisdom. "Spit it out, old man."

"The other night on the west side…had to do it?"

"They came after me and killed a kid. No second chances. You taught me that."

Wisdom nodded and went back to writing citations. Pone got inside the Yaris and eased on down the road.

Wisdom lived in a modest light green two story home. The house didn't have a white picket fence, but a varnish tall wooden fence kept things private in the back yard. The front open to the public, but the rear said mind your business.

Front and backyards looked like a Mister Rogers neighborhood. Lawns cut concise, trimmed hedges, one oak tree in the middle of the facade and there in the rear two rose bushes enhanced the landscape during the limited spring and summer.

The neighborhood knew nothing about Wisdom's background and accepted him as a neighbor living a simple life.

Pone parked on the side of the street and strode up to the door. He pushed the bell then entered.

"Make yourself at home," said Wisdom from the kitchen.

It's been a while since Pone set foot in Wisdom's house. He and Wisdom would talk too much about the past. The antiquity being Shelia Green. The repartee weighed down both their hearts. Pone felt the need to stay away because neither he or Wisdom needed the forgone to be burden on their lives since no matter how much they talked about her she would not walk through that door.

Pots and pans clanged and the aroma of spices brought him back to the present. Pone smiled, it had been time since he had either of Wisdom's Shepherd's pie and goulash.

The old man made both dishes and some type vegetable to boot. Pone saw the table set for three. He would wait until time to eat to ask or see the dinner guest.

He strolled around the room looking at pictures of himself, Birdie, and Jade as kids. Pictures of Sheila Green by herself both young and old and two pictures she took with Wisdom. They looked so young and happy. Other photos decorated the cream color walls: Wisdom's siblings and parents in dramatic black and white.

He didn't talk much; as part of a killers code you separate yourself from loved ones to protect them.

His parents dead, but as far as his siblings Pone didn't know. Pone shook his head about the lifestyle of making blood money. Nine to five jobs no thank you; at least you had a better chance of living to see another day. Most jobs have perks, but who would considered killing people a profession. You made more money than some people see in a life-time. Pone never felt good about taking out perpetrators who deserve to die. People good, bad, and ugly, it didn't matter because killing fell under the Bible as a sin. Pone committed a lot of sins and heaven wouldn't be rolling out the red carpet for him. The only comfort in his soul he worked for Red as her personal troubleshooter.

The doorbell rang, and Pone felt relieved when he heard it. Now he'd meet the mystery dinner guest. Pone opened the door.

"Hey, Chub…" said Birdie. Her surprised expression rivaled his own.

She stepped inside taking off her tan jacket and wore a red blouse underneath, skinny leg blue jean, and brown slip on loafers. She wore her hair pulled back leaving a tail between her shoulder blades. Pone recognized her smile, which ended up with a question.

Pone glanced back at the table. "So you're the extra mouth."

Birdie gave him a playful slap on his jaw. "Always had a way with words. When did he invite you?"

"A spur-of-the-moment invitation. You?"

"Likewise. You think nothing's wrong do you?"

Pone shrugged. "We use to do this a lot."

"It's been awhile, Chub."

Pone nodded. They all kept busy, he running around town for Red responding to her every call, Birdie managing her club, and keeping Tony in the loop, and Wisdom dealing with a humbling life as a working class civilian working an unappreciative job being insulted daily. They used to get together for dinner a lot before Shelia died. After her death, the feast gathering faded like the smell of a new car.

It became an afterthought. Wisdom broke the cycle and both Pone and Birdie shared a dubious look.

Wisdom sprung from the kitchen carrying a bowl of steaming greens. "What you two standing around looking like you lost something? Sit on down before the food gets cold."

Food covered the mahogany rectangle table. Wisdom went with his famous Shepherd's pie and later said because the macaroni to make the goulash would have been too much starch, both Birdie and Pone didn't mind the choice Wisdom made, they tore into the Shepherd's pie. The creamy buttery mashed potatoes with sharp cheddar cheese baked into it covered the ground chicken, sweet peas, corn, carrots, and onions sautéed in butter. Two steaming bowls featured green beans and collard greens with diced red onions on top. A pitcher of both water and sweet Lipton iced tea to wash down every morsel. Wisdom's desert Apple Crumble topped off the meal with a scoop of vanilla ice cream. All three ended up rubbing their stomachs. Wisdom cleared the table with Birdie's help while Pone sat at the table manipulating a tooth-pick in his mouth.

Wisdom and Birdie joined Pone back at the table. Pone gave Birdie a look. "Wisdom thank you for a delicious meal," said Birdie.

Wisdom cleared his throat. "How's baby girl doing?" Pone exhaled. "I already told you."

"She will make us proud. Even thinking about going to grad school," said Birdie.

Wisdom nodded. "That's what I'm talking about, instead of singing at that club."

Birdie straightened in her chair. "What do you mean that club?"

"I worry about the company you keep. You're sitting on a powder keg with the who's who rogue's gallery."

"That company I keep as you so put it has made me very successful and nobody gets inside without a thorough body search." Birdie rested her arms on the table. "Get caught packing and you're banned for life."

"You got a college degree, you should marry and start a family of your own. Tony is a good man…"

"Should've known something was behind this dinner, but I wanted to give you the benefit of a doubt. I'm a grown woman and so far I'm doing a damn good job living my life how I want, the way I want and need none advice from you."

"You got to think about the future." Wisdom shook his head. "I'm proud of you. Don't make the mistake of waiting on something too long and then when you want it, it's gone. Tony going to tire of hanging around and find somebody else."

Wisdom drank water. "I'm sure he's had enough of the criminal element."

Birdie laughed. "What do you want me to do? Tell them oh no you've killed too many people and your kind i s not welcome here. You know how many establishments in this city or any other place that are not aware they are entertaining killers?"

"But you do, and you keep on doing it."

"It's a successful business, its legal," said Pone.

You got a lot of nerve, thought Pone. He wanted to tell his mentor they didn't need his opinion on how he and Birdie lived their adult lives. "And you…" Wisdom shook his head. "You still killing people."

Birdie sat back and folded her arms then stretched her eyes nodding to Pone. A tag team wrestling match. His turn to enter the ring.

"You know my situation," responded Pone.

"Talk to Red. She understands…have her find you something else."

"Do I look like a pencil pusher? I'm not a desk jockey. There's no white picket fence fantasy. Besides, did it ever occur to you I like what I do?"

"Yeah, yeah…a damn troubleshooter."

Pone stood taking the tooth-pick out of his mouth. He snapped it between his fingers tossing it across the room. "I sure as hell don't plan on being a valet to the city."

Wisdom inhaled. "You're still young enough to put your degree to work." Birdie rose from her seat. "Let's…"

Pone held up his hand to silence Birdie. He glared at Wisdom. "Yeah, I got the face for news anchor of the year, but I got where I am because I had to man up."

"Chubby, don't," said Birdie.

Wisdom stood face to face with Pone. "Say it, you've waited seven years. Hell, I blame myself every day, but you go on ahead and get it off your chest, boy."

"I was a boy who had to do a man's job because you weren't man enough to…"

Pone could have stopped the punch. Old age slowed Wisdom. Pone figured he'd give him a freebie since he deflated the old man's ego bringing up Sheila's death.

The room went silent. Pone nodded and headed for the door. Birdie sat in her chair looking toward the floor.

Pone walked outside, he stood on the step inhaling the cold air to clear his head. Then made a beeline to Lucille. Before he could take another step, a father's voice stopped him in his tracks.

"Chubby," said Wisdom.

Out of respect, Pone turned and faced Wisdom.

"Did you invite us here to criticize our life choices?" asked Pone.

"That wasn't the plan. It's been a long time, and I got sentimental, so sue me."

Pone smiled. "Remember that fable you told me when I was a boy?"

Wisdom snorted. "You said it was your favorite."

"It made sense. I was trying to be friends with that asshole."

Wisdom nodded. "Mervin Roomer."

"No matter what I did to be nice he'd still pick a fight with me, and you sat me down to explain why he and some people do the things they do."

Pone glanced around the yard highlighted by the moonlight. "You said the scorpion was the star, and the costars were sometimes a turtle, otter, beaver, frog, and a snake."

Wisdom folded his arms to keep warm. "And your favorite costar?"

"The Beaver."

Wisdom and Pone laughed.

"You paired the scorpion with the turtle," said Pone.

"Only because you use to be in a shell when you were younger."

"Yeah. You broke me out of it. Anyway, you said the scorpion wanted to get across the river, but couldn't swim. A turtle came by, asked him for a ride across the river. The turtle said no because he feared the scorpion would sting him half way across. The scorpion laughed and said that would be absurd since they'd both drown. The turtle nodded thinking the scorpion wouldn't be crazy enough to put his own life in danger, so he agreed to give him a ride across the river. As the scorpion sat on the turtle's back, sure enough half way across the river, he stung him. As the turtle and scorpion sink beneath the water, the turtle asked him why he'd done such a foolish thing and the scorpion said, It's my nature."

Wisdom shook his head. "You are not…"

"Killing those boys made me the scorpion. I'll see you around old man. No more dinners, okay?"

Wisdom walked back inside to the warmth of his house. Birdie placed a gentle hand on his shoulder.

"What did you do?" She asked.

"I said goodbye."

Seven

"Everything all right, sweetie?" asked Lorna.

Out of the frying pan into the fire, thought Pone. Back to back dinners and the one Wisdom threw together a hard one to swallow. Like trying to hit a Wifle ball. Pone tried piecing together what was Wisdom doing telling he and Birdie about their lifestyles. He must have had a point, but what? Did he think going after the both of them would level the playing field? It didn't work ending up with Wisdom giving him a right cross after an ill-advised remark about Shelia.

Pone didn't need the moon-eye look and frown Birdie gave him to know his wisecrack crossed the line. A low blow he traded for a blow to his jaw. For now Wisdom's dinner a thing of the past. Time to focus on the Brigands.

"A beautiful woman under my arm; what could be better," replied Pone.

Lorna giggled. "You make an old gal feel young again."

"Age ain't nothing but a number."

"Wait till you get there and you'll change that thought," said Lorna.

Killers never think about getting old. A bullet, blade, bomb, and poison don't discriminate.

Stay in the game too long after your twilight years and you will get your ticket punched.

"You trying to scare me?" asked Pone.

"Better if you have children. Marty's my favorite of all my brothers and sisters children. He's the closes I have to a son. He took to Math the way I did. If I had known he would get in this deep I would have never introduced him to Macone."

Does she know Marty's gay? Pone snorted. "He's a grown man."

"I feel like the pot calling the kettle black."

Lorna exhaled. "Sweetie your situation is different."

"Thanks to Red. I use my talents to help people and…" Pone smirked. "Hurt people who deserve it."

"You're still young. You need a woman and not that tall red head," said Lorna. "You talking about heartbreak hotel. No woman or man deserves to be kept in the dark or caught in the cross-fire when things heat up."

"If there's a way in then there's a way out."

"Go postal on the Brigand band and spare Red… yeah that will go over well."

Lorna placed her hand on his knee. "Do something that would put them in your debt. You're a gambler you'll know when to play that card and trump their assess."

Pone gave Lorna a moon-eye look.

"I can spit fire when I have too," she smiled.

Shelia was gone, but her dear friend Lorna gave a surrogate mother appeal. Pone didn't ask for her advice; when they talked she gave it any way knowing when he needed another point of view. Pone beamed anticipating the surprise look on the Brigands faces. Linda's expression would be priceless. Linda glaring at him trying to make him feel like a valet for the family. Red sat next to him to offset Linda though Pone didn't need her too.

Bringing Lorna the first fly in the ointment. He smiled thinking about his next guest.

"How do I look?" she asked. Gray hair dominated her black strands she wore pulled back in a bun, light blue eye-shadow, red lipstick, pearls, royal blue dress and white hosiery and heels.

"A vision," smiled Pone.

"Aren't you sweet," Lorna blushed. "Why; am I your arm candy?"

Pone pursed his lips. "I sensed you were tired of being cooped up and getting some fresh air would do you some good."

"Hogwash!" blurted Lorna.

Pone laughed. "Where did that come from?"

"They picking on you?"

"Is that what you think?"

"No. She raised you to be strong."

"Not for this," said Pone.

"Don't worry, sweetie," she touched his arm. "Am I too old to say I got your back?"

Pone winked. "Never."

"Heavens no," laughed Lorna. "A couple of old gals like us can't left the young ones have all the fun now can we?"

"I couldn't agree more?" Mary giggled and toasted her cup of tea. "So your nephew works for Macone?"

"Marty's a good boy," said Lorna.

Pone twirled his bowler watching the two old gals reminiscence about the old days. He traded his bowler for a cue stick and scanned the lounging room. It rivaled a country club for space and recreation. Sofa chairs, love seats and Lazy-boy recliners Linda glared at him and he smiled. Red informed her about his guest. The room's ambiance resembled a boys club for smoking cigars, but served as a family and friends get-together before dinner. Pone relaxed at the pool table working on his trick shots.

Pone enjoyed his moment alone. A trait he developed as a young boy being teased by the other kids about his bald head. Pone exhaled sending the cue ball crashing and breaking the triangle shape of solid and stripe colored numbered balls in every direction. He smiled thinking the cue ball symbolized his child hood; not many friends to speak of.

White, round, smooth, and conglobate like his head when he was a boy. The difference…the cue ball got to be a bully. Knocking the hell out of the other balls till he got to the king, the eight-ball. Black, smooth, glossy, and beautiful. Pone didn't get punched or kicked.

Harsh words his pain. Getting teased every day, but as time went on the words became rain drops rolling of an umbrella. Pone bend stroking his stick between his fingers holding it steady with his thumb. Ready to play bully with the white ball.

A soothing voice interrupted his private party.

"Can I play?" asked Red.

Pone inhaled wishing the other participants would not disturbed his game. He glanced around and sure enough all eyes on them. Pone played pool like he played poker. He was a natural when it came to sports and games.

Pone stood up straight supported by the cue stick. "If you don't mind losing."

Red grabbed a stick. "I might surprise you."

"You already have," remarked Pone.

"Lighten up, Pony." She sunk her first ball. A solid color. "You're supposed to mingle."

Red moved around the table getting into position sinking her second ball. "Talk about college."

"No fraternities or wild parties," said Pone.

Red frowned and sunk her third ball. "Boring."

Pone shrugged. "All about the books."

Red gave a look. "Trying to distract me?"

It's not working, thought Pone. He watched her immaculate body glide around the table sinking ball after ball.

"Did I motivate you?" asked Pone.

Red winked. "You think this is a boy's game?" She sunk another ball. "I can miss so you can keep your ego."

"No thanks." Pone looked toward the bar. "You already brought your charity work with you."

Red swallowed hard. "You'll pay for that."

She ran the table leaving one solid, the eight ball. It sat on the edge of the left corner pocket at the head of the table. The cue ball thirteen inches away with the number nine ball between them. Jump the nine-ball and hit the eight-ball making it bounce out of the pocket, hit the cue ball too hard sending it off the table or scratch having the cue ball follow the eight-ball down the hole.

Red flash a smile at Pone hitting the right bank then top bank. The cue ball rolled in a diagonal path kissing the eight-ball into the pocket.

Red exhaled. "Game." She batted her eyelashes.

"I got next," said Maxwell.

Red put her stick back on the rack. "You boys play nice." She strolled back over joining the her sisters and sister-in-law.

The miniature district attorney grabbed a cue. Pone smirked after he saw the stick taller than Maxwell.

"You break," said Maxwell. "Give you a chance to win your pride back."

Pone got moon-eye hearing the little man's trash talk. He racked the balls and got the same result he did with Red. Pone underestimated her and if he played her again he'd take her to school like she did him. He wanted to see what kind of game Maxwell had in him.

The cue ball three inches away from a solid on the edge of a side pocket. He sunk the ball. Maxwell twisted his neck, snorted using his free hand to balance himself on the table moving around it trying to find a better shot. He lined up with the cue ball for a longer shot to a corner pocket. Twisting his neck, rotating his shoulders he aimed and hit the cue ball which hit the solid sending it bouncing off the table walls towards the pile of balls holding a junction of their own scattering them and helping a couple of stripes find a hole.

"Been playing pool…billiard long?" Pone took his first shot sending a stripe to the upper corner pocket. He got ready for his next shot.

"Don't know why you're here?' said Maxwell."

"I'm family." He sunk another ball. "What? You don't see the resemblance?"

"I've dated Red four years and this is my first invite," said Maxwell.

Tonight will be a first for a lot of things, thought Pone. "Do I look like I want to be here?"

"Then why?" asked Maxwell.

Pone banked a shot off the right side of the table to the left side pocket. "I'm family."

"You said that already," remarked Maxwell.

Pone caught Red eyeing him and Maxwell. He placed a ball in a corner pocket.

Maxwell looked at Pone and exhaled. "I shouldn't be here."

"Get no argument from me," Pone strolled around the table looking for his next shot. "A man of the court around criminals."

"Sounds like blackmail," said Maxwell.

"Yeah. Pone chuckled. "I'll add that to my resume." Maxwell swallowed hard. "What Brooke and I have is real."

"Did I say anything?" questioned Pone.

"You were thinking it," said Maxwell.

"You wouldn't survive a second inside my head," smirked Pone.

"She could have her pick of anyone. Four years… nothing to blink at," said Maxwell.

"True that," said Pone. Bending over and sinking the eight-ball. "Game."

"What?" asked Maxwell. Looking at the table he saw his solid color balls, but the stripes and eight-ball gone.

Maxwell tossed his cue on the table and Pone did the same.

Before Maxwell could utter another word the Butler walked in with the last dinner guest.

"Bolden," whispered Pone.

"Is everything to your liking Mister Bolden?" asked Mary.

The police captain tried to show good manners, he frowned away the roast duck and vegetables. Bolden a meat and potatoes man eating bacon wrapped meat loaf and garlic mashed potatoes smothered in brown gravy.

Pone nodded at Mary for being a gracious host.

Bolden swallowed. "Best meatloaf, potatoes, and gravy I've ever eaten."

"Your appetite reminds me of my late husband," smiled Mary.

Linda inhaled. "He's noting like my…"

Mary cleared her throat and sipped wine. Linda straighten and smiled.

"I had the same meal at a Wolfgang Puck's cafe in California," said Pone. "Delicious." Linda inhaled cutting her eye at Pone like a hot knife through butter.

The seating arrangement at the table changed with the three unexpected dinner guest.

Linda kept her seat next to Mary the matriarch sitting at her rightful place the head of the table where J Paul once occupied. Sue moved down a seat making room for Mary's new friend Lorna. Pone didn't know if the duplicates flipped a coin deciding who would give up their seat, but Sue more ungrudging than Linda. Linda on the right and Sue on the left, but not tonight.

Pone observed the two golden gals eating like birds, raising their hands over their mouth controlling their giggles. The husbands stayed in place; Stanley the stockbroker beside Linda. And Murray the Realtor next to Sue. Both showing better table manners than the previous dinners. Food and beverage on the lips, chin, talking out of turn with chewed food in the mouth. A pinch and smack on the thigh under the table came from Linda reminding Stanley of his table manners. Sue said oh and babied Murray wiping his chin, but not tonight. The portly brothers chewed, swallowed, and wiped their own mouths and residue on their chins. Pone nodded his approval of the two men graduating from Mary's school of etiquette. Sitting next to Murray, Maxwell sipped his wine, diced his duck breast placing it on his fork with veggies escorting them into his pie-hole. He wiped the corners of his mouth. Bolden sat across the table from the DA next to Stanley. Bolden faced down in his plate using his fork to cut the meatloaf mixing it with the mashed potatoes making it look like an Army dish called shit on the shingle. He shoveled the food into his mouth chewing with his mouth closed. Bravo, thought Pone.

Red sandwiched between Maxwell and Pone as her bookends. Wiped her mouth after every bite and sip. The dwarf DA peeked around his scarlet hair goddess giving Pone the evil eye.

Jealous little fucker, thought Pone. Across the table Paul J sat beside Bolden wincing at the police captain's table manners. Angel at his side used the long model legs playing footsies with Pone's privates while nibbling on a carrot staked on her fork. Pone acknowledge her doing the same to his carrot.

"Captain Bolden, do you desire seconds?" inquired Mary.

"I believe it's his third plate," snorted Linda. She sipped her wine giving Pone a dagger look.

"Nothing wrong with a healthy appetite…kind of refreshing," said Paul J.

Pone caught an slight wink from Paul J to Bolden. The police captain straightened in his chair wiping his mouth and clearing his throat.

"If it's no bother I'd like to take some home?" Bolden looking toward Mary.

Mary smiled. "No bother at all. I'll have Rita fix you a plate to take home." Bolden nodded and smiled.

"We'll have her give it all to you." blurted Linda scrounging up her nose. "It smells. Don't know why we have red meat. It's poison."

"To annoy, you dear sister." said Paul J, toasting her.

Linda blushed. "Oh Paul."

Pone and Red shared a glance. Red tilted her head raising an eyebrow as if to say now you know why I do not live here. Pone pursed his lip, inhaled and stiffened.

"Are you all right?" asked Red.

Pone tapped his chest. "Must've been that last carrot I ate." He glanced down between his legs. A silk black hosed foot rested on his groin. Looking up and exhaling he saw a brown-eyed Angel brushing back her raven hair.

Everyone retired to the all-boys club lounge room. To honor her late husband who used the room to woo potential business partners, Mary left it with the masculine appeal. The two golden girls did a contagious yawn. Mary gave Lorna her driver to take her home after they exchanged numbers made a date to meet up sometime next week in the city for breakfast. They hugged and kissed cheek to cheek. Lorna told Pone she'd be fine with Mary's driver thanking him for the invite.

Sue escorted Mary upstairs while her other children with their spouses and date sat on the sofas drinking and chatting. Pone perched himself at the bar to observe.

"Did you enjoy yourself Mister Pone?" asked Linda. She strolled over to the bar to grab a bottle of brandy. "Don't be rude, please join us for some eau de vie."

"Cognac…so many names for a drink that takes me an hour to finish. I'll pass." Felt like someone lit a match inside him when he first tasted Brandy and he vowed never again.

Linda smiled. "Your Kryptonite?"

"That pleasure is yours," remarked Pone.

Linda batted her eyelashes. "You're not afraid of little old me?"

Pone snorted. "You're mature."

"How sweet," said Linda.

Pone swallowed hard. "I fear you more than sleeping in a bed of spiders and snakes."

"I don't know whether to slap you or be flattered," said Linda.

"I have a soft spot for feisty women," remarked Pone.

"Go on," said Linda.

Pone smiled. "I'm a man of mystery."

Linda moved in closer eye to eye with Pone leaning back against the bar sitting on his stool The awkward moment broken…

"But why murder innocent kids?" questioned Maxwell loud enough to wake the dead waving his arms like a politician making a point. Red touched his arm calming him down.

"Is this your poker face Mister Pone?" asked Linda. "I play a mean game of pool too," replied Pone. "You flatter me," said Linda.

Pone raised any eyebrow. "You want me dead."

Linda nodded. "I'm a bitch and I love it." She gazed into Pone's eyes then glanced over at Red engaged in the teen tragedy debate. "You're a valuable commodity. You served my father well."

A long inhale, rising chest, tensing body, and piercing eyes.

"Got your attention." She looked between his legs. "Well…not all of you."

"I work for Red," said Pone.

"You know too much and we just can't let you walk away." Looking over her shoulder at Red. "She needs you."

"And your death threat is to keep me at her side," snorted Pone.

"She's my baby sister and she doesn't live here. I know you'll keep her safe," said Linda.

"Baby brother doesn't live here either," said Pone.

Linda rolled her eyes. "Married with children." Giving a Cheshire cat grin. "We worry about him too."

His extracurricular activities , thought Pone . "Troubleshooter not body guard or hired hit-man." He glanced over at Maxwell. "She has her little man to watch over her."

"Anyone ever told you you have a smart mouth?" asked Linda.

Pone pursed his lips. "Get in line."

"Guess you do make a lot of enemies," said Linda "And kudos on your dinner guest."

Pone smiled. "Had to do something to liven things up."

"The Lorna woman and the captain of police," said Linda.

Pone exhaled. "Your mother made a new friend and I'm sure you'll find some use for Bolden."

Pone figured Bolden desperate for a home cooked meal and the way he devoured the meatloaf he was right. Bolden not ignorant knowing the history of the Brigand family, but came to dinner any way eating himself into a conflict of interest. Giving the Brigands if they don't already have one with the police a blind eye advantage to a minimal crime. Pone wondered if Maxwell knew dating Red and coming to a crime family function set himself up to be a pocket politician if he decided to run for a higher office.

Linda nodded. "Well played, Mister Pone."

"Games people play," remarked Pone.

Linda tilted her head. "Charming. I understand what she sees in you."

"But you still want me dead?" asked Pone.

"About that…" replied Linda.

"What's keeping you?" asked Red towering over Linda. "We're running dry."

"Being entertained by Mister Pone." Linda gave an over-the-shoulder-glance heading back to the group. Red followed giving Pone a bewildered look. He shrugged.

Pone was glad his conversation with Linda ended. Hopped off his and stool strolled over to the billiard table hoping to play solo.

"Was this a botched hit that could escalate to an all-out gang war?" questioned Maxwell. Bolden shrugged and the first to break in the bottle of brandy. "I graduated from the academy when black Halloween tore up this city." He frowned allowing the stinger to settle in his body. "Now that I'm captain I'll make damn sure that won't happen again."

"Tough task," remarked Paul J.

Bolden took another sip of his applejack. "No thanks to you."

"What's that supposed to mean?' intervened Linda.

"Put me in coach, I'm ready to play?" said Bolden. We're supposed to sit on the sidelines."

Linda crossed her legs. "You do know accepting an invite to our dinner from Mister Pone…"

"I'm sure the police is hard at work," said Red. "Captain Bolden wants to make sure no further damage comes from this."

"The important thing is finding the monster murdered this," said Angel. Sitting beside Paul J holding his hand in her lap.

"Any suspects Captain Bolden?" asked Paul J.

"No, but it smells like a mob hit," replied Bolden.

"How can you be certain?" asked Maxwell.

Bolden pursed his lips. "Gut feeling."

"Red meat will do that to you," giggled Linda swirling her brandy.

Bolden toasted. "Respect to you in your home, Mrs.… you use your married or maiden name?"

Linda straightened in her chair. Stanley rubbed her back. Pone cleared his throat making a trick shot.

"Anything you'd like to add Mister Pone?" asked Maxwell.

"Sounds like police business to me," remarked Pone bending over the table examining his next shot.

Maxwell twisting his body to face Pone. "Nothing you can add at all? I mean you…"

An airborne cue-ball torpedoed toward Maxwell made the DA duck for cover. It hit the lower back of the sofa.

"Oops…" Pone snapped his finger. "Got to work on that." He scooped up the cue-ball like a shortstop after it ricochet back to him. "If a black man or woman waltz through that door am I supposed to know their name?"

"Keep practicing your trick shots?' said Red giving Pone a side-way look."

Maxwell straightened his tie and sat like a quiet little boy. Pone tossed the ball in the air catching and placing it on the table. He sunk a ball in the corner pocket.

"Have you spoke to the families Captain Bolden?" asked Angel.

Bolden nodded. "They were unaware of their children dating."

"Romeo and Juliet," said Paul J.

"Except they didn't commit suicide," remarked Pone.

"So you do have an opinion," said Red.

"When it counts," said Pone.

A game of deception keeping them guessing Pone played with Red. Her jealous boyfriend threw a sucker punch at Pone bringing up his past and got a cue-ball shot at his head for it Red came to her man's aid.

Paul J shook his head. "Makes your job harder if the two families weren't making a move on each other."

Bolden leaned forward. "Yeah…no secret your father laying down the law and the Prohibitions and Hip-Hoppers agreeing to the terms drawn out." He rubbed his chin. "Somebody kept a close eye to know the teens dated." Bolden looked at Linda, Paul J and Red."

"Are we suspects?" asked Red. The room got quiet.

Bolden swallowed hard. "Let's not be naive. Teens from crime families dying in a car bomb…if that's not a mob hit then I don't know what is. Everybody's a suspect until I get substantial evidence. It's just police business and part of my job."

Well said, thought Pone.

Paul J rose from the sofa. "It's getting late. I think we all had enough excitement for one night." He helped Angel to her feet and looked at Linda. "Tell mother and Sue goodnight for me and Angel."

Linda smiled. "Drive safely"

Pone stood with Bolden outside next to his 1985 black Cadillac Seville. Pone folded his arms rocking back and forth. "So if Red hadn't invited you…"

"I'd be sitting in my boxers on the couch in front of my wide-screen eating a TV dinner drinking Coors."

"You could've left out the boxers part."

"I'm a cop. A sucker for details," said Bolden. "Listen, I ain't the first po po to sit in a house of demons. Accepting Red's invite…she didn't pick her family and she's clean."

Pone nodded. Despite turning over a new leaf being a troubleshooter instead of a hired hit-man wouldn't look good for Bolden and him being chummy. Red knew him better than he knew himself. Inviting Bolden would irritate the hell out of Linda and it worked.

"See you got your doggy bag," said Pone.

A full face smile. "Going to make this last the rest of week," said Bolden.

Pone got moon-eyed. "Yeah, right."

"Who am I kidding," laughed Bolden. "Finish this shit soon as I get home."

"You can say that and still eat it?" questioned Pone.

Bolden frowned. "Stop acting squeamish. The proper folks have gone to bed."

"You had a good time, huh?" asked Pone.

"A home cook meal and ramming a stick up their tight asses… yeah." Bolden leaned in. "Is the brother a fairy?"

Pone laughed. "You're not his type."

Bolden shrugged. "Either way I ain't no faggot." He snorted. "How does he keep that gorgeous wife of his satisfied?"

"So you think the hit on the teens was a mob job?"

Bolden nodded. "Gut feeling and it ain't the red meat."

"Heard you say you spoke to the families?" asked Pone.

"Police procedure and they had no clue. Despite who they are I feel for them."

"You do know if it's gang related and they catch the culprit they won't hand him over to the police." said Pone.

Bolden knew that meant cement shoes or food for the pork. A gangster style execution.

"Whoever the scum that did this deserves to get what's coming to him." Bolden pursed his lips. "We hate paperwork."

The sound of high heels on the pavement got their attention.

"That sound gives me a hard on," said Bolden.

Pone shook his head. "Too much information."

"Squeamish," remarked Bolden.

"What are you boys talking about this time of night?" asked Red.

"Wrapping things up," said Pone.

"Thank you for a lovely dinner, Miss Brigand." Bolden gestured, got into his car and drove off.

Pone exhaled turning to Red. "Thank, you."

"Lorna looked nice," said Red. "Didn't see that one coming. My mother enjoyed her." Red smiled. "It was fun watching Linda get humbled."

Red punched Pone's arm. He rubbed it looking around. "I see the Saab still here. You tuck the little guyin?"

Red made a fist.

Pone held up his hands surrendering. "Okay. Okay."

"Why did you do that?' asked Red."

Pone glared. "He asked for it."

Red nodded. "Fair enough."

"So he is crashing here?"

"After the scare he drank more. Thought he had too much to drink."

Pone observed Red dressed in her tan trench coat and black purse on her shoulder. "You're not staying?" he asked.

Red shook her head. "If you're not married, you don't share the same room and I don't want to deal with Linda asking about our dinner guest."

She looked down at Pone's crotch. "Your boy's okay?"

He blushed. "Caught that, huh?"

"Thought her foot was glued to your groin," giggled Red.

Red knew Paul J and Angel's marriage a business arrangement . The former supermodel knew thirty a retirement age in the business and wanted to keep her hands callus free.

"Innocent flirt," said Pone.

Red nodded. "PJ's lucky to have her."

Pone gave a look. "She doesn't…"

"She supports his habit."

A faithful wife to a gay cheating husband…wow, thought Pone. "Is it okay for me to say it hurt so good I didn't understand?"

They laughed.

"Was Linda bothering you?" asked Red.

Pone snorted. "She hinted the mark of death was overrated. You all just couldn't let me walk away. She said you needed me and I'm okay with that."

"What did I interrupt between you and Bolden?"

"I'm not going to step on his toes," said Pone.

Bolden wanted to go back to the days when law enforcement struck fear in the heart of the criminal element. Pone wondered in those days ever existed.

"The more eyes the better. We're in the discrete business," said Red.

"I told him if the families get their hands on whoever did this they won't turn him over to the police."

Red checked the time on her cell-phone. "Getting late."

Pone swallowed hard. "Who knows what I used to do for J Paul?"

Red stepped to Pone. "You were a salesman."

Pone smirked. "I sold death to those who deserved it." He nodded. "My briefcase a Tommy-gun."

"Dad played it safe in case he had a rat in his stable. To make business deal he bend but didn't break. My father business not a secret but not all his employees got dirt under their nails."

"My hands aren't clean," remarked Pone.

Red inhaled. "Wisdom was his top salesman and when he retired you took his place."

"I was his… I became…"

"And now you're mine," said Red. "Not in that…"

"It's okay," said Pone. "These people in our circle bought this?"

"They have no choice."

Pone scowled. "What do you mean?"

"Everyone has skeletons in their closet, Pony."

"Crowe?"

"He works close to the mayor."

Pone shook his head. "That's why he was being so bold."

"Flexing muscles he don't have," said Red. "Trying to get under your skin."

"Still doesn't answer my question."

"Winslow is incumbent but not stupid. He and dad compromised."

Pone snorted. "I'm expendable."

"He worked hard to build his empire."

Pone nodded. He knew a lot of business ventures were approved through the Mayor's office.

Red cleared her throat. "You're a salesman for the Brigand corporation."

"Maxwell?" asked Pone.

"He's not , but jealous."

Pone sighed. "I don't want to be around people who know more about me than they should."

Red grabbed Pone by the shoulders. "Escort me home?"

Eight

A slow smokey Saxophone harmony in a dim lighted night-club; a smidgen of people lingering made the atmosphere on a late Sunday night at Nadine melancholic. The left-overs, five guys and six dames not counting Birdie and Red perched at the bar sipping their signature drinks. Birdie had her Strawberry Daiquiri and Red nursed a Long Island ice tea.

"Your sax man knows how to set the mood," said Red.

"We call him, play it again Sam," said Birdie.

Red chuckled. "Not original."

"You want authentic? Ask him to play the piano."

Red toasted Sam. "A man with many talents comes in handy."

"Including one with restraints."

Red twisted her lips then sipped her long island. She didn't have to say I didn't see that one coming. The moment Red walked inside the cabaret and spotted Birdie perched at the bar with her back to her she felt tension before sitting down next to the woman Pone called his sister. Not by blood, but raised together as siblings.

Red met Jade the younger sister, a quick smile followed by a handshake then back off to college.

Birdie greeted her with a smile: her eyes and spread lips didn't match. The glower look Red got from Birdie after meeting her; how deep are your claws inside him?

Birdie acted like a protecting older sister. Pone told her Birdie an eye-blink older, but responsible for helping him build his self-esteem.

"Thought we had our cat fight?" questioned Red.

"I lost," remarked Birdie.

Red sipped her drink. "I don't feel like a winner."

"You still got your claws in him and don't tell me he has a choice." Red smirks crossing her legs. "If he has any scratches they didn't come from me."

Birdie straightened up. "Linda… Sue… Paul J… or mommy dearest and mandatory dinners?"

"Don't talk about my mother?" said Red.

"My bad." Birdie held up her hand. "I know how precious mothers are."

Yes you do naming the club after the woman who raised you and Pony, thought Red. "You'll be happy to know he broke the restraints if he had any this year."

"I'm listening," said Birdie.

Red pursed her lips. "How much has he told you about the dinners?" Birdie shrugged. "Tasty dishes and bad table manners."

"We have a world class chef and my brothers-in-law graduated this year from mother's school of etiquette."

"How much can one man eat?' murmured Birdie.

Red batted her eyes. "Pardon?"

"We had a hard to swallow dinner before your shindig."

"Pony marveled about Wisdom's cooking," said Red.

Birdie inhaled. "It was the after dinner convention that was difficult to digest."

Red sipped her drink. "Want to talk about it?"

"He'll tell you in good time." Birdie took a drink of her Daiquiri. "What about your no restraint banquet?"

"He'll tell you in good time," replied Red.

Birdie toasted. "Touché."

"A truce?" questioned Red.

"Linda?" questioned Birdie holding up a finger.

"The oldest. Thirty minutes older than Sue."

Red snorted. "Bossy, straight-forward and Sue follows her…" She rolled her eyes. "Because she's a follower."

Birdie nodded. "Okay, Paul J?"

Red smiled. "Couldn't ask for a better big brother and a the twins are protective of him. They'll scratch your eyes out."

"They want to hurt Chub?" asked Birdie.

Red gave a look. "Who says I'm protecting him from them?"

"I don't like your arrangement."

"You sure he's not your jazzbo?" Red batted her eyes.

"You going slang, huh?" Smiled Birdie. "I ain't his boo boo, main squeeze, or tenderoni. Can you say the same?"

"I didn't hear, brother," remarked Red.

Birdie made a check mark in the air. "Is that how you see him?"

"Touché," said Red.

"Are we fencing?" questioned Birdie.

"On Guard," Red looked around the club. "Sure these guys would love seeing a cat-fight."

"In their dreams."

"I know, right?"

Birdie rested her arm on the counter. "Can't blame me for worrying."

"We both care about Pony."

"I don't have a leash on him."

"Call it what you want."

Birdie glared. "What would you call it?"

"Complicated," said Red. "How's Wisdom?"

"Decaying," Birdie swallowed hard. "He's embarrassed issuing citations and booting cars."

"We all get old," Red nursed her drink. "Just have to embrace it."

"How did your father handle it?"

Red smiled. "Grand-kids."

Paul J's eyes lit up seeing his grandchildren. Christmas was his favorite time watching them open their presents and showering him with hugs and kisses. They gave him an escape from his imperfect world.

Birdie exhaled. "Yeah…me, Jade, and Chub…ain't going to happen anytime soon or ever."

"What about you and that hot Italian?"

"Excuse me?" Birdie rolled her eyes. "Honey, I don't see a ring on your finger."

Red cleared her throat. "Career woman."

Birdie got moon-eye. "What am I, chop liver?" The ladies laughed.

"Wisdom's not bitter," said Birdie. "He wanted retirement to be more."

"Grand-kids," remarked Red.

"Nobody's knocking me up and I'm happy he's no longer ending somebody. Chub…"

Red uncrossed her legs. "I don't think he's a pencil pusher do you?"

Birdie frowned. "I don't want to say this type of life suits…"

"Nobody's born to be a killer. Animals maybe and that's for survival."

Birdie exhaled. "Like you said…"

Red nodded. "Complicated."

Birdie shook her head. "Damn code of ethics…either stay in the game," She took a gulp of her drink. "Thought your sisters and brother adore you?"

"This is business."

"Poor Chub," said Birdie.

Red giggled.

"What?" asked Birdie.

"There's not an ounce of fat on him."

"It's a play name "

"So is Pony."

Both women smiled. They had companions, but pondered the thought of Pone being more than amicable.

"Thank you," said Birdie.

"I didn't do anything," replied Red.

"He's no longer a killer-for-hire."

"He sees you as a sister," said Red.

"We're both forbidden fruit." retorted Birdie.

Red surveyed the club. "Nadine."

"Her middle name."

"Pony mentioned her. Was she special?"

"More than you know," Birdie looked at the Budweiser digital clock above the bar. "He's late."

Red touched Birdie's hand. "I worry about him too."

Lucille pulled up in the VIP parking lot section of Nadine. Pone smiled. He felt good riding in his baby. A truck man. He got out and headed to the club entrance when a colossal shadow engulfed him.

On a chilly night, a normal man would have wet his pants; Pone recognized the shadow.

"Damn Ben…you should know better."

"Sorry to bother you, but thought you forgot about me," said Ben in his baritone voice.

Pone loved the sound of Ben's voice. It reminded him of those R & B groups of the nineteen seventies. One member could swoon the hearts of women with his deep bedroom bass voice. A la Barry White.

"Look, this thing I'm doing now won't give me a lot of wiggles room, so…"

Pone pulled out a business card. A basic red line with an ink stamp name and phone number. He handed it to Ben.

Ben studied it. "Mercury Slim?"

Pone snorted. "Yeah, mention my name, tell him your situation, and he takes cash, nothing less than a thousand depending on how serious your case. Then again he might work for free."

Ben frowned. "Shit'd."

"In your case…" Pone shrugged.

"All right. Will do," said Ben.

Pone entered Nadine and scanned the sparse crowd. Greeted by two gorgeous women each taking an arm.

"I'm touched you two waited for me," said Pone.

"Shut up," said Red.

Pone glanced at Birdie.

"What she said," said Birdie.

Pone smiled and kept quiet. He knew better to argue with women. His chaperons took him for a ride on the elevator.

Pone stepped off the elevator with his two lovely escorts. The gambling room occupied by three others: Deputy Mayor Harvey Crowe, Hip-Hop lieutenant Rufus Brown, and Prohibition lieutenant

Martin Boysenberry. Crowe sat at the head of rectangular mahogany table while Brown and Boysenberry sat across from each other in a stalemate stare down. Pone, relieved the block sidebar gave them breathing room. A round table console too close for comfort. Knights of the round table, not tonight.

The dames released Pone taking their places at the table. Red sat next to the former stock broker Boysenberry. An inch under six foot, stocky build, early forties and crude oil hair slicked back looking like a Bela Lugosi Dracula in his pin striped gray suit.

Boysenberry used his degree to work with his Aunt Lorna who worked for and kept track of Macone's books. As she got older, she convinced Macone her nephew a chip off the old block and would make an excellent replacement .

Macone liked what he saw in Boysenberry, gave him more authority, and in no time the investment paid off, Macone treated Boysenberry like a son. Birdie sat next to the average height Brown, late thirties, he sported a tan suit with a pink shirt. A fade style haircut, and silver strand goatee. Brown didn't go to college, but Harvard street smart, Brown a cliche` raised by his grandmother his father's mother and once upon a time G's girlfriend. G wasn't older than Brown's grandmother, but when the two met, the rumor around town made her a primeval cougar back in the day.

His father a street hustler and not a great one; it got him killed. His mother a fast in the ass hoochie ran off with a gangster whose name not worth mentioning, he hated kids, and so she left town with him leaving Brown in the care of his grandmother.

As a favor to his grandmother, G took young Rufus under his wing and from that day on, Brown's gratitude turned into one-hundred percent true loyalty. Pone strode over to the other end of the table opposite Crowe.

"About time," said Brown.

"I know right," said Boysenberry.

Pone smiled at the two men agreeing with each other. So far a good start, thought Pone.

Red stood in her body-hugging scarlet dress, black hose, and pumps. "It's a sad occasion that brings us here tonight; we can put the mayor's office at ease about a possible gang war." Red paused. Eye-balling Brown and Boysenberry. "We don't want that to happen which is why Mister Pone is the assign investigator on this tragedy."

Pone rested his chin on his cupped hands and studied the lieutenants. Despite putting bullets in both Probonos and Hip-Hoppers, he never crossed paths with the two of them. He couldn't explain why himself, except maybe they both had nothing to do with the hits put on him. Like cats and dogs, they would never be close friends, but when they had a conversation, mutual respect came from their voices.

Boysenberry took center stage. "Mister M devastated by the news of his daughter. He read about it on the front header of the blab sheet."

Pone shook his head. Boysenberry represented using probono dialect. It sounded cool to hear him referring to the newspaper .

"We got no beef with the hoppers. Besides, they wouldn't be that brainless to kill one of their own," said Boysenberry.

Here we go, thought Pone.

Brown cleared his throat. "Same here except the brainless part. We don't make it a point targeting children to make a point," remarked Brown.

"You need to view that scene in Scar Face when Tony said I ain't killing no kids," said Boysenberry.

"You ain't Italian," said Brown.

Pone knew the importance having mediators; glad for presence of Red and Birdie. They weren't there for eye candy, but to whether the storm and both played their part well. A placed hand on the shoulder and a one handed rub on the back soothed the beast in both men.

A crooked smile came across Boysenberry's face. "Good thing we got these two broads." Red smacked the back of Boysenberry's head. "Hey, whoa! Did I say something wrong?"

Birdie swallowed hard. "If you prefer to refer to us in cant, please refrain from calling us broads, shorties, ho, hoochie, puta, skank. Skeezer, and any other disrespectful female vulgarity."

Birdie raised an eye to Brown.

Brown shrugged "I respect females, women, ladies?"

Boysenberry looked as though he needed a smoke. "Apologies to you both. Is dames okay?"

Red and Birdie nodded.

"If the dames don't mind," Pone ignored the icy glare from the femme fatale. "How did G get the news?"

"Me," said Brown. "Hit him hard."

Boysenberry grunted. "Might have too much lard in those collard greens, salty fat-back, and too much sugar in that red glass of Kool-Aid."

Brown snorted. "Must be tough eating linguine on all four."

"What's the difference between hip-hop slang and Ebonics?" asked Boysenberry.

"Gentlemen!" Pone rose from his seat. "If you two want to off each other, fine by me. Hell, I'll help you kill each other, but this is not about you. It's about two teens who lost their lives for what reason we do not know. I give you my word, I will find the culprit, but I need your cooperation, okay?"

Both men agreed.

"Before I get started, let's get one thing straight…no more surprises like the morning of last week," said Pone.

Boysenberry looked like a kid trying to figure out an algebra problem. "What are you talking about?"

"Not you," Pone gave Brown a stern look. "Somebody put a hit on me using youngsters."

"Swear from the cross it wasn't me, boss," said Brown putting his hand over his heart.

"On my grandmother's grave, Pone. On my grandmother's grave."

Pone didn't know which of brown's grandmothers bit the dust. The one G. use to drill or his mother's mother, and he didn't bother to ask. It proved to him this would be a get together with crossed fingers.

"Can't help you if I'm dead," said Pone.

"We don't send boys to do a man's job," said Boysenberry. "You have. But I'm still standing," said Brown.

Pone pursed his lips. "Helen and Reggie didn't expect to die. Like any teenager they enjoyed a Friday night at the movies. Both headed off to college and their lives cut short and here you two grown as men acting like children on this important matter. Again, I will help you two kill each other, but make up your minds because right now you're wasting my time."

"G wants closure," said Brown.

"Likewise for Mister M," said Boysenberry.

"That's all we want, gentlemen," said Red. "We need to make sure this does not escalate into a gang war."

Red made eye contact with both men.

"Nadine is where you air out your differences, bullets flying back-and-forth won't solve this," said Birdie.

"This ain't the old days," said Brown.

"We're more civilized than you give us credit for," said Boysenberry.

Crowe stood up and cleared his throat. "I assume we're all good here? Mister Pone will have parlay so he can keep havoc from running amok in the city? He is working on behalf of the mayor's office."

All eyes on the deputy mayor, but not one reflected respect. "We don't want another Black Halloween!" blurted Crowe.

"Well what do you know? The pencil neck can talk," said Boysenberry.

Crowe glared. "And none of that gibberish you two talk."

"You ain't at the state house," said Brown.

"Got balls mouthing off like that," said Boysenberry. "He has immunity," said Pone.

"Inside here," stated Boysenberry. "Free game outside," remarked Brown.

Red rose from the table. "State official." She pointed to Crowe. "Lawyer and this is my city."

Brown snorted. "Just fooling around."

"Lighten the mood," said Boysenberry. Red exhaled and sat back down.

Crowe eyed both men. "You remember Black Halloween?"

Both Brown and Boysenberry were young boys playing marbles and video games before getting involved in organized crime. Though both schooled about what took place that day in Metro City. The bloodbath and tragedy changing lives.

Brown straightened in his chair. "Times were different then."

Boysenberry looked at Red. "Your old man set the table." He adjusted his tie. "We know our place."

"Any idea who could have done this?" asked Crowe. "Because I am serious about not having another Black Halloween."

Brown glared. "No man. We don't do kids. Reggie was G's son…"

Birdie inhaled. "Don't mean it can't be from within."

Brown leaned forward. "We run a tight ship."

"Don't mean it leaks," said Pone.

Boysenberry looked at Crowe. "No clue. Insane to think a prohibition would do in Helen. She was an angel."

Brown stood. "But you could do Reggie right?"

Boysenberry pointed at Brown. "That ain't what I mean and you know it."

Pone cleared his throat. "And there you have it guys. Pointing fingers at one another. That's why we're here to try to keep this from escalating." Birdie touched Brown's arm gesturing him to sit down. Pone shook his head at both men. Brown exhaled taking his seat.

Pone leaned back folding his arms. "I believe both sides are innocent, but I need to be able to find who the guilty party is." Pone shrugged. "What's it going to be?"

Boysenberry checked his watch. "Pone, you have immunity."

"So we cool?" asked Pone.

"Straight from the fridge," said Boysenberry.

"Solid as a block of ice," said Brown.

Hip-hop and Prohibition hipster slang. Prohibitions call their slang probono instead of hipster and maybe a pot shot toward the hoppers to each his own. Pone understood Brown's and Boysenberry's lingo. Take something from the fridge long enough and it won't stay cool and a block of ice melts. After the job done, he'd have to watch his back.

After the meeting, only Pone and Brown stayed behind to talk.

They settled on stools at the bar. Neither ordered a drink. "If you didn't send those boys, then who did?" asked Pone. "That's the point, they were boys," said Brown.

"Who wanted to be men."

"Now they'll never get the chance." retorted Brown.

"Tell that to the mother of the eight-year-old boy they took out. What you call that, friendly fire?" responded Pone.

Silence took over for a few seconds. Brown stared at Pone. He knew Pone's reputation as a poker player and studied his face. He saw a killer.

"They had relatives," said Brown.

"So did that boy. His mother grieving too." Pone glared at Brown. "What if they had taken me out? Who would handle this situation between you and the Prohibitions? Somebody wants a gang war."

"Wouldn't jive you, man, we had nothing to do with that shit."

"Got that…yeah, swear from the cross boss," remarked Pone.

Brown laughed. "A Rage In Harlem. One of my favorite movies."

Old movies from back in the day on the cable movie channels; Pone didn't have as much free time as Brown.

"They were trying to impress somebody. You know you have to do something big to get in the good graces, and they had hip-hop brand," said Pone.

Brown look as though he could use a smoke or a drink; he didn't want to stick around Nadine longer than he had to. Nostrils flared, words became wood put on the fire. Pone breathed heavy.

"I promise. If somebody in my group did this…they will pay."

"Nothing worse than looking up to someone who carries a gun for a living." Brown raised an eyebrow. "You talking about the Po Po?"

"It's part of their tool box," said Pone.

"I understand where you coming from, but you crossed a line." Pone cracked his knuckle. "They tried to kill me."

"You burned the bodies, man." argued Brown.

"Sending a message." stated Pone.

"Loud and clear." Brown glared. "Those boys had mamas."

"Then they should've raised them right."

Brown let out a frustrated laugh. "They wanted one last look at their babies." Pone gave a stern look. "That's why you have pictures."

"You a cold ass brother…you know?"

"A block of ice."

"They wanted to bum rush your ass, but G's word is golden."

"Live by the sword, die by the sword." Pone leaned in. "Somebody in your click sent those boys to their graves… instead of sitting here preaching about guilt, you might try looking for that snake in the grass."

Brown swallowed hard. "Nobody will fuck with you. My word."

"As long as I'm on the job."

"Man, you got trust issues."

Pone straightened up. "Too much trust can get you kill."

Brown stuck out his hand. Pone didn't like hand-shakes with adversaries. Then again opposing athletic teams shook hands after the game and politicians; democrats and republicans before and after a heated debate. Pone indulged him. Sure enough, Brown gave a vice grip, and Pone returned one of his own.

Brown drew closer. Pone knew Brown to be a heavy smoker; he turned his head for a moment taking a deep breath. He wasn't in the mood for halitosis.

"One day a bullet will have your name on it," said Brown.

Pone pulled back and smiled. "Yeah, well, boy…when I die, I'm going to miss me."

A stare. A few seconds of silence, Then a release of hands followed by loud laughter.

Nine

Pone wasn't ready to pack it in, he joined a small crowd lingering around closing time. Pone sat at a corner table to his own thoughts listening to Sam on his sax playing a slow noir tune. Sam's body language wanted to call it a night. Barkeep wiping down the bar gave a look toward patrons to go home.

Sam and the bartender knew Pone owned stock in Nadine. He could stay pass the twilight hour plus he knew the owner. Pone pondered Wisdom's dinner. A mystery why Wisdom ambushed he and Birdie telling them how to live their lives.

The evening felt like a man trying to clear his conscience. Maybe the old man lost it. No pop in his punch, back in the day Pone knew he would've ended up on his ass seeing stars. Getting old sucked. Grandkids transitioned to the golden years worthwhile, Pone shrugged at the thought of it and the only way Wisdom could get any simulation of grand kids would be through Birdie and Jade. Pone not interested in settling down. Jade needed to concentrate on college and he didn't know if she dated or not.

What game Birdie played with Tony gave him a headache. Marriage a bad word in this family.

Wisdom and Sheila never married though they acted like a couple. So why would he expect the same from them? Pone sighed, bringing up Sheila a low blow. He knew he owed the old man an apology.

Pone held up his finger telling the guys it won't be much longer. He went back to his thoughts; laughing to himself about how the diminutive Crowe looked escorted by the statuesque Red like his personal body guard. Red dwarfed her boyfriend Thomas Maxwell the District Attorney whom didn't care much for Pone. Boysenberry long gone and Brown scanned the area before hitting the road. Pone waited to say goodbye to Birdie in her office with Tony and he didn't want to disturb them. He'd kill time until she came back inside the cabaret. Pone took out a small black pouch sounding like bells. Two Chinese exercise balls twirled in his hand to stimulate vital acupuncture points in his fingers increasing vital energy and blood circulation. The manufacturer included a disclaimer with instructions to protect them from lawsuits.

Pone whirled the balls until one escaped his grasp rolling up to the bar. Pone bent done to retrieve it; he noticed a lady's shoe revealing twig shape pointy toes. Pone looked up and saw puffed bug eyes glaring at him.

"Trying to check the engine?" Asked the bug-eyed woman. She crossed her chicken legs, almost kicking him in the face.

Pone rose to his feet. "Say what?"

"Don't play dumb. Dropping that ball, letting it roll near me so you can get a look."

Pone wanted to laugh and vomit. The woman resembled an ostrich: short hair greased back on her head like a helmet, beak nose, long turkey neck, dirty brown complexion like an Egyptian, and looked nothing like Cleopatra.

"I was picking up my ball, and that's all."

"Negro please…you trying to see what I got."

Pone shook his head. The woman looked like a human hanger wearing a dress. "If you are a woman, I already know what's under your dress. I've used it from time to time and it's not that special. Now if you'll excuse me."

Pone felt a presence behind him. He looked at the bug-eyed witch; she displayed a crooked smile. He glanced over his shoulder and saw an average height, bullish hairless man in a black shirt and charcoal suit. In a fairy tale, he would be the witch's troll.

"I go to the John to take a shit and this happens," said the troll.

Pone squeezed the balls. "Keep your business to yourself." He nodded . "I apologize for any misunderstanding."

He showed the man the Chinese balls. "I'll go back to my table and play with my balls…"

The man spun Pone around; Pone put the balls in his pocket. The man pointed his stubby finger. "You think this is funny?"

"I guess not since you're not laughing," said Pone.

"He got a smart-ass mouth," said the bug-eyed woman.

"Don't worry, baby I will change that…wait a minute… your face, I've seen it some place."

"I doubt that. It's where it is," said Pone.

"He still got jokes," said the bug-eyed woman.

By then the bartender stopped wiping and Sam stopped playing. The sparse crowd cleared out. Pone decided to do the same. He said adios to the bartender and told Sam to say bye to Birdie.

Pone didn't head straight to Lucille, instead he played the Pied Piper. He recognized the bullish man in the club. Arnold Pratt. The name itself struck no fear, Arnold not confused with Schwarzenegger, thought Pone.

Arnold a low rent hood. The guy wanted a piece of the action to build a resume`.

To get into the click: you either knock off a cop, rob a bank or take out a guy with a bug reputation. Arnold started out small with pawnshops, liquor, and convenience stores.

Five years ago, Pone met Pratt in a wrong place wrong time scenario 2 a.m. at a 7-Eleven. Pratt robbed a third-shift clerk safeguarded by the MPD. Most cops want no part of playing bodyguard for a convenience store clerk. The copper left after midnight thinking nothing would happen despite convenience stores being robbed the in thing.

Pratt already pulled off the job. He stepped outside the store and spotted Pone. He figured Pone a cop and got the jitters and fired shots.

Before Sally became his companion, Pone's best friend in those days a Smith & Wesson bodyguard 38. special (a favorite of detectives) with a wing-sight laser.

It carried six rounds. He should have adopted a Glock since it carried more , but the revolver gave him an old style gangster appeal and it made him feel cool.

Pratt fired and Pone returned in kind. Having a revolver, you count your shots and make them count because reloading in a gunfight could be a bitch.

Speed loaders. Pone didn't have one because he didn't expect to be in a gunfight.

Pone found cover in case he had to reload, but he didn't bring extra bullets. If he owned a Glock bullets would not be a problem; he heard stories of Glock guns jamming and in his profession he needed a tool he could count on. Revolver's, six shots, but reliable. Both men scrammed to safety; Pone behind Lucille and Pratt on the side of a dumpster. A store near a plant where they made pesticides and fertilizer.

Every store a sitting duck for robberies on Rozelle Ferry road the bad side of town.

The police made a few rounds in the area and why the officer made a quick departure from the store before midnight because of the troublesome neighborhood. Pone didn't fire another shot, he hoped Pratt would run out of bullets. Pratt kept firing which meant he possessed a Glock. Pone wanted a 40-ounce Polar pop and a bag of Funyuns not bullets. He hid behind Lucille for cover to keep from getting lead poisoning. Pone wanted to get away from Lucille since her body at the time didn't repel bullets.

He saw a thick round cement pillar with a light pole, but that was a no go since the light would make him an easy target. He decided Lucille had to take one for the team. Pone wished for sirens despite being on the other side of the law, but instead he heard bullets hitting

Lucille, and that made him angry. Damn. How many bullets does that gun hold? Pratt stopped firing; Pone figured he needed to reload or the damn thing jammed. Pone peeked around the front bumper and like a mouse sticking his head out of a hole Pratt leaned his head out from cover. Pone fired two shots causing sparks from the metal blinding Pratt. Things got a little more dicey when a young girl six or seven appeared on the scene. Pratt had a daughter and maybe he and his old lady divorced or the kid was a love child. in either case the cretin brought a child along on a nickel and dime hold up job.

Pone didn't notice the Chevy Lumina until he saw the girl. He wanted to tackle the kid but too late. Pratt must have seen a shadow, got startled, and shot his daughter. The lass curious about the gunshots. Curiosity killed the cat. Pratt stood over the body, his gun slipped through his fingers like melted butter. He cried like a baby holding his child.

Pone could have ended it there, a bullet to the back of the head; he pitied the man for killing his offspring. He kept his attention on the grieving man until he climbed inside Lucille and drove away. He hadn't seen Pratt until now.

Pone led Pratt to an alley fifty yards from Nadine. He kept his back to Pratt to make him believed he didn't notice him.

"You killed my little girl!"

"Been a long time. Enough time for you to realize that your daughter's blood is on your hands," said Pone.

Pratt got into a fighting stance; he impressed Pone flipping open his butterfly knife. Pratt must have hidden the knife in a secured place on his body for him to get pass the metal detectors, thought Pone.

He remembered Pratt coming back from the restroom and frowned. Pone beat the metal detectors wearing and insulated vest with paper and wood to keep his blades from being detected inside the club. Birdie would have his head if she knew.

She didn't believe in bending the rules even for him. Despite the club rules Pone took nothing for granted and would continue to get away with breaching Birdie's security by concealing his straight razor. Pone reached inside his vest and took out the razor.

He preferred it over a knife because easier to conceal. Pone trained himself to become one with the razor like a part of his body. Fighting with a knife meant extending your arm giving your opponent a chance to grab it and ending up with a broken elbow.

Pone encountered assassins holding a knife like a boxer and watched them trip over their own feet falling on the blade trying to break their fall.

Pratt held the butterfly flat extended with the elbow bent; he looked uncomfortable doing it. Should have gotten out of the game, thought Pone.

"You good with that thing?" asked Pone.

"You'll find out soon enough," Pratt glared.

The two combatants circled each other. Pone observed Pratt who proved he had no business in the killing business. Pone dodged all the forehand and backhand motions Pratt delivered like a tennis player; Pone evaded his telegraphed thrust. Pratt held the butterfly like a rapier. Pone knew Pratt didn't take fencing lessons. The man a puppet to his anger and it made him careless.

Pone put the razor away making Pratt angrier. He panted like a dog in heat. Age, booze, bad diet, and perhaps too many ugly cheapass women took their toll on him.

Pone put distance between Pratt and himself. "Walk away. You will never be part of any cartel. I know a restaurant owner looking for a dish-washer."

Pratt screamed. "Motherfucker!" He charged like a raging bull. Pone rock steady; he concentrated on the knee cap. The knee hyperextended. Pratt stiffened making an ill-advised thrust. He got another unwanted anatomy lesson from Pone bending his elbow in the wrong direction. Pratt looked like a lame horse. Pone analyzed Pratt.

He saw a broken man, and not by bones alone…his spirit. Pone felt the need to end his misery. He never grasped why you put a horse to sleep after a broken leg. Maybe horses could no longer pull a plow or carry its master around with a hitch in his step, or the animal felt a low self-esteem because it couldn't perform like it used to. Pratt would not get another chance to come after him.

Pratt laid on his side in pain and whimpering. He didn't notice Pone picking up his butterfly knife slipping behind him placing the knife under his chin. The cut clean and quick, Pone laid him down. A witch-like figure got his attention.

The bug-eyed woman from the club. Pone wiped the blade and wondered why the broad followed. He strode without a glance. The woman spoke under her breath, but he heard her disturbing words.

"Fool ain't worth a shit. Got to do this my damn self."

A rufled purse followed by a shadow of an extended arm holding a small caliber pistol aimed to do damage. A hundred times a day practicing knife throwing. Pone moved with cat quickness turning in time tossing the six inch butterfly blade like a Frisbee hitting her in the larynx.

A hard thud against bone. She resembled a skeleton covered a thin sheet of flesh. Bug-eyes went down with the look of surprise in her eyes without firing a shot. Pone took no pride in killing a woman and she became his first. A trend he hoped to break. The young men at the rundown club and now a woman suffering the same fate as her succumbed counterpart. He left the blade in her throat; the bodies would descry in the morning. He realized walking back to the parking lot Pratt and this broad hired to put a hit on him. Pratt, Bug-eyes, and the young men…hired to put a hit on him, thought Pone.

"You know baseball players don't make it to the big leagues unless they can hit a curve-ball," said the man on the phone. "It's getting close to the ninth inning, and you're down two runs."

"What the fuck?" White swallowed hard. Frustrated and tired of hearing damn baseball shit. He wanted to crush the cell against the pavement and stomp the life out of it.

Enough of the baseball crap, thought White. He played the game, but was not good at it.

He lost his second cousin in a matter of weeks and the reason he hired her a career crack head to take out a pro like Pone so she could continue her cocaine habit. She had an on and off thing with Arnold Pratt whom White and almost every hip-hopper knew the wannabe loser-hood rat trying to be a gangster would remember Pone and inspired to ice him after their first encounter.

"Told you Pone was a seasoned pro, man," said White.

"And you keep reaching in the minors?"

White shook his head. Only if he could talk to this son of a bitch in person. He'd put a stop to those baseball terms. "Two strikes, huh?"

A chuckle on the phone. "You catching on. I'm impressed. You want more money? I'll think about it because I don't want to read about another fuck up in the blab sheet. You don't need another fuck up if you know what I mean?"

White wanted to say fuck you. He'd lost two cousins to this gig and wasn't about to sacrifice another one. Three on his conscience, no way.

He thought of little buck-teeth Bucky, White told the youth what he needed to do to be a gangster; he ended up barbecued and in an early grave. Wanda? He pondered.

Eyes bulging out of her sockets, wobbled knees and elbows looked at any moment to penetrate through her flesh…he did her a favor. White blinked. Wanda looked like a dried up twig with arms and legs. Killing herself. Committing suicide and she didn't know it. Rest in peace cousin. He thought about his unwanted partner, Krasko. Hell, he might know somebody to be Pone's equal on the prohibition side.

White held two strikes, he gritted his teeth. Krasko anointed his designated hitter. White hated thinking about strikes because now the bastard lived inside his head. He needed to buy time, no more sacrificing any more of his peeps. Let Krasko have a try, thought White. He might get lucky and put Pone down. "Look…let me talk to Krasko. He may know somebody who can take out Pone. But it'll take greenbacks." White didn't need any more cash, but he wanted to bleed the man for all its worth. Two dead cousins.

"Love the way you assholes butcher the English language. I give you more currency you better not run out on me."

"Wouldn't dream of it. I owe you for getting me out of the pen."

Bastard might be the one who set my ass up, thought White.

"Krasko better know what's at stake."

"Whatever, man," remarked White.

"What's that?"

"You lead, I follow."

The man hung up. White exhaled relief when the conversation ended. The voice on the phone burned in his ear like acid. White wished to tell the jerk to go fuck himself, but the mystery fellow controlled his balls. The bloke knew White and Krasko, and he kept them in the dark.

Ten

A photo album on display. A handsome male teen flashed pearly whites. The picture admired by an elderly man shaking his head. G observed his eldest child's photo.

He sat somber in his chair clothed in a blue satin robe and white cotton pajamas his attire of late. Reggie received a full scholarship both academic and athletic to a school on the west coast.

He loved his father, but knew they lived a dark and dangerous lifestyle he wanted no part of. Reggie desired a legit respectable way to make a living. He could have gone to an in state college or a university close to home; Reggie distanced himself from his father's world. G sensed his son's discretion, but never questioned him about it.

G a proud parent; Reggie the first in the family to go to college. His younger siblings destined to follow; Reggie would lead the way. Everything in place for it to happen destroyed by a horrific car bombing. G laid out plans for all his children, but for Reggie, those plans were over. The trip down memory lane interrupted by a knock on the door.

"Come in," said G.

Brown entered the home office. A miniature library with the wall to wall books. G wasn't educated, but loved books. His street smarts got him wealth which intrigued him about Brown. He saw a little of himself in Brown. He took the hood-rat under his wing molding a man capable of taking over if something happened to him. G didn't want his children to inherit his life. He felt Brown better suited being a thug.

Brown didn't cringe about G doing his grandmother. G never mentioned her, a show of class, thought Brown.

Brown observed the pictures of Reggie; he would not have followed in his father's foot-steps.

G would have made sure of that and Brown would assist him to keep the young man on the right path. Brown smiled thinking how talented Reggie was on the hard-wood. He had a bright future. The kid a wizard on the court and watching him play magical. A five-star recruit destined to play professional. Brown joked with him about buying court-side seats in NBA cities. He also admired Reggie for conquering the class-room.

Yeah, the kid was like Halley's Comet, a once in a lifetime phenom. Brown had none brothers or sisters, so he became a big brother to all of G's kids.

He pondered over how he should have been there to protect Reggie, he should have given him a detail to watch his back, the two youths knew how to ditch and sneak around and always came back home safe and sound except for the night they lost their lives. Brown played Reggie's confidant. He promised Reggie to keep his relationship with Macone's daughter a secret. Brown kept nothing from G and now with Reggie's death he would take it to his grave in fear of what G would do if he found out he knew about the two. Brown remembered his grandmother telling him how funny life can be and what happened to Reggie and the Macone girl was so true. Both dying at a young age, innocent and pure, but flawed by sins only of their fathers, Brown frowned thinking if Pone didn't find the perpetrators, then he sure as hell would and make them pay.

He cleared his throat to get G's attention.

"What's the deal?" asked G.

"Pone's working for the mayor. He'll be handling things,"

G nodded. "He's still under the royal family?"

Brown took a seat in front of G's desk. "He wanted to make sure nobody interfered with the investigation."

G closed the family album. "Make sure the boys know."

"Already talked to the crew. They know how important this is… Pone admitted to the house cleaning. Said they tried to kill him and instead offed a little boy."

G clenched his fist. "More children dying…he knows we had nothing to do with that?"

Brown nodded.

"Make sure the families don't touch Pone or they'll deal with me. I want to know who killed my boy."

"He mentioned somebody in our crew pulled those boys strings," said Brown.

"You looking into that?" asked G.

"On top of it." Brown stood and left G to his thoughts.

An average height grief-stricken late middle-aged man stood over the fire-place. He stared at pictures of family members on the mantel. Relatives old and young decorated the solid mahogany stained wood support. The star in Macone's teary eyes, a picture of a young girl on the verge of blossoming into a beautiful young woman. Helen, his eldest had golden hair felt like velvet every time she gave him a hug and her smile lit up a room. All gone in a senseless unexplained death. He swore once he found the culprit, he would make him beg for death.

Boysenberry stayed silent in the background letting Macone have his moment of grief. Boysenberry took his own moment to remember the golden hair, porcelain skin rosy-cheeked lass whose smile reminded him of the Swiss Miss girl. Helen had a bright future; engineering, and law school awaited her, she had a knack for problem solving. Boysenberry used to tease her by giving her Trigonometry problems to solve.

It was child's play. She teased him to be more challenging. Helen loved life. Boysenberry missed her natural pearly white smile and harmony voice. Being Macone's, lieutenant, he felt responsible for protecting her and he failed because now she was dead. So young to end up in the bone-yard. Boysenberry felt selfish; young people met unexpected death. The Grim Reaper did not discriminate. He wished for a rule in place for dying, but then people would panic knowing they approached their age for mortality. Logan's Run, he thought. Boysenberry lived in the real world and no such rules.

Things happen for a reason. He shook his head what a load of crap. He couldn't think or see any reason or good behind her death.

Macone glanced over his shoulder.

"How did it go?" Macone asked.

Boysenberry strolled toward his boss. "Pone in his role as a troubleshooter on behalf of the mayor will handle the investigation. I told him he would have immunity from us."

Macone nodded. "I take it the rug-heads complied?"

Macone stood with his back to Boysenberry. He focused on Helen's picture. He didn't noticed Boysenberry's raised eyebrow. Macone referred to the blacks as spades. But when he found out that his beloved daughter was involved with his rival's son, he approved. Any black on the verge of something good he considered them not a regular black in his eye. He smiled thinking about having a jock in his blood-line if the two got real serious. He would not mind having permanent tan grand-kids blessed with athletic ability. Macone a sport fanatic, father of three boys and none of his sons possessed a lick of athleticism in their bones which they inherited from him. He followed the exploits of G's boy Reggie. He would had relished having the young man as part of his family.

Boysenberry saw Macone taking baby steps changing from his bigotry.

He allowed a few minorities; blacks and Latinos in the fold saying good for business. "The hip-hoppers are on the same page as us. Find the rat who did this."

Macone turned and nodded. "Stay in touch with Pone. Let him know I want to ice the piece of shit when he finds him."

"Heard from Brown, he's looking to see if this was an inside job. Suggest we might want to do the same."

"What do you mean?" Macone asked.

"Think about it? Somebody knew they were dating before we did."

Macone collapsed in his brown leather lazy-boy. He gripped the arm of the chair pointing at Boysenberry.

"You saying one of mine put my kid in the bone yard?" Macone gave a stern look. "Somebody on my pay-roll is the reason my daughter is taking the big sleep?"

Boysenberry shrugged. "Something we might want to look into." Boysenberry read the old man's body language when he leaned back in his recliner. He left to start his own investigation.

Eleven

The Penn Station East Coast sub shop on Remont road ten miles outside Metro. Not your ordinary deli. Similar to the defunct Quiznos for hot subs though not toasted, but nothing like Sub-way because of its lack of, meat, vegetables, breads, and assortment of sauces. You could order a regular cold cut sandwich they called the Dagwood: a Philly cheese steak, Chicken Parmesan, Teriyaki Chicken, Chicken Philly, freshly squeezed lemonade, ice tea sweet, unsweetened, and a soda fountain. Chips complimented your sandwich.

The meat cooked on a hot griddle like a Japanese steak house. You heard spatulas clanging and mixing meats and vegetables. You couldn't see them prepare the food` because of a mid-size red tile wall.

Pone preferred Quiznos' toasted Chicken Carbonara with bacon. No other sub restaurant made the submarine and Quiznos now extinct. He went to Sub-way for the turkey breast and peanut butter cookies. Jersey Mike, Sub-station II, Blimpie subs didn't appeal to him. Sub shops an alternative to the high-calorie greasy burger joints. Pone tired of the marquee burger displays showing fresh veggies, cheese, juicy beef between a bun and once you got it…the burger looked nothing like advertised: tomatoes and lettuce sliding between the bun in opposite directions, sandwich pressed together and soggy.

Pone stood at the counter and ordered two Teriyaki chicken subs without the Teriyaki turning the sandwich into a chicken Philly. The Teriyaki sauce too strong and the chicken seasoned enough to provide flavor. He preferred the Penn Station for hot subs. They made one cold sub, the Dagwood. An under the radar eatery and few customers. Pone wondered how they stayed in business.

He glanced at the man making the sandwiches, bald and sweat balls the size of quarters on his head. He cringed thinking the perspiration rolling off the head onto the griddle blending in with the meat and vegetables.

Pone looked around the place and decided this would be the last time he'd come here for a hoagie. He joined Sonny at one of the booth in a dark secluded corner.

"Ordered two Chicken Philly," said Pone.

"What? No Teriyaki?" asked Sonny.

Pone snorted. "Don't you worry; you'll get plenty of flavor and then some." He thought about the cook with the quarter size sweat balls dripping into the food. "Did you a favor considering your stomach. The Teriyaki not sweet like that Bridgeford beef jerky."

Sonny waved Pone off. "Should've gone to a burger joint."

"You don't need red meat. How you think I keep my girlish figure?"

"Dodging bullets," said Sonny.

Pone laughed. The old timer told it straight pulling no punches.

Hated hearing you say sir more than twice. (I ain't a knight and that ain't what my folks named me.) A TV station showed only classic dramas and comedies from the 1960s to the 2000s. Pone watched the network because he saw it as a history lesson. He liked Sanford and Son. Sonny could be a clone of the character Fred Sanford played by the late entertainer Redd Foxx.

"Any sauce going to be on it?" asked Sonny.

Pone shook his head. "Caramelized onion, Swiss cheese, salt, and pepper." Sonny smiled. "Mouthwatering already."

"Who do you know in town willing to do a car bombing job?" Sonny shrugged and rubbed his thick cotton head of hair.

"Talking about them kids, right?"

"Yeah."

"That's something I ain't never done is kill kids. Couldn't pay me enough for that shit. Blown up snitches, cars, and building for insurance frauds, but no kids.."

"Going to ask you a dumb question."

Before Pone could ask, the sandwiches placed near the cashier. Pone came back to the table with two-foot longs and large soft drinks.

Sonny looked seventy years old. Owned all his teeth; he tore into the sandwich and sipped his soda, closed his eyes, and sighed like he died and gone to heaven.

Pone didn't touch his food. He couldn't get those quarter size sweat balls out of his head.

"Damn good sandwich," said Sonny.

If he only knew, thought Pone. "Moist and extra salty?" Sonny gave a dubious look.

Pone inhaled. "You know anybody who'd be cold enough to take out kids?"

Sonny swallowed hard. "Depends on who don't want a day job. Any low life who wants to make a fast buck got to know what he doing or he might blow his own ass up."

"Come on, Sonny."

"Most of the guys I knew pushing up daisies. They got a taste of their own medicine, old age; you name it. Don't know nothing about the young bloods. What you need to do is find out who knew those kids dated."

"A needle in a haystack." said Pone.

"You can put that haystack in two piles."

"Prohibition and hip-hop."

Sonny smiled and winked. "You got it college boy."

"Already got Brown and Boysenberry thinking it might be an inside job."

Sonny moved his tongue around his teeth. "Playing with a double edged sword."

"Almost got cut twice."

Sonny took another sip of his drink. "Now that's shit. They want you to solve this mess and dead too? Damn."

Pone shove his sandwich toward Sonny. He knew Sonny didn't do much cooking.

"You sure?" questioned Sonny

"They'll wrap it for you." replied Pone.

"All right, this is a good sandwich."

"Got too much on my mind to eat." retorted Pone.

"You and the other two fools the only friends I got. I want you boys to see me in the ground and not the other way around."

"Can't make any promises," said Pone.

"Ain't that the truth," remarked Sonny.

"We your kids now?"

"Maybe you. The other two too damn ugly." remarked Sonny.

Pone bit his bottom lip to control his laughter. "Guess I better keep my head on a swivel."

Sonny washed down his last bite, and Pone gave him his drink.

"This lunch was for my benefit?" asked Sonny.

"I wanted to pick your brain."

"Whoever did this ain't going to be staying in the city."

Pone leaned back folding his arms. "I think we both can agree that this one of those inside out job."

Inside job meant somebody knew the families, but hired outside help, thought Pone.

Sonny nodded. "Somebody pulling the strings."

"Find the puppeteer and there won't be a gang war."

"If you had to, which would you rather be, a puppet or a dummy?"asked Sonny.

"Something about being a dummy don't sit well with me," said Pone.

Sonny nodded. "Don't want nobody's hand up my ass."

Twelve

The landscape once fertile farm land overran with greenery compared to a rain-forest Rock Hill resembled its namesake after the falling star gave the world a make-over.

A weathered white ranch house, stone steps, three bedrooms, and bath sat on hard rock. During the day an eyesore, but at night just damn creepy. Inside the dump, cobwebs, dust, worn out furniture, stained carpet, dirty dishes, cupboards with one door missing on one of the sink cabinets, and a permanent smudge on a filthy kitchen floor.

A corduroy beige sofa, matching recliner in front of an old fashioned 42 inch. Box style TV. Next to the sofa a small brown wobbly coffee table. Electricity ran through the pigsty thanks to the puppet master, but no cable. A relic VCR/DVD player to play VHS tapes from the past and DVD.

Staring at the boob tube watching a DVD was a disgruntled James Krasko. Unkempt brown hair, pale chiseled malnutrition crater stubble face. Average height wearing a white sweat-shirt, blue jeans, and black classic high-top Converse sneakers with Chuck Taylor written on them. Chuck Taylor a basketball player? Krasko didn't care.

The hovel turned his stomach. He wondered if he would have been better off in prison than living in a smelly moldy hole. Before he could finished the thought, he heard the Chevy S-10 pulling up behind the house. Coming through the kitchen door was his partner in crime Roland White. A low-class hip-hopper in the same situation as he. His crony: average height, dark brown skin, hair on his head, and face looked like little black beads.

White always cringe-combed his hair. It sounded like popping bubble wrap. White needed a haircut and a shave. Krasko hated talking to White and though he despised the moldy smell of the house it countered White's horrific breath.

White came back from a food run carrying a plastic bag containing two square Styrofoam boxes. He dropped them on the mid-sized wooden brown square table surrounded by an assortment of chairs: two blue, one white, and the other green.

"Better come and get this shit while it's hot," said White.

Krasko strode over to the table with his index finger under his nostrils to fend off the breath of death. "It would help if you didn't call it shit."

White opened both boxes. Popcorn shrimp spilled out onto the table. "Damn!" said Krasko.

"I know right," said White. "This hole in the wall will load your ass up with shellfish. Under the shrimp is cocktail sauce and hush puppies."

White put a brown paper bag on the table and took out two 32 ounces of Polar pop cups.

"What flavor of soda?" asked Krasko.

"You thirsty?"

"Hell, yeah."

"Then drink the shit."

White settled at the table while Krasko placed himself on the coffee table in front of the telly. "Fuck…"

White shook his head. "What's your problem, man?"

"I can't live like this. This place is ugly, it smells…when I eat I need something good to look at, some place that smells nice you know?"

"Pop something in the damn VCR and look at that and this is temporary."

"Damn! Got us living out in the middle of nowhere. Shit! Is the name of this place, nowhere?" questioned Krasko.

White didn't like living in his family's house and didn't want Krasko to be his roommate. It was the best he could do and Krasko didn't offer them an alternative. They needed to lie low and ravage off the radar. Krasko didn't know this use to be White's family home. They abandoned the rickety after the meteor metamorphose the abundant land into a solid desert rock without an oasis. A dead farm. The family packed up and left.

"Your punk ass need to stop complaining. You should've stayed your ass in the joint." demanded White.

Krasko was clueless how he had ended up in the slammer. He remembered getting his drink on in a bar when he woke up behind iron bars wearing an orange jump-suit. Someone slipped a Mickey Finn in his drink. Krasko's talent, blowing things up; he and White outcast from their prestigious gangs and both bomb experts.

Ending up in lockup on some trumped charges. In the can, Krasko became everyone's Maytag. He washed too many skid marks out of tidy whites and droopy drawers; staying in this scrap made him home-sick for his cell. Krasko came back to reality; at least he wasn't a caged animal anymore. Krasko thrilled when White told him some man he didn't know and yet to meet pulled strings to get them out.

Krasko gave White the look of you don't have to ask me twice. Orange wasn't his color, so he had no problem ditching the threads. White promised a big pay-day which gave him plenty of motivation to blow up two kids belonging to the prominent crime families. Things though not so good on the outside as he hoped. He looked around his environment and realized he left a hell hole for another.

Krasko swallowed hard. "Look, all I'm saying is the accommodations could be better. Glad we got electricity and can take a bath, but no cable? I've seen all these tapes and DVD's more times than I can count."

White pursed his lips. "Okay, I'll tell the man about your complaints, but he might put your ass back in prison."

"He'd do that?"

White shrugged popping shrimp into his mouth. "Think about it? He got us out…who's to say if I tell him about your bitching he might consider you ungrateful and incarcerate your ass again."

White saw Krasko squirm like a worm thinking about being sent back to the pen, he smiled. White hated Krasko because he bled prohibition. He enjoyed keeping secrets from the dunce.

He told his cell-mate what he needed to know and kept him in the dark.

He showed his fellow lifer a burner phone. Krasko believed White talked to someone on the outside. Since things weren't going as planned. Krasko knew nothing about the baseball terminology, and a strike away from heading back behind bars or worse. It's been a frustrating day and White would mourn in private the relatives he lost trying to ice Pone. The man needed him to take care of the troubleshooter. Krasko unaware of their situation and White planned to keep it that way. So he'd just sit back and devour his popcorn seafood.

"Damn that… I ain't going back to the Hoosegow. I'll roll with the punches. Tell me the plan and don't give me hooey."

White glared. "What the hell is a hooey?"

"Lies, rubbish…tell me the truth." replied Krasko.

"I told you to speak English when you talk." said White.

"You do the same gabbling that hip-hop shit."

"You can understand my shit better than your prohibition shit."

"Enough of this shit! Just fill in the blanks, will ya?"

White shook his head.

"The man said one more job, and we get paid in full and go where we damn well please. For now, he'll give us enough loot for food and gas."

"One more job? What does he want us to do now?"

"When I know, you'll know."

"Yeah, yeah…sit tight, right?"

"You catching on."

"You trust this cat? We should roll in dough after the job you pulled."

White rose from the table. "Hold up! I push the button, you planted the bomb, and that makes you accountable too."

"All I'm saying is we need to agitate the gravel…that means…"

White held up his hand. "I know what you mean, and I agree. But I need my bread, dividends before I dash off. You feel me?"

Krasko nodded giving white a sharp look. He knew the hip-hop slang for money. Krasko threw up his hands.

"What do you suggest?"

White glared. "Shut the hell up. You weren't too happy being everyone's Maytag."

"No. They can wash their own damn laundry."

"That's what I thought," White sat down and took out a plastic bag of rolled joints.

"Hey! Give me one of them jive sticks," said Krasko.

"If it'll make you shut up."

Thirteen

No matter how many times Pone walked inside the Ritz building, the ceiling mesmerized him. Detailed workmanship, artistic vision; beautiful captivating colors. Pone's serene moment interrupted by an abrade poke between the shoulder blades. He turned looking down on the diminutive District Attorney, Thomas Maxwell. Red's annoying boyfriend. In a Wonder Woman comic book, he'd be Steve Trevor and she Wonder Woman saving his ass from danger. The slight endomorphic man, thin hair crossed over to cover a bald spot; stubble on his upper lip trying to grow a mustache. Pone wondered what Red saw in the guy.

Maybe she dated Maxwell to improve her family's image, thought Pone. The city knew the Brigand family played a big part in organized crime.

Red warned Pone to be careful around the district attorney. She found a file on him in Maxwell's apartment. Pone pondered if the little fellow used it to keep Red on his arm.

Pone felt like Gulliver's Travel: Lars Lambert, the janitor, Harvey Crowe, the deputy mayor, and Thomas Maxwell, the district attorney, short antropos who didn't care for him and he thought the same about them. He understood why Lambert hated him. Ungrateful twerp should thank him. Pone rescued Lambert from a cement burial, pork food, and a monster truck pull. J. Paul wanted to rip him apart.

Crowe and Maxwell worked in law enforcement and Pone a former killer-for-hire.

Pone couldn't figure out what a statuesque beauty like Red saw in a five-foot-nothing like Thomas Maxwell. A District Attorney his calling card; short and thinning hair; his suits wore him. Red could carry the guy on her hip like a child. Pone knew Red could have her choice of bucks, but told him she liked Maxwell's bravado. Pone concluded she dated the shrimp to protect him. Maxwell made it no secret he wanted Pone off the streets Maxwell killed the headlights and put it in neutral because he dated a goddess and feared he'd lose her.

"What are you doing here?" asked Maxwell.

"Business. None of yours," said Pone.

Maxwell pointed. "You do anything to hurt her…"

"It's the other way around."

Maxwell had a dubious look. "What we have is special."

"You're both lawyers, and you both do charity work." Pone stared down at the little imp. "She does a lot of charity."

Maxwell glared, and Pone smiled then made his way to the elevator.

Black two inch pumps propped up on a grand Mahogany desk; long legs in silky black hose, leading up to a dark gray hemmed at the knee of a sleeveless dress displaying toned arms, smooth hands, and manicured nails holding a Kindle. Red sat reading a novel about a serial killer and a werewolf wreaking murderous havoc in a city.

Romance novels bored her, but blood and gore she liked. Red deep into it when Pone busted in.

"You wearing the right attire for the occasion," said Pone.

Red stood putting down the Kindle. "What are you talking about?"

"My funeral."

"Look who's talking. I should take you shopping before they call you the Grim Reaper."

"I'll do the jokes."

"What's wrong, Pony?"

"You want me to do this job?"

"Did you run into Maxwell?"

"I stepped and scraped him off my shoe. Your munchkin's an itch I can scratch, but damn this shit!"

Pone hunched over Red's desk using both hands to support his weight.

"What happened? She asked."

"No more meetings if the plan is for me to end up dead before or after I attend them."

Red stood beside Pone placing her hand on his arm. Her touch always sent his heart racing, and he believed she felt the same. He inhaled counting to ten making things professional again.

"So, the man and woman I read about in the paper found dead in the alley…"

Pone exhaled and took off his bowler placing it on the desk. "He was a blast from the past that should have never taken up the criminal trade, and she looked like the walking dead."

"You think there's a rat in our circle?"

"This is not a coincidence," stated Pone. Red shrugged.

"No one comes to mind."

"You and Birdie are in the clear."

Red's nostrils flared. She smiled reaching inside her desk grabbing a pink stress ball squeezing it five times before putting in back inside the drawer.

Pone gave her a look.

"Better than getting slapped," said Red.

Pone chuckled. "So far it's been amateur night and yeah, both hits after midnight. Boys in the Crown Victoria and a guy partnering up with a witch."

"Oh Pony… I'll pull the plug on this. I had no right to ask you."

"No. I'm doing this for those kids. They were innocent," Pone snorted. "I I believe their spirits are restless."

Red twisted her face. "Seeing ghosts, now?"

Pone waved her off.

Red got behind Pone giving him a hug. Pone moved away. He ended up facing an expensive painting.

"I know it's not…" said Pone.

Red shook her head. She took a seat behind her desk. Pone turned staring at her. Red studied Pone. She knew him long enough to perceive he concluded.

"Okay Pony, spill it."

"I'm a gambler. I never put all my cards on the table."

"You don't trust me?"

"You're my guardian angel."

A smile creased her ruby lips. Red hated being called an angel. Her family built their empire on blood and evil. A part of her felt good being Pone's protector.

"Pony…"

Pone held up his hand. He walked over to the desk grabbing his bowler. "We'll meet on Sundays at Nadine during the day."

"Sounds like a plan."

"Not yet, but I'm working on it." He headed for the door. "The important thing is staying alive and finishing the job."

Red grabbed her Kindle swinging her gams atop her desk. "What are you reading?"

"A thriller horror."

"You love blood and gore."

"A serial killer and a werewolf terrorize a city."

"Sounds like a page turner."

"You read, Pony?"

"Let me know how it turns out."

Fourteen

Cruising down South Tryon, the city's Parking Enforcement restricted the heart of the city; for sporting events, parades and festivals. Red and orange the wardrobe worn by poles, parking meters, and pay stations. Orange signs on the poles displaying no parking anytime, and sometimes days of the week (Friday, Saturday, and Sunday) depending on the occasion of a special event. Red bags the color for meters and pay stations.

Large red bags engulfed the pay stations with a capital P in a circle and slanted line over it meaning no parking which some people ignored.

Like signs, the bags also had days of the week and their own identity; Friday yellow, Saturday orange, and Sunday blue. Red bags and orange signs with anytime on them dominated the streets today. Two cars disregarded the banners.

Drivers left their parked vehicles despite warning showing their lack of respect for parking enforcement. Tickets rested on the windshields held down by wiper blades.

A twenty-five dollar mulct made violators angry. The citation a city penalty confused citizens into thinking it affected their insurance and driver's license.

You could not tear the paper though some tried. A populace considered the notice not real because they knew it had nothing to do with their car insurance or license; dense thinking and a carefree attitude toward city laws. Any vehicle with a fine over a hundred dollars ended up wearing a boot and if not paid their car got towed. Cars on the tow truck's flatbed made the tickets real.

Pone shook his head and smiled strolling down Tryon. He searched for Wisdom. Instead he found and settled for his four-foot-eight coworker, Carmen Valdez.

There she stood weighing in at one-hundred-and-twenty-eight pounds though she looked smaller. Lucille pulled up and the parking enforcer, Carmen turned to face her adversary. Pone hopped out with a grin.

"Excuse me, sir. You can't park here," said Carmen with a cunning smirk. She gave Pone a strong hug.

"Better be careful, people might think I'm trying to get out of a ticket," joked Pone returning the embrace. The diminutive woman released him and looked toward a few patrons walking by.

"Forget them," glared Carmen.

Wisdom convinced the single mother of two she need a city job with a pension than being a cashier at the 7-Eleven. Carmen agreed, she tired of asking customers if they wanted paper or plastic.

"Looking for the old man," said Pone.

"He took time off," said Carmen.

In all the time Pone knew Wisdom, he never took a day off

The man needed to be busy.

"Wisdom said nothing, but I could tell something was wrong," said Carmen. "Always hung around after getting off the clock to shoot the breeze."

"Stopped coming to work…no notice or anything?" asked Pone.

Carmen shrugged. "I'm sure management knows, but they said nothing to us." Carmen knew nothing about Wisdom's past. She saw him as a kindhearted middle-aged man.

"How long has he…?"

"Since last Friday," said Carmen.

Pone nodded. "Don't worry I'll check on him." Pone climbed into Lucille and, waved to Carmen. Wisdom not at work and being antisocial. Something wasn't right.

A mid-day brandy not too early for Harvey Crowe. Taking over the duties running Metro City since Mayor Winslow tucked his tail between his legs to go on an extended vacation after the deaths of two youths from powerful crime families. Crowe circled his office observing pictures and paintings to help pass the time with his stinger. He rubbed his chest and stomach caressing the warm cognac. Applejack tasted and felt better in the winter. Cold weather seemed to last longer since the great meteor. Another sip and a long exhale made him realize this is how it should be. He should be king of Metro once this mess gets cleaned up; he'd try to make Winslow's vacation permanent, he thought.

Static from the intercom. "Excuse me, sir."

Crowe startled. "Mary…"

"Miss Brigand is here to see you."

An unexpected visit out of the blue. No phone call, email, or text. What's going on, he thought? Crowe took another sip. "Sir?"

Crowe got comfortable behind his desk. "Send her in."

The door creaked open to the sound of elegant heels moving with deliberate grace over wooden parquet floor. The secretary closed the door leaving Crowe to gaze upon the statuesque beauty. A fantasy for men like him. She stood in front of his desk. Hair worn in a prohibition bun. Her eyes piercing, and body hidden by the conservative black trench coat gave her a bewitching look.

"Change of plans."

Crowe bit his lower lip and raised an eyebrow. "Okay… you want to sit down and tell me what you're talking about?"

"This won't take long."

"Sounds serious."

"We'll continue to meet on Sundays when there is something to talk about, but it will be during the day."

Crowe rose from his chair. "We agreed to be discrete."

"Man up and grow a pair. Stop riding around in the limo, besides you always travel around the city with one of your goons. You have nothing to worry about as long as you come in the club's back door."

Crowe sat down behind his desk. "Why the sudden change?"

Red smiled and batted her eyelashes. She learned from her late gangster father to treat trust like walking on egg shells. Trusting a politician like putting your hand in fire and not expecting to get burned. Pone her man, and a dear friend caught between a rock, and a hard place. She plan to keep him in a soft spot. Pone educated, gave up a life as a regular citizen to get revenge for a loved one luring him into a life of organized crime.

"It will be safer for us all. Unless there's a reason you want to keep meeting at night?"

Crowe shrugged "No one else knows about our conclave, but if you say it's best to get together during the day then fine by me. All I want is to make sure there will not be a gang war." Crowe poured himself another glass of Marc. "Your family has a lot of enemies."

"High and low," said Red.

"Can't picture a powerful woman like yourself rattled."

Red pursed her lips engaging Crowe in a stare down. He looked away. "Predators come out at night. They're cowards during the day."

Crowe nodded. "Anything else?"

Red smiled, pivoted, and exited the office.

Crowe got on his cell. "Change of plans."

Fifteen

Pone inhaled then exhaled through his nostrils. He left Lucille inside a parking deck on 100 East 6th. He made a beeline toward 200 North College. No parking between the hours of 4:00 p.m. and 6:00 p.m. because of rush hour. Pone witnessed cars ticketed and towed off the street for obstructing traffic. He didn't want to see Lucille on a flatbed for violating city rules.

A usual day in Metro; gray skies with no rain in sight keeping the sun from making an appearance. Pone now at his destination wasn't ready to go inside the bistro.

He stood in front of the doorway in his own thoughts. Pone was angry at Red texting him about an impromptu meeting with Crowe. It didn't surprise him she picked up the vibe about the two attacks he endured or who might be behind them.

She being a brilliant attorney. But she made a mistake moving on Crowe without consulting him first. She should have waited till he made things concrete before taking it upon herself to confront the deputy mayor. If he engineered the attacks and picked up they knew about it, he might cover his tracks.

Pone didn't want to give wind of being on to him, but that ship sailed thanks to Red.

Then again maybe she bought time making Crowe rethink his plan now they will no longer meet at night, In a case scenario three would have been the magic number. Three times the charm or three strikes and you're out terms. Two hits on his life before and after a moot with the second-in-command too coincidental.

Pone gambled telling Red he smelled a rat in their clique; pondered if he made a miscue. A gambler never puts all his cards on the table, thought Pone. A young couple muttered excuse us entering the brasserie known as Mert's.

Mert's a soul food restaurant at 200 North College. The only soul food eatery inside the city. Other soulful joints dwell on the outskirts of Metro. Mert's the only one brave enough to venture and lay foundation inside the megalopolis. White and blue collar class adored the cafe`. Pone stepped inside the mid-sized establishment. He took off his bowler surveying the rathskeller; small square brown tables, chairs all wood, sandy tan stone smooth walls smothered by photos of African-Americans past and present. Family members, no one knew except the owner. Pone spotted Brown in a corner wolfing down food. Pone sat down to the sound of finger licking and lip smacking.

Brown had a nice spread; honey glazed barbecue ribs, side bowls of collard greens with bits of chopped ham, black-eye peas, cheesy macaroni, a plate of buttery corn bread and to wash it down a big glass of ice tea.

"Want some? Plenty to go around," said Brown. Pone waved him off.

Pone scanned and saw dagger eyes glaring his way from the kitchen. "Too many enemies. "Don't want my food with the flavor of saliva,"

Brown grunted. "You paranoid."

"Better safe than sorry. You going to talk or keep feeding your pie hole?" Brown washed down a mouthful of mac and cheese. "Okay man, shoot."

"Don't tempt me," said Pone.

"You going to talk or make jokes?"

"Another hit on my life after a meeting."

"A bony ass broad and that loser, Pratt."

"How you…"

"Put two and two together after reading the blab sheet." Pone gave Brown a dubious look.

Brown smiled. "I like what they call the newspaper." Brown studied Pone. "Hold up now, I know you ain't thinking I tried to dust you?"

"The Probonos didn't know Arnold Pratt."

Brown straightened. "You living under a rock? The probonos done open their membership, they got blacks and Latinos in their crew now."

"Pratt wanted to be a hip-hopper fucking bad. He even had a walking dead partner."

"They both dead now." Brown took a bite of his collards and made a face.. "Damn cold." He motioned to a waitress. "Baby, could you warm these up for me?"

She smiled and also took the black-eye peas and mac and cheese. The waitress short, stocky, full lips with a gold piercing wedge on the side of her nose, multicolored braided weave draped around her full face, and her blue jeans looked painted on her thunder thighs.

When she carried the food to the kitchen, Brown hypnotized by her big round bouncy ass. Pone exchanged icy glares with woman wiping down tables.

She had a full face and glossy hair wrapped around it looking glued to her head. Googly eyes and enormous bosom exposing deep cleavage. Pone wasn't a breast man.

An average man would use the melons like a pillow and sleep in paradise. Thunder thighs returned with Brown's food. He attacked it as if afraid it would get cold again.

"A lot of eye-balling going around," said Pone.

Brown swallowed hard. "You're a pretty man." He sipped his tea. "Light skin, got that hairless boyish look, white people type curly hair, and one brown and blue eye. Damn."

"Wanda Rembert. Did you know her?" Pone figured he'd throw the dead woman's name at Brown.

Brown wolfed down a mouthful of collards. "See that woman with the googly eyes glaring at you?"

"You mean bug eyes," said Pone.

Brown laughed. "Same thing…anyway that was her cousin, but that ain't the only reason she got eyes for you."

"What do you mean?" asked Pone. "She know I clipped her?"

Brown shook his head. "One of them boys you clipped was her own."

"The whole family stupid?"

"Show respect man."

"Wanda worked as a hired killer?" asked Pone.

"Skinny ass Wanda…fuck no. She was heavy on the eight-ball."

Eight-ball a slang for two things: malt liquor and cocaine. The way Wanda looked, she snorted blow.

"You're not talking about malt liquor are you?"

Brown shook his head. "You saw her."

Pone glowered. The woman looked like a carbon skeleton. "That hard up, huh? That means somebody in your neck of the woods put her up to it."

"I wish you cut that shit out. Something to look into, but G gave you a parlay. But some cold-hearten fucker knew she was a coke-head and convinced her to come after you."

"Guess I need to talk to bug eyes."

Pone was about to get up, but Brown motioned for him to stay seated. "Leave Ella alone."

"Maybe she knows something?"

"All she knows is that Wanda was a coke-head and good giving head." Brown snorted. "Hell the way she looked, if yo dick saw her, it would jump off your body and run and hide."

"You got a rat in your house." said Pone. "I'll put down cheese."

"Works better with peanut butter." retorted Brown.

"Do me a favor," said Pone.

"When the time is right. I'll holler at Ella."

Pone nodded, and Brown winked. Pone made it to the sidewalk outside of Mert's. He took out his phone and text. Pone received his response and put his phone away. He felt eyes on the back of his head.

"Excuse me, sir."

Pone focused on the Spirit Square building across the street. A haven for bankers, brokers, and attorneys. One of many buildings in the city catering to working professionals. Two types of security guards posted at the building; one group dressed like enforcers wearing black baseball caps, tan shirts, black slacks, boots. Badges, cuffs, and guns.

The other guards wore blue blazers, white shirts, red ties, black shoes, and gray slacks. Both worked for the same company, The suits acted like doormen and the welcoming committee and the armed guards, storm-troopers. Pone pondered who considered more important, the doorman or gunmen? Armed guards controlled the parking deck and loading docks. They checked vehicles for bombs and anything dangerous. He smiled because he answered his own question. The building had an upper-class restaurant called Blue, but replaced by a Mexican eatery. Fuel pizza with its gas station theme, Chinese food, and a Greek gyradiko took up residence. Pone used the scenery as a distraction for the coming storm.

"Sir," Followed by a poke between the shoulder blades. Another poke, somebody will lose a finger, he thought.

"Yes, ma'am," said Pone.

A glare and one hand on her hip. "So you got manners," she sneered. "Wanted to meet the man who kill babies."

"Babies with loaded pacifiers." Pone glared. "Tried to kill me. Instead, they murdered an eight-year-old boy."

Her body deflated like a balloon losing air.

Pone knew his words leveled the battlefield.

"You didn't have to burn them..." Her eyes welled up. "They didn't deserve that."

"A message to any-body young or old trying to take me out."

The woman looked as though she wanted to slap Pone. "Mister bad ass tough man."

"When I need to be."

"You a cold hearten hoodlum. Ain't worth a shit."

Pone wanted to tear into the woman. The profession cemented no pity in his heart. "Pot calling the kettle black. Those boys were on the road to being a piece of shit."

Rage and anger made the woman strong; Pone held her at bay till Brown came out of the restaurant grabbing her around the waist swinging her away from Pone. Pone stared then headed toward the parking garage.

Sixteen

The banging on the door loud enough to wake the dead. An hour before midnight. Krasko startled from a good deep sleep. He watched a DVD, *The Good, the Bad and the Ugly*. The spaghetti western anything but boring with its landscape, dramatic scene setting music, and the coolness of Clint Eastwood, what's not to like. The pounding ended with a car skidding like a getaway from a bank robbery.

Krasko got off the recliner and headed to the kitchen. He grabbed the butcher knife for a weapon. No gun in the house.

Krasko stood at the door. No peep-hole to look through which would prove futile since there wasn't a streetlight out in the middle of nowhere. Hell, they didn't have a porch for a porch bulb, just three gray stone steps.

Krasko opened the door clutching the knife. The moon went into hiding, and the illumination came from the living room lamp shining into the abyss. When the lunar appeared it didn't ease the conscience. During the day the landscape harder than cement, desert dust, tumble weeds, sand storms caused by howling winds making the nights spooky.

A large dead oak tree with a hollow black hole the size of a watermelon. A snake would have made the tree it's home. The barren land scared away wildlife and grass afraid to grow on the concrete dirt. At night a beam from the lunate made the lifeless tree look like Sleepy Hollow. The living room glimmer made the tree look as if teasing Krasko to come out wanting to grab him by its tentacles of dead branches.

No wonder who-ever came to the door sped off like his life depended on it.

The only positive thing Krasko saw at his feet a large black athletic dufle bag on the top step. He yanked it inside slamming the door. He carried the bag to the sofa and laid it on the stained floor. Krasko looked around glad he didn't wake White. Not in the mood to deal with his breath of death.

He stretched out on the sofa, turned off the lamp, and closed his eyes.

Seventeen

Twelve p.m. Pone picked up Stick on Sharon road.

"I'm hungry as a motherfucker," said Stick.

Stick hungry, nothing new and he ate his food without the fear of counting calories.

"Where does it go?" asked Pone.

Stick flashed a canine smile. "Maybe I got a tape worm."

"And you cool with that?"

Stick shrugged.

"Where do the two of you want to go?" asked Pone.

Pone hated eating lunch with Stick; he didn't have bad table manners, but peculiar about his restaurants. If it's Chinese or Japanese, he needed to see Asians preparing the food. Pone took him to Taco Bell once, and the string bean man said hell no when he saw all blacks. In his mind something Pone never wanted to enter; what the hell do blacks know about making Mexican food? Stick walked out of a Sub-Way shop claiming Latinos couldn't make him a proper sub sandwich. Pone told Stick Latinos own Sub-way franchises and used their own people. Stick replied they needed to hire more white people.

Any place that served fried chicken whether it a hole in the wall like Chicken King or commercial establishments: Kentucky Fried Chicken, Bojangles, Churches, and Popeye's, he didn't care as long as he saw plenty of blacks handling the chicken.

He loved soul food joints because of the culture. Stick loved big boned black women; settled for smaller ones from time to time and they loved him.

"Decided yet?" asked Pone.

"In the mood for some fried chicken."

Pone sighed. "Kentucky fried chicken it is."

"You black and don't love chicken? What the fuck is wrong with you?" asked Stick. "Don't care for Watermelon and Red Kool-Aid either."

Both men laughed. They arrived at the king of fast food chicken on Freedom drive.

Stick carried his tray of food while Pone lagged empty handed when they sat at a table near the back.

"I'm eating alone?" asked Stick.

Pone snorted. "Fine if it will make you feel better I'll get one of those bowls they make."

"You sure you black?"

"Till the day I die."

Pone returned to the table with his chicken, gravy, cheese, corn, and mashed potato bowl. While Stick boned his chicken, Pone examined his meal with a frown.

"It's food in case you've forgotten," said Stick.

"It's supposed to be popcorn chicken," remarked Pone.

Stick shrugged. "Looks like chicken."

"They cut up a breast and mixed it within."

"I fail to see the problem."

"It's not popcorn chicken." Pone shoved the bowl to Stick, and he dove right in.

"You met with Brown," Stick faced down in the bowl. "Why not Boysenberry?"

"The enemy of my enemy is not my friend."

"The other might get jealous," said Stick.

"You can get cut playing with a double edge sword."

"You trust one guy, but not the other?"

"I trust you."

Stick blushed. "What can I do you for?"

Stick worked freelance, but still recruited hard by Boysenberry and company. He turned down the invitation to join because he felt he could make more money working as a free agent.

"I need information."

"You expect me to go where you can't to get it? You know they don't like me."

"You can only say no but so many times."

Stick flashed a ghoulish grin. "How can I Help?"

There were times Stick gave Pone the chills when he flashed those canine teeth. Bad enough looking into those eyes; yellow iris, and black pupils. Pone imagined the horror his victims faced before their death looking into Stick's eyes.

"I know you can be straight with me." Stick nodded. "Need a shadow?"

"Ask around…you still got people?"

"Where you going with this, Pone?"

Pone connected with Stick over a bar fight: not with each other. Some of the locals didn't warm up to Stick's bizarre looks and Stick being human took all the insults he could take and a fight broke out. Stick outnumbered and Pone knew how it felt being picked on about a condition that was not your fault. Pone's dilemma, Alopecia. He didn't know the cause of Stick's predicament; he saw the odds against Stick so he joined in on the raucous. When the smoke cleared he and stick the last two standing and they became friends.

"I think outside talent took out those kids." Pone swallowed hard. "I don't think they were always on the outside, know what I mean?"

Stick nodded. "You talking about outcast after getting caught. Lost their club card going inside the hoosegow."

"Can you help?"

"I know people in the pen."

"A lot of information lock up inside the big house," said Pone.

"A library under lock and key." Stick finished the chicken bowl. "Sometimes information seep through the cracks."

"Now you feeling me," said Pone.

"Yeah…got a cousin who loves it inside, never want to get out. I'll hook up with him. Might take a day or two."

Pone got moon-eye "What's his deal?"

"Free food, room and board," Stick shrugged. "Got himself a law degree."

Pone heard about bestselling novels written and getting an education while doing time. He shook his head.

"The quicker the better."

Stick downed his coke. "Got your back."

Eighteen

Both windows in the living room cracked open to help combat the breath from hell. Late afternoon and White asleep in his room. Drinking forty ounces of malt liquor and smoking pot will make you sleep like the dead.

Krasko put on some coffee hoping it would act like the Pied Piper bringing White out of his coma. It worked, a creaking door followed by a long yawn and White made a beeline to the kitchen.

Krasko grabbed some Febreeze and spayed the room. White frowned at him for asking to buy the air freshener. Krasko wore a jacket to fight off the chill from the opened windows. White entered the living room with his steaming cup of coffee. He sniffed then glared at Krasko. "You farted?" asked White.

"Hell no, motherfucker!" Krasko returned the glare.

White pulled his robe closer around his neck. "Why you got the windows cracked and wearing a jacket?"

"This house is old and smells," said Krasko.

White shook his head…crazy ass cracker.

This fool nose-blind to his own breath? Thought, Krasko. Even if he passed gas the aroma would smell better than his ozostomia.

White sipped his coffee then displayed a decayed toothy smile when he saw the bag. "It came." He sat down putting his coffee on the table and opened the haversack.

Wrapped money fell out. Krasko acted like a kid on Christmas day. "What the hell? You knew about this?" asked Krasko.

White ignored Krasko. He liked keeping his probono partner in the dark. His way of letting Krasko know who's in charge. The cellphone in his possession, keys to the S-10, the power to come and go as he please where-as Krasko got a reminder of being in prison without the bars. White compared Krasko to an insect and not a fly.

The worst insect he ever encountered his childhood in the summer time living in Rock Hill. This insect he considered dumb as hell. It's attraction to pig shit made it real dense because after all the creatures like a fly seemed to need shit. On those hot summer days when the fan blew out hot humid air making it worse, you place the fan in the window at night hoping to attract cool air to no avail.

A mosquito disturbing your sleep with their wings' sound in your ear letting you know they wanted to taste your blood like a vampire. The mosquito was a smart bug, it attack you at night like a vampire and ninja in your slumber. White admired the insect for wanting hemoglobin and not shit. Yeah, summer nights were like hell in the dark. He remembered as a boy in school the teacher showed a film about the cruelty of-the desert.

The narrator said during the day, the desert would roast you to a crisp, but at night freeze your ass off. The narrator didn't say it in so many words; you got the picture. And he never visited Rock Hill in the summer because it was hot at night as it was during the day. What insect irritated him more than an aedes and a fly. This insect adore shit and wanted to get inside the human eye.

A mystery to White and was what made it so dumb (beside craving feces), even though there are people with beautiful clear eyes making you stare and admire it, it has fluid to keep it moist and what this insect don't realize once inside the orb it will irritate it for a moment, but the dumb ass will realize too late it can't swim and drown. A twisted and rolled up tissue will remove it from the pupil. White considered Krasko a Gnat.

Those uncomfortable irritating summer days now gone thanks to the Great Meteor turning Rock Hill into its namesake.

"Easy." White gathered the money. "The man was upset the job didn't get done. So I convinced him we needed more capital to hire better help."

"What're you talking about? The kids are dead."

White shook his head. "You dumb ass cracker."

Krasko glared. He wanted to drop the N-bomb, but knew blacks to be more sensitive than whites hearing racial slurs.

"Did you think it would be that easy?" White rolled his eyes. "There's still work to do and whether or not you like it we done shit and stepped in it."

"If this ain't a payoff then what the fuck is going on?" asked Krasko.

White sipped his coffee . "We got two strikes."

Krasko strode around the room. "I know we from different sides of the tracks…speaking slang what not, but I'm in the dark."

Where your ass need to be, thought White. "He wants us to take out Pone."

"What the fuck? Chubby Pone. Thought we were supposed to off the kids and split. What's this shit?"

"Turns out that was just the appetizer."

"No. No. You told me…" Krasko got moon-eye. "I doubt if I can swallow the main course!"

White pulled out a jive stick and lit it. "You need to chill."

"You telling me to calm down and you the one going steady with Mary Jane."

"Want one?"

Krasko scratched his head. "Need to keep a clear head. Didn't figure this shit."

"We're just keys on the piano," said White closing his eyes savoring the herb. "Yeah, I get it I'm white, and your ass is black, but I'm tired of being played on. Chubby Pone ain't no joke. There's a reason they call him leave him alone Pone."

White nodded and thanks to the marijuana he was as high as a kite. "He put down two of my family members."

Krasko marched over to White. "You got your family involved? Are you crazy?" White reached in his pocket tossing the phone to Krasko.

"What the hell am I supposed to do?" asked Krasko "Batter up."

"I'd should have stayed in the bucket."

White took a long drag from his reefer. "Ain't no going back to prison. You want to get in good with the man, you step to the plate and hit a home run."

"I ain't involving my family."

"Ain't no monkey see, monkey do," remarked White. Krasko stared at the bag. "Look at all that money."

"Way ahead of you. If your man fucks up then we split the loot and make tracks."

"Now you talking. Agitate the gravel," said Krasko.

White inhaled. "Speak fucking English."

"Take the money and run." Krasko shrugged. "Same as make tracks. "

White nodded. "Only if whoever you get fails."

"I'll get on it." Krasko stared at the money. "How much is that?"

"Don't know. The man must be desperate and being desperate makes you stupid."

Nineteen

The pinball ring tone of Pone's cell kept him from falling asleep while waiting in Birdie's office.

"What's going on, Stick?"

"Got what you wanted," said Stick.

"That was quick."

"Got your back, Jack."

Pone rolled his eyes. "Lay it on me."

"My cousin said two guys, a black and a white from his cell block got released with no static, if you know what I mean."

Somebody with big balls moving and shaking, thought Pone. "Got any names?"

"James Krasko and Roland White. Krasko was a Probono and White a Hip-Hopper."

"What were they in for?"

"Petty arson shit ending up with casualties," said Stick. "My cousin said he spoke to them being a lawyer and shit. He said they told him they didn't know people were in the buildings. Smells like a set up."

"So they're not cold-bloodied killers?"

"Only when things went boom. They were cell mates and according to my cousin they had a bad habit bragging who could set off the best bomb."

"Somebody did their homework. These guys were hand-picked."

"My cousin said it's like they were never there."

"Politics rearing its ugly head."

"What's your plan?" asked Stick.

"Find the head of the snake and cut it off."

"Those guys are like a burner phone," said Stick.

"Untraceable and expendable. I know they're not in the city," said Pone.

"When you find them…"

"I'll let their own decide their fate. Macone and G. deserve satisfaction on the men who took the lives of their posterity."

"I'd hate to be them," said Stick.

"Way to come through."

"Anytime, friend." Stick clicked off just as the doorknob turned. Birdie walked in, catching Pone put away his phone.

"Talking about me?" she asked. Pone smiled.

"Always."

Birdie sat down behind her desk. "Okay…what's with the surprise visit?"

"When did dropping by become a surprise?"

Birdie smiled. "Just playing. Why so serious?"

"Have you heard from Wisdom?"

"Not since that weird dinner."

"True that."

"Is something wrong?"

"I was hoping you could tell me."

Birdie shrugged. "You know as much as I do."

"You stayed behind as I walked out."

"Somebody had to help do the dishes…it brought back memories when we were kids. You always had a way of getting out of chores." Birdie watched Pone nod and smile. "Why did you bring up Shelia?"

Pone swallowed hard. "I have been driving around trying to find him. He inhaled"I want to apologize… I don't want to go to his house. Memory lane is not good for me."

"No doubt. Did you go by his job?"

"He took a leave of absence…don't sound like Wisdom."

Birdie shook her head. "That is strange. Everybody knows Wisdom is a busy body." Pone looked toward the ceiling.

"What Chubby?"

"I didn't mean to upset him. He's not answering his phone," Pone snorted. "To hell with memories, I'll drop by."

"You know Wisdom's rule. Don't come by unless invited."

Pone frowned. Wisdom used the rule when he worked as a hatchet-man. He didn't trust a lot of people and worried about innocents getting caught in a cross-fire in case his enemies found out where he lived.

"This is different, got a strange feeling something's wrong. So you just helped him clean up? No talking?"

"He's not angry, he still loves us, but just want us to make a new lease on life."

"So you talked."

"Sometimes people need time to themselves, besides he'd want you to concentrate on your job. Remember, he always said an occupied mind gets you killed."

"I'll talk to him after I'm done."

Birdie leaned on her desk. "He don't want you to worry about him."

Pone studied Birdie. He felt she knew something and didn't want him to know. He cleared his throat. "Need a moot here today."

"Office or basement?" asked Birdie.

Pone loved Birdie for her no questions ask support. No matter the situation he could count on her.

Brown escorted Ella. She walked in the office acting like if anything touched her would contaminate. Ella glared at Pone when she saw him sitting behind the Ebony desk.

"Please have a seat," said Pone.

"Had I known it was you, I'd never come." She glared at Brown. "You lied. Luring me into this place of sin."

Pone shook his head. He never understood why women like Ella brought the presence of God with them.

"Trust me when I say this is important," said Brown.

"This is a respectable night-club. Nothing sleazy or sinful about it," said Pone.

He knew Ella's assumption correct about a house of sin. Nadine catered to the world of organized crime, gangsters, thugs, thieves, hit men, assassins, and what not.

It became a place where Prohibition and Hip-Hoppers could call a truce instead of being rivals; Ella did not need to know the club history. Felony ended with housing murderers. Birdie a business woman did not allow prostitution inside Nadine.

Ella and Brown sat in chairs put in place for them in front of the desk. Ella took out a crucifix of Jesus, closed her eyes, murmured a prayer, and crossed her heart. Brown rolled his eyes and shook his head.

"You good now?" asked Pone.

"Got to prepare myself when facing the devil," said Ella.

Pone smiled. "I've been call worse."

Ella slapped Brown's arm. "Got me meeting with the demon who killed my boy."

"He tried to kill me and an eight-year-old boy lost his life," said Pone.

Ella rose from her seat and pointed at Pone. "May God strike…"

Brown grabbed Ella easing her back down in her seat. "I told you to listen to the man for closure."

Ella folded her arms. "Ain't nothing he can say."

"Roland White," said Pone.

Ella got moon-eye.

Brown straightened in his chair. "First cousins."

Again with the family theme, thought Pone. "You don't say?"

Ella stood up. "You trying to be funny Mister Pone 'cause I don't have put up with your nonsense."

Pone had 101 insults dancing around in his head, but he needed information about White from Ella.

"I meant no disrespect. Please…sit down."

Ella batted her eyes as if to say all right, but one more insult and she would leave. Pone leaned back and studied the grieving mother. She did what most women did when thinking men eye-balling their rack. Ella closed up her sweater.

Pone didn't find her attractive by no stretch of the imagination, but he would give her this one.

"What can you tell me about your cousin?" asked Pone. "Much like yourself, a no good for nothing."

Pone gave a stern look. "No more insults goes both ways. Listen to what I have to say and it might shed light on the recent tragedies. Can you sit and listen?"

Ella nodded.

"I believe your cousin influenced your son."

"From prison?" asked Ella.

Pone watched Brown raise an eyebrow and crossed his legs.

"I'm not sure, but I don't think he's in prison," said Pone.

Brown leaned forward. "What the fuc…" Brown caught himself when Ella gave him a look. "What's going on, Pone?"

Pone held up his hand and looked at Ella. "Was he ever in the service?"

"Two years in the Army," she said.

"Enough time to learn a trade," remarked Pone.

"Surprised us all when he enlisted. Then when he got out he…" Ella gave Brown a somber look. "He ended up in prison."

"You never noticed your son talking to anybody strange or even acting strange?" asked Pone.

"I work and Bucky was out of school." She choked back tears. "Not book smart, but he graduated." Her eyes brightened. "I had a rule; if you ain't going to school or have a job then you can't lay your ass around my house. Father forgive me," she said looking toward the ceiling crossing her heart. "Thought he had enough sense to know right from wrong," Ella shook her head.

A buck-teeth youth flashed in Pone's head. Eyes wide, mouth dropped open shaking like a leaf before Pone ghosted him. Pone exhaled.

Brown sat up straight. "Now Pone, what do you mean…"

"Thank you, Ella. I know how difficult that was for you. Thank you again for your time" Pone nodded at Brown. "You mind getting her a cab?"

Ella rose from her chair like she sat on a tack. She glared at Pone walking out. He returned a sullen look. Pone realized Ella considered her son an innocent child. Pone saw a delinquent holding an automatic weapon. Brown gave Pone the I shall be back look and returned as quick as he left.

He sat down and leaned toward Pone. "Give me the scoop on Roland."

"What? You don't keep tabs on your boys when they go inside?"

"Hell no… Roland knew the rules. You on your own when you get busted.

It was his own damn fault messing with a snow white and got collared by a white Po Po." Pone gave Brown a dubious look. "What is this the civil rights movement?" He knew Roland didn't get sent up the river for dating a white woman, but Pone played ignorant.

Brown laughed. "No man, I'm just fucking with you. We found out he was doing shit on the side. We paid him good, but his ass got greedy and you know sometimes indulgence can be the end of you. He blew up a building, some people ended up dead and he got fucked."

Pone snorted and leaned back. Stick told him about the bombing and the casualties. "And it didn't bother you he put his talents on the market?" asked Pone.

"We weren't sorry to see his ass go."

"Why?"

Brown frowned. "His breath. That fucker's breath was so bad… whew! I remember it was cold and windy. He stood a few feet across from me, the wind blew between us and I kid you not his breath penetrated the wind and burned my nostril hairs."

Pone almost fell on the floor laughing. "He was your bomber?"

"He had mad skills if nothing else," said Brown. "Could make a bomb out of a pack of cigarettes."

Pone pursed his lips. "Out of curiosity, if his breath was so bad, how did he get that white gal?"

"She was a bow wow, chicken head, trailer trash. The man couldn't afford to be choosy," said Brown.

"Yeah, well, that hire bit you in the ass," remarked Pone.

"What are you trying to say?"

Pone wanted to tell Brown that Roland and a Probono blew up the kids, but figured if he did then Brown would put out an all-points bulletin on White and shake down Ella for information on her cousin's whereabouts. Pone wanted to do the shaking.

Pone knew G cared about Brown. "G might alienate you."

"So you know something and going to hold it over my head?"

"Ella has enough on her plate," said Pone.

Brown flashed a Cheshire cat grin. "The man has a heart."

"When it suits me. I'll fill you in when I know more, until then I need you to be discrete."

Brown nodded. "We solid, brother. Solid."

Twenty

Reflexes, muscle tone, endurance, hand and eye coordination—the reasons boxers loved the speed bag. Pone boxed to stay in shape and combat stress. His fighting style based simulated a boxer, thanks to Wisdom. Pone wanted to make amends with his mentor, Wisdom the closes thing to a father. Shelia never mentioned his parents and he didn't bother to ask. Shelia and Wisdom made he, Birdie, and Jade feel like family. Pone needed to speak to Wisdom. He hit the man below the belt bringing up Shelia.

He couldn't figure out why Wisdom used a long awaited dinner invite to convince he and Birdie to change their lifestyles. Birdie could transition a lot easier than he could, but then again how would her audience take it if she didn't have Nadine for them to unwind after a hard day of blowing up, shooting, stabbing, and making illegal business deals what not after making people lives miserable. Birdie's cortege would get paranoid thinking she knows too much about them if she shut down her haven of organized crime club. Her transition to recreate herself if she did so easier than his.

Pone shook off the thought weighing in on his life. Hit-man paid to kill and troubleshooter stopping trouble before it gets worse. Pone left the speed bag and put the hits on the heavy bag. Where the speed bag used for speed, hand, and eye coordination. The heavy bag made for power. Pone wasn't working out of anger though hitting the heavy bag, anger came out thinking about Wisdom suggesting he change his lifestyle. No longer a hit man or assassin for hire. His job now handing out parking citations; a hell of a lot different than before when J. Paul use to order him to off a person whether they deserved to die or not.

Pone hit the bag harder and harder; beads of sweat ran down his forehead and his workout clothes drenched and weighed on him. He loved every minute of working out on the heavy and speed bags. He wasn't about to ask Red to make him a parking enforcer. Talk about an unappreciative job; no respect from patrons or the city itself. Besides he had a college degree, but he was no pencil pusher.

Pone cringed thinking about getting up every morning going to an office or worse a cubicle feeling trapped a trash compactor. Wearing a tie also bothered him.

Pone had no problem playing dress up, but a fancy noose tied around his neck on a daily bases not for him.

He admitted to himself his college degree wasted, but entrenched working as a troubleshooter. The freedom like a leaf in the wind with more control. Red the tree he fell from; she gave him an assignment, and how he handled it up to him as long as he got the job done. He couldn't have asked for a better boss, the woman put herself out on the limb for him against her own family.

Red took up a special place in Pone's heart. Comparing his relationship with Red to peanut butter and jelly meant nothing romantic. Forbidden fruit, if one tasted the other it would be Brigand band poison. Pone didn't want to come between Red and her family.

Temptation filled the air when they occupied the same room, but keeping their relationship professional better for both.

His arms ached, knuckles sore; flow of blood through his body made his mind more than alert so he decided that both the speed and heavy bag had had enough pounding for one day. Pone took off his gloves and grabbed a bottled water from his basement mini fridge and sat on his seldom used weight bench.

Sweat plopped on the smooth cracked burnt orange concrete floor. Pone thought about his conversation with Brown and Ella. White and his Prohibition partner blew up the teens. Pone glad he didn't tell them. A gambler never puts all his cards on the table, he thought. Pone would have to keep a poker face dealing with the lieutenants of both gangs. The enemy of his enemy not his friend Pone a nemesis to Prohibitions and Hip-Hoppers. He associated more with Brown than Boysenberry because the hits on his life came from Brown's neck of the woods. White a former Hip-Hopper and a fool for convincing his relatives to take him out.

Ella hit the nail on the head about her cousin being a piece of shit sending his kin to a guaranteed death going up against him. Brown smart not to tell Ella he took out her cousin Wanda. Pone didn't know if Wanda was close to Ella, but they were family just the same and even though Ella wanted nothing to do with Roland, he saw it made her proud he enlisted in the Army, but disappointed he got out by the way she looked at Brown. Ella must have known about their association. Pone wondered why she seemed comfortable around Brown. She did the lord Jesus, crossing her heart and clutching her crucifix; yet paraded around with not the devil, but Brown at least a demon. Maybe a secret connection to do with the restaurant. Ella didn't own Mert's, but feared losing her job if she failed to comply with Brown. A middle-aged woman and the walls of opportunity closed.

After all there's a reason they call it organized crime and then again she may have been dumb for her son, but smart enough to keep her mouth shut about Brown.

A blind-eye and tight lips the best way to stay alive around a gangster even when she got wind of her son trying to get an entry level job with the Hip-Hoppers.

Pone believe Ella the mother who struggled all her life and no matter how much she prayed, and try to live right, she still got the short end of the stick and willing to look the other way if her son had become a successful gangster she would take the blood money just to get a taste of how the other half lived. She being human would accept gangster lifestyle taking away her son's innocence which it did, the buck-tooth youth responsible for putting an eight-year-old boy in an early grave.

The thought of Ella's son made Pone focus on Macone's and G's progeny. They were innocent, but suffered because of their fathers trangressions. Pone embraced the responsibility of finding out who would be cruel enough to snuff out two youths with bright futures. At least he knew who planted the bomb; Roland White and James Krasko, but the man behind them calling the shots still a mystery. Pone's gut feeling took over and the man that came to mind none other than ex District Attorney Harvey Crowe. He put a lot of criminals away giving him a Rolodex of names to manipulate and he chose White and Krasko, bomb makers. The hits on his life both came before and after meetings with Crowe during the night.

What puzzled Pone the most, why would he target two adolescence of powerful fathers and not the fathers themselves? Pone pondered why Crowe wanted to stop him from solving the case. He wants a war between the Prohibitions and Hip-Hoppers. He took the lives of Reggie and Helen to get the ball rolling.

Twenty-One

The Mimosa Grill at 300 S. Tryon sounded like a diner; the sophisticated brasserie made a greasy-spoon look like an outhouse The grill name gave it a diner appeal and it ended there. Living on the south side of the city where the elite class: lawyers, brokers, and bankers a who's who the Mimosa Grill served. White collars loved the corporate cafe. Lawyers entertained potential clients, made business deals, and welcomed new employees to their firm.

Mimosa furnished with booths, tables, and bar stools to sit while watching flat screens above the bar. The restaurant's seating area near the windows gave its patrons a great view of the city. One citizen enjoying his window scene, Deputy Mayor Harvey Crowe. He sat looking out into the municipality waiting for his lunch guest. A sparse lunch crowd; how he liked it while indulging himself on bread and butter. Man cannot live by bread alone and a leggy waitress with the name tag Lori brought an appetizer plate of eight deviled eggs made of grain mustard, and crispy bacon. Tall and her crisp white blouse gloved her upper torso, her black skirt hemmed three inches above the knee showed enough black panty-hose thigh, and black two inch pumps enhanced her bulging toned calves.

Crowe smiled watching her head back to the kitchen. He knew his lunch guest would enjoy the view once he got a load of her. He wasted no time indulging himself with the eggs before the leggy waitress interrupted his moment with the tasty morsel by escorting his lunch guest to the table.

"Here you go sir," She filled their glasses with water. "I'll give you a few minutes before I take your order."

Thomas Maxwell took his seat at the window view table while watching the waitress switch her way back to the kitchen. He took a long drink water.

"Down boy, you already have a lap to sit on," said Crowe. "Have yourself a deviled egg, I guarantee the taste will take your mind off the land of the giants."

Maxwell took a deviled egg glaring at Crowe. He stood five-three, a generous height assumption by his peers. He never understood why people like Crowe made short people jokes considering he'd never play in the NBA. Crowe maybe four-inches taller if that, but still a small man by any standard. Crowe knew Maxwell conscience about his height; stretching his neck to the limit when standing, the diminutive district attorney put lifts in his shoes for height increase when attending social events. Everyone saw a stunted man with lifts in his shoes.

"Is that why you asked me to lunch to make fun of my height? You're short too you know," suggested Maxwell.

Crowe snickered. "I'm taller than you." Rubbing his chest and shoulders.

"Kudos though for dating an amazon."

Maxwell rose from the table. "Thanks for wasting my time."

"Come on Tommy, can't you take a joke?" Crowe took a bite of his egg. "But this does involved you and your tall drink of water." Crowe took a sip of water from his glass.

"What are you talking about, Harvey?"

"Pone."

Maxwell sat back down and straightened in his chair. "Thought I'd get your attention," smiled Crowe.

Before Maxwell could comment the leggy waitress returned.

"Hi, I'm Lori and I will be your waitress. Are you ready to order?" She took out her order pad.

"I'll have the Shrimp and Grits," assured Crowe without looking at the menu winking at Maxwell.

Maxwell inhaled twisting his lips. "I'll have your patty melt with crinkle fries."

"And what will you be drinking?" asked the waitress.

Crowe smiled. "Bring us a bottle of your best red wine."

"Superb," approved the waitress. She grabbed the menus and headed for the kitchen to place their orders.

Maxwell held up a finger. "Heineken for me."

Crowe snorted. "Never understood why some people order a burger at a fancy restaurant?"

"Because it's on the menu," remarked Maxwell.

"We eating at the Waffle House?" questioned Crowe.

"It's just lunch Harvey." Maxwell shook his head and rolled his eyes. "What's the big deal?"

"Guess I'm just different, but we do have something in common."

"Pone," retorted Maxwell.

"You want him off the street as much as I do."

"He's clean and working for you."

"A soapy Brillo pad couldn't scrub the dirt off him."

"You're talking about past transgressions."

"He killed a lot of innocent people for J. Paul."

Maxwell frowned. "I thought you wanted him to find out who killed those kids and stop a potential gang war?"

"I do, but I still believe in justice. He being a troubleshooter doesn't change who he once was in my book. Just because he's working for your girl doesn't give him a clean slate." Crowe leaned forward. "Two birds with one stone."

Maxwell sat back folding his arms. "How do you plan to proceed with this, huh? You plan to make a move before he solves the case?"

"If I was a criminal, I would love for you to prosecute me. Am I wrong to think you're not cut out for this?"

"I'm tiring of your insults, but what I'm hearing here is that you want to go after a man you hired through the mayor's office to stop two gangs from wreaking havoc on this city. I'm confused on where you're going with this."

Crowe finished off the last egg. "I want to move on him as soon as he solves the case. There…are you happy now?"

"Happy that you still have your priority straight, but he is no longer a criminal."

"We're politicians, Tommy."

"I won't do anything shady."

"You know when you succeeded me, I thought you had potential."

"To be a crooked politician? Glad to disappoint, in fact the more you talk the more I'm losing my appetite."

"The district attorney was a stepping stone for me and look at me now," Crowe sipped his water. "This isn't the end of it."

"Winslow's the mayor."

Crowe snorted. "You think this city wants a mayor who runs from the first sign of trouble. No pun intended. He left me to handle this mess and you think I'm not going to ride this thing."

"If that's your goal, I don't see how I can help you and you do know…"

Crowe rolled his eyes. "I know the public advocate if the regular Mayor's incapacitated. I do however…"

Maxwell took a swill of his water. "You can wait that long?"

"Like fine wine," Crowe sipped. "Patience is a virtue."

Maxwell shrugged. "If you say so."

"Don't you tire of Pone being around Red? I mean…"

The waitress returned with their food. She placed the Shrimp and Grits in front of Crowe and gave Maxwell his patty melt and Heineken. A waiter followed her with a bottle of red wine. He poured and Crowe motioned for him to leave the bottle.

"Enjoy…let me know if you need anything," she said then headed back to the kitchen with the waiter. Maxwell eyed her all the way.

Crowe cleared his throat. "She's a knockout, but not in Red's league and neither are you. You both being lawyers can only go but so far."

"Brooke and I have a strong relationship."

Crowe smiled. He enjoyed his shrimp and grits. The shrimp sauteed in garlic butter, sweet onions, charred peppers, smoked tomatoes and red gravy. Crowe closed his eyes to savor the flavor. "I get this dish every time I come here because it's so sentimental."

"What do you mean?" asked Maxwell with a mouthful of patty melt.

"These grits are just how my mother use to make it, not too stiff and not too soupy with just the right of amount of garlic butter mixed in. How's your patty melt?"

Maxwell toasted. "Waffle House don't serve beer."

"I was eight when my mother died."

Maxwell took a drink of his beer to wash down the patty melt. "Excuse, me?"

"My mother…she died when I was eight."

"That must have been hard?"

"I used it as motivation."

"If I'm not being too forward, how did she die?" asked Maxwell. "A casualty in a gang shoot out."

There had been several gang shoot outs throughout the years in the city, Maxwell didn't want to push any further realizing how hard it must have been for Crowe to lose his mother.

"You mentioned motivation?"

"Guilty, that's why I go so hard at mobsters while I was the DA and why I can't leave Pone untouched despite him working on behalf of the mayor's office."

Maxwell finished his patty melt. "I still don't see how you going to do this without some kind of fall out," He attacked his fries dipping them in ketchup.

"Why'd you think I hired him? Who better to deal with gangsters then a former gangster hit man."

"Pone's holding a double-edged sword," said Maxwell.

"He's expendable," remarked Crowe.

"Can't argue with you there, but I still don't see what this have to do with me."

"Winslow picked me as his deputy mayor not because of my looks, but how I went after mob activity and though I didn't get the big boys," Crowe swallowed hard. "I let them know …" He cracked his knuckles. "The mayor figured I would strengthen his office and he was right."

Maxwell nursed his beer. He heard whispers around the office Crowe ran a tight ship and went after mobsters with reckless abandon. Maxwell didn't like Crowe, but admitted Crowe stuck his nose in their business and put some of their key players in the pen.

Maxwell didn't know the deputy mayor's ambition, political or personal why he went after the mob so hard, but Maxwell's flaw, no signature case to make the office forget the former District Attorney.

"What can I do to help?" asked Maxwell.

Crowe use his fork to poach two shrimp out of the sea of grits. "If you say you're not jealous, then you're lying. He spends more time with her then you do. Have you seen them together? I have and they have a hard time keeping things professional."

Maxwell finished off his beer to Crowe's delight chewing the shrimp. "I can't make her fire the guy," stated Maxwell.

"So you do want to get rid of him. Good, but it needs to be discrete."

"He's a killer and I want to protect her, but what can I do?"

"It's no secret you haven't made a big splash sitting in my old seat. You nail Pone and you will be the all the rave. You know I'm right and you know you need to win a big case. A mob case. What Pone did in the past can only hurt him, but help you make your doubters believe you are the right man for the job."

"I can't tell Brooke what to do."

"I said be discrete, you don't talk to her about this at all."

"Guess it's a good thing we see each other when it suits her."

Crowe gave Maxwell a Cheshire cat grin. "You're whipped."

Maxwell shrugged. "She's an amazing woman."

"You're afraid she'll dump you and I can understand that, because if I had a woman like her I'd walk around on egg shells too, but you need to think about your career. You become a big time DA and that leggy blonde waitress depending if she likes powerful men could be a side dish unless Red has your heart."

Maxwell frowned holding his empty bottle wishing for another beer. "You're a cliche."

"A lot of small, but powerful men have more than one woman." Crowe smirked. "How hungry are you?"

"I'm not that kind of guy."

Crowe downed his wine. "Then let me handle things, you sit on the bench and I'll let you know when to go in."

Crowe's phone buzzed. He checked his text. "Bottom of the ninth," he murmured.

"What's that?" asked Maxwell.

"Are you on board?" asked Crowe putting away his phone.

Maxwell grabbed the wine bottle and extra glass. He emptied the vino; swirled it, sniff the aroma then took more than a sip letting it settle on his tongue before swallowing. The taste of grapes the only thing making sense to him of this bizarre lunch with Crowe. Who did that text come from and what did Crowe mean bottom of the ninth, thought Maxwell. He didn't wait for Crowe to end their lunch. Maxwell rose from the table finishing his wine nodding count me in.

Twenty-Two

Everyone has a foresight like Spider-man's Spidey sense warning him something bad about to happen. In Pone's business, an awareness can be life and death.

Seven blocks stood between Pone and Nadine. He wanted to grill Birdie about Wisdom because he felt she wasn't telling him everything. He took a walk to clear his head and to relax. Pone got tired sitting home worrying about his mentor making him want to interrogate Birdie. He thought she gave him the run around and figured a walk through the city letting the cool breeze clear his head would do him good.

His intuition told him he wasn't walking alone. Other patrons shared the side walk moving in the same and opposite direction. Pone got an itch he couldn't scratch. He knew better than to look back spooking his pursuer. He hoped whoever followed him wouldn't involve gun-play because innocents paraded the streets. Shooting into civilians a no-no. Men, women, and children doing their daily routine.

Not the time for a few casualties; so what?

Pone continued his journey till he spotted an old watering hole he hadn't been to for a long time. An average sized establishment on the outbound of Metro city. A black Gothic building in the metropolis art district. Square in front and back with a rectangular body wedge between two new built apartment complex several blocks away from the urine stench Greyhound bus station at 900 Trade Street. Before the new condos, the area donned a nickname, cutthroat lane. Men got drunk and flashed their loot only to get their throat slit once outside the bar.

Pone stepped inside the tavern hoping his tag along would follow and stick out like a sore thumb. Pone wasn't Gothic, but he wore black and that made him close enough. He stood at the entrance staring at what kept him from this side of town. A five-eight one-hundred and fifty-five pounds of dancer muscle behind the soot bar. Queen Garret. Queen's features hard, but beautiful.

Raised by a hard nose father and no mother. Queen's dad, a retired MMA fighter who gave as good as he got inside the octagon and used his earnings to purchase a taproom which he named The Raven Cavern. He took too many hits to the head and placed in a retirement home leaving the saloon in Queen's care forcing her to quit the exotic dancing circuit making her old man happy.

Queen a strong woman. She slid beer across the bar to a patron spotting Pone at the entrance. Queen motioned to a tall, muscular Gothic man who looked like Mister Clean except for the ebony lips and eye liner. He adorn a black leather vest and leather pants.

Pone scoped out the place making sure it didn't turn into a gay club. Not quite dark and gloomy Goth, tattoos, body piercing, men looking like women growing their hair from shoulder to the butt and women resembling men with close to the scalp buzz cuts decked out in black with a handful of normal looking people in T-shirts and blue jeans. When Queen finished talking to Mister Clean, she used her eyes to motion Pone into following her to the back of the lounge. He obliged.

Queen stood with her back to Pone in the Gothic dark hall-way. Enough light shone for him to get a close up on Queen's body from behind. Tanning booths not her thing; pale as a ghost highlighted by Goth darkness with raven shoulder length hair. She kept her signature Moe Stooge bang cut above her eyes. Tattoos decorated most of her body to the point she may have joined the Yakuza, thought Pone. Her outfit all black; sports bra top, spandex leggings, and pumps.

The walk to her office wasn't like the green mile, and many convicts would've loved to journey behind her. Pone smiled thinking all the women in his life strong and independent.

Inside the office, pale white walls and jet black furniture. Small and cozy with three goth-like paintings on the wall. The floor sandalwood and clean. She dimmed the light, went to her desk drawer took out a mirror, wiped her lips with tissue only to paint them again. She strode over to Pone. Her lips glossy rose red.

She tilted her head sideways. "I am a lady, Chubby."

In a gentle manner, Pone took off his bowler and tossed it on the sofa. "Can you tell me what that painting is?" asked Queen.

Pone looked to the right wall and studied the painting; orange, red, black. And yellow colors smeared on rectangle, square, triangle, and circle shapes. "Picasso," said Pone.

"No," said Queen.

Pone analyzed the painting a little closer. "Well, I always thought Picasso overrated." He turned back toward her greeted by a powerful right cross knocking him back against the door. Before he could recover, she rushed forward pressing him tight against the egress with her muscular arms.

"Two years. Two fucking years and you bring your ass to my bar. What the fuck do you want?"

Pone shook off the cobwebs. "First…ow and damn you're strong for a woman."

Queen released him.

"I need your help," said Pone.

A quick powerful left cross sent Pone to the sofa almost landing on his derby. Queen straddled him.

"I gave you my number…was I a notch in your belt?"

Pone rubbed his jaw. "No…look there are three women in my life."

Queen glared.

Pone held up his hand. "They're family, okay. I fear for their lives every day. I don't need a fourth."

"I'm a big girl. I can take care of myself," said Queen sitting beside Pone. "Sisters, huh?"

"Grew up with two of them."

"So the other could be more?"

"She's my boss, Red…"

"Brigand." confirmed Queen.

"You've heard of her?"

"Perks of owning a bar. People drink and talk. You know you're a good looking man?"

"I'm not a womanizer. A special lady taught me how to treat women."

"She never told you how one night stands could hurt?"

"I had my reasons."

"So you didn't lie?"

Pone smiled. "You took my virginity."

Queen blushed. "So trouble brought you back into my life?"

"Not if you're using me as a punching bag."

"I felt used…you hurt me, and I wanted to hurt you."

Pone rubbed his face. "You happy now?"

"What's going on, Chubby?"

"I think I'm being followed."

"Okay." shrugged Queen

"Need you to go out to the bar and see who sticks out like a sore thumb." Pone was mesmerized how the ruby lips and eye-shadow emphasized Queen's face. "I know it's a stretch."

"I got this, I can tell a fish out of water." she smiled.

Queen sneaked in a quick erotic kiss ending with her biting his lower lip before she left.

Pone tasted blood and shook his head. She likes it rough And so did he in deep thought:

All the women in his life were strong and independent; Shelia Green took a bullet because of her connection to Wisdom and it ate at him like cancer. Red, Birdie, and Jade connected to him and he promised to protect the glamorous trio. Queen's beauty came from the school of hard knocks streetwise tough. Ridge in stress, chiseled facial features.

Queen came back and sat next to Pone. "Okay, Milt thinks you're hot."

Pone pursed his lips. "Your bartender?"

"Don't worry, he knows you don't swing that way."

Pone smiled. Never trust a man comfortable wearing leather.

"And he said some tall blonde guy wearing jeans, Khaki breaker, and a red flannel shirt sat down surveying the place from a corner table like he's looking for someone."

"Must be him," said Pone. He looked into Queen's eyes realizing she could be woman number four in his life.

"Does he want to kill you?" asked Queen.

"Welcome to my world."

"How can I help?" She held his hand.

"You got that mandatory drinking policy?"

"Don't every bar?" Shrugged Queen. "Got to make money."

"I need you to get him seated at the bar drinking. Tell him tables are for couples and give me five minutes. Engage him in a conversation until I leave. Look toward thedoor making sure he follows your eyes."

"You want him to follow you?"

"You want to clean up the mess in your bar?"

"He'll be right behind you?"

Before Queen could exit, Pone grabbed her arm. "Are the police more visible since they put up those condos?"

Queen snorted. "It ain't cut-throat alley, but we still at the bottom of the society pool."

Five minutes can be like that traffic light when you want green you get red and vice versa. The five minutes Pone wanted went by faster than a rat crossing the room.

Pone stood in the entrance hallway. Queen did her job luring the man to the bar giving him hard liquor, Pone made it to the bar entrance tipping his hat on the way out.

"Have a nice day, sir," said Queen.

The buck saw the back of Pone's head and almost fell off his stool watching him leave. "Hey!" said Queen. "Drinks ain't free."

The buck tossed a twenty. "Keep the change."

Call it a cliche`, but fights and murders seem to go hand in hand; Gangsters, thugs, and Rogue's gallery are people who believe in street survival; they all love bars and clubs with alleys and dumpsters hidden from the public eye. The tall bloke didn't know where Pone ran off to, but he speculated down the alley between the dumpsters lined up against a black painted brick wall. He stood about five feet from the dumpsters glancing up and down the ebony brick passage

He was about to walk away.

"How much?" A voice behind a green recycle bin.

The buck stared at the recycling bin. Did he have too much to drink? He sighed relief when he saw Pone ease out from behind it.

The buck stood twenty yards away. He looked about six-five, well built, and in his mid-twenties.

"We don't have to do this…look, the guy who hired you is a nobody. So if you walk away he can't hurt you," said Pone.

The buck stared. Pone snorted and thought White sacrificed his family so it's Krasko's turn and he chose a big one to be his champion. If they were cousins, Pone did not ask.

"We talking or bopping?" asked the buck spreading his arms.

Pone couldn't help but laugh. The guy Probono saying bop for fight. Pone knew the buck didn't come to do the funky chicken or the wad-tootsie. He put up his dukes and Pone saw another Arnold Pratt.

The buck threw two quick right jabs followed by a left hook. Pone dodged with ease. The buck big and slow telegraph his punches. No weapons. Pone expected his adversary's plan to stun him with a few blows then move in and break his neck. Pone knew when fighting a bigger opponent, the smaller chap had to get in close to inflict damage.

The buck went for a hay-maker with his left, Pone ducked and saw his right leg planted. He hit the shin with a stamping blow. Scraping down the shin followed by a stamp onto the instep. The buck buckled to the ground grimacing in pain, but had enough instinct to protect his left jaw from Pone's backhanded fist and caught Pone with a solid uppercut to the chin. Pone stunned ending on his back.

For a brief moment, Pone remembered a conversation of a retired boxer who said though no longer quick; if he connected…a right hook on the chin. Pone down but not out. The buck saw Pone groggy. He pounced on him.

Just as Pone thought, the plan to stun then get those big mitts around his neck.

Mission accomplished, but Wisdom always said when falling to the ground be sure to keep your arms free. Pone did just that.

The buck's body weight forced air from Pone's body making him winded. Things got worse when he squeezed his larynx. Pone used his left hand grabbing one wrist to loosen the buck's grip and with his right causing an eruption of blood hitting the buck in his nose with a palm-heel strike. The buck felt the blows; being bigger. stronger, and younger. He kept on squeezing. Pone felt his lungs burning, but kept hammering away at the buck's face until he heard a bop and the buck fell to the side against the wall.

Pone sat up gasping for air rubbing his throat. He looked up, saw another giant clad in black leather. Milt. He swung a Louisville slugger. Pone shook his head.

Boy these Goths enjoyed wearing black. Milt raised the bat looking to hit a home run. "No!" Pone rose shaking his head, "Let him live."

"You sure, 'cause he was going to ghost you," said Milt.

Pone nodded. "Let's see if you knocked sense into him."

Milt held the bat like a baseball player. "Your call."

The buck sat up against the wall eyes glossyrubbing his head. He used the sleeve of his arm to wipe blood from his nose. He looked at Pone.

"I had you."

"Shut up and listen or I'll have my friend here swing away," The buck glared at Pone.

"A broken nose and that comment alone proves you're not cut out for this."

Pone took out his wallet grabbing a hand full of hundred dollar bills tossed them at his feet.

"Take that and there's a Greyhound station a few blocks inbound and get the hell out of town. If I see you in town… if I see you at a hot dog stand I will kill you."

The buck observe the money.

"Get set up else-where and send for your love ones if you got any, I gave a bloke a second chance like I'm giving you and now he's in the bone yard."

The buck picked up the money and walked away.

Milt rested the bat on his shoulder giving Pone a look.

"Some people aren't as dumb as others," said Pone.

Twenty-Three

A song lyric by a famous rock star way back in the day said it best. Hurt so good I don't understand. Pone pinned on the sofa bed in a luscious lip lock and straddled by a tattooed Gothic vixen. His nipples caressed then pinched with just the right pressure to give a pleasure sensation. He inhaled with the pain The fore play technique gave a whole new meaning to pleasurable sadism and an effect on his friend down below.

Every tweak like pushing a button building pressure until his volcano erupted its lava of ecstasy for both participants.

The only problem inflicted by Queen drawing blood from Pone's lips putting an exclamation point on the night. Pone sat on the edge of the sofa bed examining the hemoglobin from his lip on his finger.

"What's wrong, baby? Not satisfied?" asked Queen.

Pone didn't dabble in sexual encounters often; didn't consider himself a womanizer.

He could count on both hands how many times he indulge in intercourse. Queen though, his first rodeo. Several one nighties after her while doing his job along the way.

Queen took his virginity. He studied her as she rolled over for a cat nap. Could he adapt to a life with a Goth. His heart raced around her confusing him. It's not like they see each other every day. His buddy down below liked her a lot getting excited without his help and then again he got excited about a few women; the ones in his circle; Pone would never have sex with them because it would complicate things. Queen for now the only one he could have pleasure with and not feel guilty except for not seeing her for two years.

Pone shook his head and came back to reality, with his lifestyle too many damn enemies; then again a lot gangsters married, girlfriends, mistresses and so on; he no longer a gangster, but troubleshooter for Metro City.

Queen an eccentric woman with an eerie Vampirella look about her. A little rough around the edges and she liked his company. Pone wondered if she held a torch for him. Two years and not married. He never thought about tying the knot and trusted she wasn't wasting her time thinking he would someday be her husband.

If that's the case then she needed to find someone not involved in his world.

"Everything okay, babe?" She asked stretching and yawning.

"Since when did you become a vampire?"

She looked away embarrassed. "Sorry, sometimes I get carried away."

"Other men, huh?"

"I ain't a nun if that's what you're asking. But I'll cut back on the blood lust next time."

Pone exhaled. Good, she's been with other men.

Queen sat up in bed. "There will be a next time, right?" Pone didn't answer.

"You motherfucker!"

Pone took a rabbit punch to the back of the head.

"What the hell!" said Pone. "Not if it will be an abusive relationship."

"Sorry, lost my temper."

"Told you my life's complicated."

"So we're right for each other,"

Pone winked and smiled.

Queen smiled. "Okay then…let me throw this at you. We don't have to hold hands in public. I'm okay with being discreet. You know on the down low."

"What are we teenagers?" Pone inhaled. "I'll think about it."

"Do that."

Queen hopped off the bed. "Right now I need to go to the bathroom…"

"What you do in there is your business, okay?"

Queen giggled. "Sure you want none details?"

"Way to kill the mood."

"You are such a prude."

"It's called class."

Queen rolled her eyes and left to handle her business. Pone relaxed on the sofa bed putting all the women in his life in perspective. He eliminated Jade. A college senior with a mad crush on him. Every time she saw him when she gave him a sucker punch kiss. He told her how inappropriate, and she'd always be his baby sister.

Jade, discreet around Birdie; Pone suspected Birdie picked up the vibes from her younger sister. He hated hearing the two argue because it always ended with you're not my mother. Pone shook off Jade to concentrate on grown women.

He almost crossed that line, but Wisdom intervened. Told Pone to think of Birdie as his sister. Don't sully their family relationship. Pone wondered why Birdie didn't committ herself to Antonio. A good man, and head over heels in love with her. She deflected the sound of wedding bells when Antonio hinted marriage and Pone hoped he wasn't the wall keeping them from holy matrimony.

Maybe if he bind himself to Queen, then maybe Birdie would jump the broom with Antonio and start a family of her own, the clock ticked and father time crept up on them. Red. Gorgeous, leggy, a goddess dating an elf. He did not grow up with Red like he did with Birdie and Jade, but the first time they saw each other sparks flew.

If he became serious with Queen, it might push Red deep into the pit-fall arms of her little district attorney? District Attorney…

"Oh shit!" said Pone. He got dressed. Queen wasn't back from blowing up the toilet. He looked around and saw a scratch pad on her desk. Pone left his number and an apology and expected she'd understand.

Pone drove on the highway at night to be discrete. He couldn't shake Queen out of his head. He knew she'd get angry he didn't stick around to say good-bye; his intuition about the case danced in his head. He realized it wouldn't work out between the two and not because of her being a Goth. but he thought about the first time they met in an exotic dancing club. She wasn't a pole dancer and she didn't dance on the stage. Pone spotted Queen high in the rafters doing stunts on an oversize ring. He couldn't take his eyes off her and not because of her beauty, but he always admire athletes and not only was she athletic, she was a good performer.

When she finished doing her act and they lowered the ring, Queen noticed Pone eye-balling her throughout her performance. When she got on the floor, she put on a robe and made a beeline to his table. She asked him to buy her a drink. He obliged. The two of them talk long enough to feel comfortable to have a one night stand. The last Pone saw Queen until today.

That trip down memory lane gave Pone an itch to scratch. The hankering took him to a place of his youth; where he met Queen. Pone went where men like him go to face their worst fears, some call it a gangsters Kryptonite; Broads and booze the weakness of most men and though Pone not being much of a drinker or playboy, he didn't cash in his player card yet. Lucille cruised down Freedom Drive; destination the House of Chantel. You wouldn't classify it as a bar and Pone didn't desire to go to another bar not worried he would run into another Queen, he smiled thinking about her. She did the job relieving his body of stress. Yeah, it felt good being wrapped in Queen's arms; rolling around on top of one another made Pone feel like a new man. He planned on making sure he would never have a long drought again.

Sex was a good exercise for stress. Pone handled anxiety hitting the speed and heavy bag and lifting his solo-flex weights. Sex took care of it this time, and he didn't mind.

Pone's head filled with doubts about him and Queen. He remembered Wisdom telling him the best way for a man to find out if he is a one woman man; go to a rump shaking club. The House of Chantel was Pone's favorite back in the day.

Pone spent little time in such establishments because putting money inside women G-strings not his thing, but when he did, he made the most of it. He met a woman named Cassie. Her stage name, Cadillac. He knew her before Queen: he did not have sex with her, instead they fuck each other's brains. Cadillac dance and talked at the same time, she put herself through college and paid her tuition by shaking her ass.

A Five-eight voluptuous, raven hair beauty. Father black and mother Latino. Pone sat at a table in a far corner a force of habit for men in his line of work. Never sit with your back to the door. Pone nursed a beer from the bar. He thought about his memorable encounter while surveying the house of tease. Women still dance on the stage and men threw money at them. Another tradition women dancing on men at their table giving them a face full of boobs and ass. He saw men escorted to private areas of the club for VIP treatment. Twenty dollars a song. Pone laughed thinking, how you could lose track of songs played because the women assets captured your attention. Better count your money while in the room.

Pone got a few offers, but turned them away.

After a few minutes, Pone decided he'd out grown cat houses. He finished his Sam Adams and straightened up to leave; there she stood; thick shapely body, bootylicious, revealing melons and ruby full lips, and raven hair in a bun leaning on his table dressed in black heels and a sleeveless blue dress.

"Look what the cat dragged in," said Cassie.

Pone smiled and cursed himself. She remembered him. "Sorry. I don't want a dance." Pone got up to leave.

"Sit your ass down and don't insult me."

Pone nodded, held up his hands and sat. Cassie joined him. "Listen, Cadillac…"

"You want to get slapped?"

Another violent woman, thought Pone.

"I gave you my real name for a reason. Use it," said Cassie.

Pone recognized something different about her. Not half dressed like the other dancers and her attire made her look more business-like.

"Cassie, dropped by to clear my head. Got somewhere else I need to be."

Cassie smiled and batted her eyelashes. "Let me guess; you came here to see if this is you. You getting married?"

Pone swallowed hard. "You majored in psychology?"

"Business, but had a few classes and your body language…you're not the only man to test temptation."

"Sworn to fun, loyal to none."

"Liar," She said in her soft-spoken voice. "You ain't in love, and I feel sorry for the woman that was your bed warmer."

"Yeah, well I'm getting too old for places like this."

"But here you are," She snorted. "Age gets us all. I don't shake my ass anymore. I told you I had goals."

"That's right…what's going on with you?"

"Graduated grad school and got hitched." She sat down resting her elbows on the table. Showed her ring finger.

Pone raised an eyebrow. "You own… I thought you wanted to get away from all of this?"

"Married the owner," she said.

Pone got moon-eye. Herman Creed owned the establishment. A five-two baby face built like a bowling-ball supporting a cue ball head, bull neck, alligator arms, and pillar legs. He weighed over three-hundred pounds. Pone saddened when he heard Herman died. He was a diabetic. Pone never knew he got married. He studied her.

Cassie glared. "Two girls and a boy."

Guess she loved him, thought Pone "Who better to run a place than a person who live the experience. Herman cared for me and the girls. I plan to keep it that way. I can do more good by encouraging them to use this as a stepping stone and maybe do what I did."

"I'm proud of you."

"Thanks dad."

Pone chuckled. "You know what I mean."

"Since I'm management, you get a freebie on the house."

"Cassie, I told you…"

"Right."

"Well, bravo and nice seeing you. I better get going." Pone stood to leave.

"Take out your cell," said Cassie.

Pone didn't know why, but he obeyed.

He watched Cassie take out her cell touching it with his. He saw a commercial where a cell phone touched another exchanging numbers.

Cassie did the same to his.

"Now you have my number. Don't be a stranger."

Pone nodded rising to leave when he heard a raucous at the stage. A large bouncer and an average sized slim black unkempt looking bloke along with a dancer argued. The bouncer and dancer both frowned and fan the air. Cassie looked toward the stage shaking her head frowning.

Pone laughed. "Guy trying to get more than a dance, huh?"

"Ugh!" Cassie pinched her nose. "Dancers complaining about his breath."

Pone observed the threesome at the stage. He focused on the unkempt man. "His breath?" questioned Pone. He saw customers led by dancers away from the tier holding their nose. Could this man about to quarantine the club with his mouth be Roland White. "Did he give his name?"

Cassie frowned. "I'll check." She motioned the dancer to come over. She looked relieved, leaving the bouncer to deal with the drama. He tried to grab her, but the bouncer engaged him.

"Thank you," said the dancer. "Whew!"

"Did he give you his name? " asked Cassie.

The dancer made a face. "R… Roll… Roland?"

"White!" blurted Pone. Pushing past the women and making a beeline toward the bloke with halitosis.

White pushed back the bouncer. His peripheral vision allowed him to see a man pushing past patrons to get to him. White recognized Pone. He escaped through the front entrance delighting the rank and file inside the club. Pone made it outside. He saw the back of a white S-10 speeding south.

Twenty-Four

Pone tailed the S-10 to Interstate-77 South on Independence Boulevard. No high speed chase, he hoped White would lead him to his hide-out. The truck looked like a used late model with a suspect engine under the hood. Mobile surveillance protocol meant staying out of target's lane, mirrors, and one car behind. On the highway Pone didn't have to worry about White making any sudden turns on the stretch road in front of them. The S-10 in the passing lane and Pone took up space on the right lane next to the by-pass. His problem, cars wanting to come off the ramp onto the interstate.

Luck smiled on Pone. Night and late, people home tucked in their beds. An 18-wheeler hid him from White's view and a black Toyota Camry on his left kept White in front of it. So far so good until a flash of light caught Pone's eye. A CR-V trying to get on the highway. Pone inhaled moving behind the Camry allowing the CR-V safe passage. Glancing ahead he got a glimpse of White holding a phone to his ear.

The CR-V moved up giving Lucille her space back. Pone settled in the right lane wondering if White made him. When did he put the phone to his ear, he thought.

Up ahead Brook-shire boulevard a left off ramp. White hit the by-pass leaving the interstate. Pone broke protocol of moving surveillance. Never mirror target's actions (changing lanes, making turns, and stops). Car horns blowing, and abusive language came from a few vehicles after Lucille cross over the lane and a median to get on Brook-shire. White now entering Metro city.

Pone spotted the S-10 fifty yards away on East Stonewall moving pass the convention center turning on South College a three lane one-way. He pursued keeping his distance he didn't want White using odd maneuvers: U-turns, stair stepping through neighborhoods, dead ends and multiple stops between home and work forcing Pone to stop following. He saw nothing out of the ordinary except White getting off the interstate as if he suspected a tail.

The S-10 hit South College heading north. Pone determined distance without a crowded street thanks to the twilight hour. White slowed than sped up crossing over West Trade to North College beating the light. Pone saw no oncoming traffic ignoring the red light. Two black Hummers from West and East Trade Street sandwiched Pone on North College a one-way three lane street. He lost track of White and figured he must have called for help. Somebody did their homework; the hummers could do a lot of damage playing bumper cars with Lucille.

Pone floored Lucille moving ahead of the Hummer on the right making a sharp turn on East 7th street. The monster vehicles chased after him. Pone headed back toward the interstate. He'd prevent another fatality like the little boy and figured it best to lead his pursuers out of the city to protect innocents.

Pone fled down the highway keeping the Hummers in his rear-view. He hated running. Pone knew of an abandoned boarded up strip mall five miles south down the interstate. Rumored to get demolished and transformed into an auto dealership, he would make his stand there.

Pone came up on the strip mall making a sharp turn heading to the back. He parked Lucille behind an old Ace hardware store. The mall built to attract out-of-towners thinking they would have needs on their travel. The assumption was wrong. Pone took off his bowler leaving it on the seat grabbed Sally and hopped out Lucille making a beeline to back door. Shot off the lock and entered using the flashlight from his cell to guide him to a counter.

Pone crouched down behind it expecting fourteen bodies inside both Hummers. Twenty-eight killers. A small army to put him in the bone orchard.

Pone thought about texting Red. She would use her contacts with the MPD, but they'd drag their feet to get to him. The file on him a former killer-for-hire. He thought of his friends: Sonny too damn old, Ben doing his own thing with Mercury, and Stick good for sneaking up on people… No.

The store cleaned out with nothing to use for a weapon. He and Sally against the world. Pone hoped they were not military trained and prayed he was wrong about how many rode in the Hummers. He turned off his cell ringer putting it inside his pants pocket. He took a deep breath and waited.

A Loud whisper gave orders to spread out. Pone heard feet moving in all directions. Three headed toward the counter. He saw three beams of light overhead. No night-vision, goggles. Maybe not ex-military. Sally a Tommy-Gun carried fifty rounds in her magazine. Forty-nine to be exact shooting off the lock. Shoot below the belt. Pone figured they wore bullet-proof vest and shooting for the head he might miss in the dark. Entering from the back a spur of the moment thought. The store big, but entrance to main lobby area average size would make a group of men be like shooting fish in a barrel. The men upon him.

Pone didn't go to church. A killer should never soil the house of the lord with his presence. Going to church did not give you a safe passage to Heaven and everyone including the choir would not be standing in front of the pearly gates. Pone inhaled and said a prayer inside his head: OUR FATHER WHICH ART IN HEAVEN HALLOWED BE THY NAME. THY KINGDOM COME THY WILL BE DONE ON EARTH AS IT IS IN HEAVEN. GIVE US THIS DAY OUR DAILY BREAD AND FORGIVE US OUR TRESSPASSES. LEAD US NOT INTO TEMPTATION DELIVER US FROM EVIL MAKE OF US SOLDIERS FOR THINE KINGDOM! FOR YOURS IS THE POWER THE GLORY FOR EVER AND EVER… AMEN.

Pone rolled out from the counter on his stomach firing at three mercenaries with lights attached to their weapons. Bullet-proof vest didn't cover private parts and much of the lower abdomen. The men went down. Blood poured like water and two whimpering sounds then silence. Light from the guns shone on Pone. He gathered the assault rifles pointing the beams toward back entrance. They'd be blind and he'd see his killers. A barrage foot-steps headed his way. Pone slipped on the blood he spilled, but made it behind a large aisle shelf. He remembered playing a video game, Fear Effect. A character faced his adversaries in a room with one entrance.

They came through the door and he picked them off. The strategy in the game worked and Pone hoped for the same results.

Pone crouched down He'd use the shelf for cover. He peeked and saw more illumination. They used the flashlights attached to their guns, but found it difficult to see with light shining back in their faces. Pone fired high and low.

The targets fell where they stood. Pone retreated behind the shelf evading shots fired by those surviving his assault. A glimmer of light came over Pone's shoulder. He fell backwards while a bullet grazed his left ear.

Pone shot upward hitting the man in the face.

A loud whisper told the remaining assassins to go night-vision. Pone moved toward the man he dropped checking his body. He gambled his assailant smoked. Pone found a lighter inside the man's chest pocket. Pone set down Sally. Reached inside his vest taking out one of his ninja knives.

He took out his phone turning on the flashlight. A prolepsis in Pone's head told him the men were not close by and if they came upon him he could buy time blinding them because they wore night-vision goggles with the light from his phone. Pone worked fast shining the light on the lighter taking it apart with his knife: Remove the flame shroud, the striker wheel, flint, and flint spring. He twisted the flint spring around the flint. Because of fluid in the lighter it produce a flame to heat the flint (thirty seconds to one minute). The red hot glow brought the remaining killers.

The men must have seen the illumine. They surrounded him. Two on his right and left. Guns clicked and Pone closed his eyes throwing the flint on the tile floor creating one brilliant spark. A flash of light in total darkness can impair the human eye for up to ten minutes. The men wore their night vision. In the past, night goggles were affected by stronger light causing temporary blindness by shining a flashlight at them. New technology reduced the danger of night blindness. Pone assumed these men did not invest in the new improved version. They didn't. Pone dove to the floor. Shots rang out inside the building.

Pone stood outside relieved he miscalculated the number of men sent to kill him. Less than twenty-eight, but more than ten. He was outgunned and lucky to be alive. Took out his cell and called Stick. The man knew how to make bodies disappear. "Need a clean-up at the old strip mall off Independence... I'll wire it to your account." Pone didn't want to burden Red with the task.

White entered the kitchen from the back door. Krasko sat at the small water stained brown table waiting for him.

"Where were you?" asked Krasko "I got worried."

White frowned. "You my fucking wife?" He gave Krasko the finger and went to bed.

Twenty-Five

"You got some nerve getting me up at this hour," said Red dressed in her cream silk robe. She sat at her dining table working on the laptop. "Give me the names again."

"James Krasko and Roland White," said Pone.

Red sipped her coffee. "What are we looking for?"

"All court cases dealing with criminals and their activities."

The information appeared on the screen. "Is this what you want?" asked Red.

Pone saw the case file of both Krasko and White. "Where's the prosecutor name?"

"Yeah, so."

"I don't see it."

Red worked the keys." Laptop's old. Give it some time," she yawned.

"Any reason you haven't gotten an upgrade?"

"It's sentimental. Got it when I passed the bar."

A gift from daddy dearest. No Maserati, Bentley or fancy jewelry. Guess he wanted to keep her humble for her accomplishment, thought Pone. He left it alone after watching Red stretching and manipulating her hair upward letting it drop down her back; Pone decided to let the little boy in him come out looking under the dining room table.

"What the hell are you doing?"

"Looking for Maxwell." Laughed Pone.

"Lay off him." said Red.

"You weren't lying when you said you slept in the buff."

Red smirked. "Like what you saw?"

Pone's attention back on the computer screen. "Shouldn't take that long."

"I take that as a yes…" Red studied Pone. "Are you glowing?"

"I'm a man."

"And men don't glow?"

"Not this man."

Red sniff the air.

"A lot of dogs do what you just did," said Pone.

"You're my bitch," responded Red. "Cheap perfume and cologne… cigarette smoke and liquor…you went to a bordello?"

Pone sniffed his jacket. "Rump shaking club to be exact."

"What's the difference?"

"To squash this debate before it gets started, black women have more ass than white women."

Red frowned. "Means more gas."

"Moving on," remarked Pone. "That's not all is there?"

"What are you talking about?"

"You got some didn't you?"

"Not from the club."

"Who is she?"

"You need a new laptop."

Red shook her head. "Oh, Pony…"

Pone looked at the computer screen. "Motherfucker!"

Red gave him a look and Pone arched an eyebrow toward the screen. Red looked and pursed he lips. "Sorry I got you into this."

Pone wanted to touch Red. He looked into her icy blues and knew there would be more than a touch going on between them.

"Poker, baby," snorted Pone.

"Is everything a game to you?"

"I'm going to need an ace up my sleeves when I meet with the two kings."

Red gave a dubious look. "Why do you want to meet with them?"

"After what we just saw, the stakes have gotten higher and I plan to cash in my chips."

"You're my guy… I want nothing to happen to you."

Red stood up to touch Pone. Her cell went off beside her laptop. "Hello…my God!"

Red turned to Pone. "Shoot-out on North Graham. Hip-Hoppers and Probonos."

The room pitch black thanks to no outside light out in the middle of nowhere. White laid in bed unable to sleep. He got what he expected, a luminous light and vibration from the burner cell phone. A call from the man. White answered.

"You're right about Pone," said the man.

Damn, thought White. "Told you he ain't no joke."

"But you are…what the fuck were you doing out in public?"

White sat up in bed. "Look man, how was I supposed to know he'd be at the same club?"

"A striptease. Can't get more public than that dumb-ass."

"Man, I got needs…looking at Krasko day and night…"

The man laughed. "You sound like a woman waiting for her period end."

"That's what I need man, women. Unless you going to send me a shortie?"

"What am I, a pimp? And don't talk hip-hop to me. Calling women shortie…stupid."

"I needed to see some ass. You can't blame a brother for that. What's the odds of me and Pone at the same…"

"Stay your ass home! You cost me money and good men died for your sorry ass."

"I fucked up."

"Give me a reason why I shouldn't erase your ass?"

White swallowed hard. "I can make it up to you, I swear."

"You shove money I gave you up those dancers asses?" asked the man.

"No. I ain't touched it. It still in the bag. I used my own money to do that."

"Bottom of the ninth."

Again with the fucking baseball terms. "On my mama's grave the next time you hear from me Pone will be dead."

The man hung up.

Twenty-Six

The pieces of the puzzle inside Pone's brain began falling in place. Like any puzzle, there's always a piece missing or won't fit.

Two exasperating pieces to the jigsaw—Prohibition and Hip-Hopper.

Pone arrived at the scene of the crime. Club Ecstasy. A rump shaking club on North Graham and Statesville Avenue. The club famous for black women with big asses.

Pone glad to see the lieutenants showing solidarity. Reluctant or not they stood together like he asked them to. A long eventful night for Pone; he went from having sex with Queen, took a trip down memory lane which he ran into the ambitious Cassie and travel to Red that would've ended with unexpected pleasure thanks to her cell putting a halt to their emotions. Yeah, his version of Charlie's Angels.

In one night he went from lead me not into temptation to deliver us from evil, a la Prohibitions and Hip-Hoppers.

Pone parked and got out of Lucille then scanned the area. A few body bags handled by the coroner. Police weaved the yellow tape like a spider web-line around the crime scene. Pone stood beside Brown and Boysenberry; before he uttered a word, MPD captain Lee E. Bolden intervened.

Bald on top, graying grass on the side giving the horse-shoe look, broad shoulders, barrel chest, soft, and round in the middle all supported by stubby legs. Looking heavier since Pone saw him last at the Brigand dinner. He wore a gray suit, white shirt, black tie, and loafers.

"Well, well, well…the gangs all here no pun intended," said Bolden with hands on hips.

"You know I don't mind you Hoppers and Probonos taking each other out… In fact, I'm all for it, but that few casualties so what shit is where I draw the line."

Pone observe the crime scene thanks to the body bags and assumed the victims were innocents caught in the cross-fire. He saw the perks, one hopper, and one Prohibition in hand cuffs involved in the gun-play. He also realized Red got the call from Bolden. A bend, but don't break kind of cop. He didn't mince words for the gangster world.

"You know the drill, some of your boys…" Bolden motioned toward the two in custody. "Going to come down to the station for questioning."

"You'll have my full cooperation," said Boysenberry.

"They need to man up to what they did," said Brown.

Pone snorted. "You seem to have everything under control Captain. Mind giving us a moment?"

"Sure, but you two," Bolden pointed to Brown and Boysenberry. "Don't go anywhere, I'm not done.."

Both men gave sarcastic nods.

"Flat foots…can't stand them," said Boysenberry.

"Your boys wanted to see some Red beans and rice, huh?" Gloated Brown.

"See, that's the difference between us and you rug heads, see. We don't shoot when you come over to check out our goods," remarked Boysenberry.

"So the shooting started over the wrong eye eye-balling ass?" asked Pone.

"Some of my boys said it was about the kids," said Boysenberry.

Brown nodded. "You better solve this shit quick."

"You two keep tighter leashes on your dogs," said Pone.

"This won't happen again," said Brown.

"I'll have another talk with the guys," remarked Boysenberry.

"Speaking of ending this thing, if I can avoid any more interference…" Pone gave both men a look.

"You mean?" asked Brown.

"Yeah, but this time it wasn't from your neck of the woods," said Pone.

"What the fuck are you talking about, Pone?" asked Boysenberry.

Pone waved him off. "I took care of it and in case you're keeping score Brown is still one up on you."

"Why do I feel like the step-child here?" said Boysenberry.

"Like I said, it's been handled. But while I got you both here I need a favor."

"Shoot," said Brown.

"Tell your bosses to expect a call from Red for a get together with me." Brown nodded. "G is getting restless."

"Mister M. don't like sitting on his hands," said Boysenberry.

"That's why I need to meet with them to put them at ease," said Pone.

Boysenberry nodded"I'll alert Mister M."

"G will look forward to hearing from you."

Boysenberry connected with l Bolden. Brown hung back to chat with Pone.

"Brown," Pone motioned. "Need to holler at you."

"What's going on?"

"Ella working tomorrow?"

"She ain't your type."

"This is serious."

Brown shrugged. "Think so."

"Tell her I'll be dropping by, need to ask something about Roland."

"I won't be there to chaperon."

"I know how to treat women."

Brown gave Pone a fist bump and headed to Bolden. Like two ships, Bolden passed by Brown on his way to Pone.

"Got a second?" asked Bolden.

Pone inhaled and snorted.

Bolden swallowed hard. "Grape-vine saw a big red truck tailing a small white truck then ended fleeing the city with two big black SUV's hot on its tail. Stopping at an abandoned strip mall off Independence and some fireworks in one of the buildings." Bolden snorted. "That building clean. No bodies, blood, bullet holes…nothing. Know anything about that?"

Pone pursed his lips. "Sounds like the MPD doing their usual job after the smoke clears." MPD protocol, observed gang activity from afar then get involve in the aftermath. He shook his head and thought of his friend's cleanup job. Stick should quit the killing gig and go full-time in the spotless trade.

"You took out the trash?" questioned Bolden.

"Thought you hated paperwork?" remarked Pone looking at Brown and Boysenberry. "Your party guest are getting restless."

"Hang on to that four leaf clover," said Bolden.

"I'm not Irish," smiled Pone.

Bolden gave a stern look. "I like you, but I can't keep a blind eye to what you do."

Pone shrugged, "Where you going with this?"

Bolden leaned in. "No more fires, okay," He placed his hand on Pone's shoulder walking away.

Twenty-Seven

A few casualties so what happened often when a drive-by took place as long as the intended target got lead poison. An unexpected tragic surprise; getting lunch, after seeing a movie, a family walking back to the car after shopping. It didn't matter if the bullet meant for you because innocents got hurt in the cross-fire. Everybody's game once the bullet takes flight. In gangland, it didn't matter as long as they get their message across. Gang violence a bitch to those who became victims.

Pone worked the keys on his computer. He didn't care for laptops. He sat at his computer desk with the keyboard on its pull out drawer and the mouse on a pad, he received from Newkadia comics for ordering a comic book online.

Metro City dot Org. the site for crimes committed long ago. Records of criminal elements from years past despite the Great Meteor changing the time structure. The accurate time periods put together by the science nerds. Pone logged into the 2050 archives gang shoot-outs. He would have asked Red, but he didn't her trust she could keep her composure after confronting Crowe when he gave her wind of his suspicion.

No more leaking faucets. Pone shook his head. Sloppy but she is human.

Pone tapped into list enumerated victims; Metro City paid tribute to the innocence of those who lost their lives to drive-by shootings. The list long and in alphabetical order.

Pone used his gambler instinct; he typed the name Crowe into the rectangle search engine. A lot of Crowes appeared on the screen spelled with and without the letter E.

Surviving relatives of the deceased mentioned along with pictures. Harvey a common and popular name.

Thank God for photos; Pone saw a young Harvey Crowe and under the picture names of his deceased family along with a nickname of the dive-by crime and the participants. In the middle of the article younger versions of Macone and G. Wisdom talked about Black Halloween. A bloody gunfight took place that day between the Hip-Hoppers and Prohibition. A lot of casualties from both sides and innocence also suffered in the bloodbath. Pone punched the computer desk. They knew. They knew. Paul J and Wisdom knew what was going down that day in uptown Metro. Sons of bitches! Damn them. Pone remembered overhearing Wisdom and Shelia arguing about that day. He didn't put it together until now.

He couldn't recall what started the argument, but it was years later when he and Birdie were around eleven and 10, Jade learning to walk and they were out back on a swing Wisdom had put together for them. Pone heard Shelia say something about him asking her to make sure the kids in the orphanage stay inside and for the teachers to do the same and she knew then that something was wrong. Shelia said Paul J would burn in hell. Ten years after Black Halloween. What Pone remembered hearing before Wisdom spotted him watching the two of them argue shutting the door. She had nothing to do with the spill bloody, but she felt the guilt.

Shelia told Pone he was a deep thinker. He never understood what she meant until he got older. Wisdom throws a weird dinner. A guilty conscience? Many people died on Black Halloween. The old man and Paul J could have prevented the massacre.

Wisdom not so much, thought Pone. Paul J could have stepped in and save lives. He knew the Prohibitions and Hip-Hoppers would bop. He wanted them to, but why? Pone wondered if Red figured it out her dad knew what was going to happen and what he had to gain. Pone thought about history: *An unqualified president. A father son act. The father okay according to the history books, but his son manipulated a war that should have never had happened. He sent his administration to investigate a country he accused of having weapons of mass destruction. When they found none; the president tried to force the dictator to leave his own country. He did not comply. He then said that same dictator used a terrorist attack on two historic buildings in New York to wage war on this country, 9/11.*

He succeeded convincing the country the dictator was behind the attacks. He used the military as pawns for his own personal gain. What did he have to gain?

Revenge for his father a former president who intervened in a war the dictator thought wasn't his concern and tried to murder him for his intervention. The dictator failed to kill him, but that president's son used his presidency to over throw the dictator and the man got hung by his own people. Pone thought another president who should have never sat in the oval office. A real estate entrepreneur came to mind. He focused back on Paul J. Pone continued digging but not in the past. He logged in Roland Whites' name.

The screen showed why White arrested. He blew up a warehouse killing three.

Pone checked out the victims: Donald Carver, 65, security guard. Retired, married, three grown children, and seven grandchildren. Felix Jones, 36 security guard married, one child, and Larry Edwards, 45, married and two children, truck driver.

A decaying drafty warehouse sat on top of a hill off Tyvola road. A real eyesore screaming for the wood pile. An insurance fraud write off causing the deaths of three innocent family men. Widows, father-less kids, and grandfather gone too soon. Pone worked the keys searching for who owned the storehouse. He inhaled and blinked. The owner Fred Shaffer's body found faced down in his pool. Drowning accident. Yeah right, thought Pone.

Krasko went to prison for a church bombing. Listed as a hate crime because it was a black church. Fatalities; Reverend Herman Pride, 50, married with four children and his assistant Emma Smith, age 32. Pone didn't bother pondering what the two were doing in the church at night. The important thing, they were both murdered in a bombing leaving behind love ones.

Crowe put in a lot of work with his plan to pull an all-out gang war. Pone took a terminology from the Hip-Hoppers using Bronco meaning breaking away from the crowd going solo.

White and Krasko wanted to be independent. How did Crowe know unless he planted a mole. Pone glad he didn't do the gang thing. Ambition a motivation both high and low in gangland. You can't trust anyone. Everyone wants to be on top no matter the cost.

Pone shook his head. Boysenberry and Brown. G and Macone treated them like their own sons. No. The lieutenants would take a different route to the top without killing kids. Pone spent enough time around them to know they seemed satisfied in their roles. Crowe found someone to keep tap on White and Krasko. Freelance bombers made more money than belonging to a gang. It's not like they were members of a union like the Teamsters what not and go on strike for money. Any rebuttal would be a bullet to the head. Thank you Red, thought Pone.

Blackmail. Why else would Krasko and White murder their former bosses offspring.

Crowe didn't framed them, but he set them up for murders they committed bombing the occupied buildings they believed vacant. MPD on Crowe's payroll and the corruption did not end there. The Warden got a fat pocket and closed his eyes on two murderers who should have gotten life or the death penalty.

Pone shook his head. No need for a headache about a world far from perfect. White and Krasko don't know Crowe is their puppet master. He no doubt threatened them with a trip back to solidarity confinement. Rather than worrying about bending over in the shower to pick up the soap. They carried out their mystery man's plan to execute children.

Before them other fatalities along the way though Pone suspected the two bombers didn't know the buildings they blew up occupants inside. A rotting drafty warehouse should have demolish to sticks long before being blown up. Pone remembered a friend attending church on Wednesday night. The night the house of worship blew up was on Monday with the preacher and one of his congregation.

Pone figured White and Krasko did not understand there would be victims and whether they felt any guilt he did not know. The important thing, people died. Helen Macone and Reggie Grant deserve to go to college and drift away from the life their fathers built. Donald Carver should have live to attend his grandchildren high school or college graduation. Felix Jones and Larry Edwards: birthday parties, little league ball games, their children weddings all gone. A sinful rendezvous or church business the Reverend Herman Price and his assistant Emma Smith dead too.

Crowe's mortality high and he wanted it to continue growing. He wants to add me to the list, thought Pone. The man wanted revenge in the worst way willing to sacrifice anyone for his cause. A gang war would destroy Metro. Pone compared Metro to a gun. A gun can't kill unless someone holds it pulling the trigger. Making the perpetrator dangerous since they possess the gun. A firearm like a snake scares people, but won't cause any harm unless provoked. A snake don't need encouraging to attack. Pone saw video of a news report where a man on a motorcycle dodging the reptile after it lunged at him.

Pone frowned understanding Crowe's anger, he lost his family in a gang war, but wrong for the way he handled it. Crowe could hired someone to ace Macone and G. Instead he wanted to make them feel his pain losing a love one and he succeeded. Pone believed he intend to off the kingpins down the road, but Pone considered himself a road block to Crowe's plan. The Deputy Mayor trying to kill him made it personal.

Karma can be a bitch. Macone and G will get what they deserve. Pone couldn't get past thinking J. Paul could have prevented Black Halloween.

Old man Brigand stepped in after the carnage meeting with Macone and G. The two men knew of Brigand's government resources and knew better than to defy him after what happened to the Webb family. He gave them options; leave, cease to exist or pick a territory. Both men planted strong roots in the city and didn't want to uproot their families. They both took the Hobson's choice. Pone logged off his computer. He didn't drink beer or Irish cream except on holidays. He did drank beer at the gentlemen club. Mandatory in clubs and bars. Pone needed another drink.

A strong drink.

Twenty-Eight

Ten a.m., enough time for bright eyes and a clear head. Mert's didn't serve breakfast, but they prepped for the noon lunch crowd. Pone entered the establishment without the dagger stares unlike the last time. The employees busy setting up tables and prepping food in the kitchen. Ella spotted Pone and motioned him for the private talk at a back wall corner. Pone sat facing the door while Ella brought a cigarette and an ash tray to the table.

Like a true waitress, she carried two mugs and a pot of coffee flanked by cream. Pone smelled the cream, French vanilla. Ella stuck the cigarette in her mouth and poured, then sat down. Pone shook his head, ignorant of him not to think the crucifix wearing woman not a smoker: yellowish eyes, leathery skin, and black lips all signs of being a tobacco kisser. Though in her defense she endured a lot of stress: a minimum wage job, dealing with the death of two family members of violent crimes and worrying about life it-self. In her case thinking what else could go wrong.

"What happened to the no smoking policy?" asked Pone.

"I'll Febreze before customers come in," said Ella blowing smoke through her nostrils.

She sat with her thick legs crossed and looked at Pone wondering why he hadn't touched his coffee. Ella sipped hers and smiled. Pone cautious about drinking anything from a potential enemy. He heard a story about an employee telling other co-workers about the morning coffee tasted funny. Soon after, management placed a hidden camera in the break room. The camera showed a disgruntled employee making coffee with his urine. The employee got fired and ordered by the court to clean building restrooms for a whole year. Pone added the French vanilla taking a sip, shrugged as if to say I'll live.

"Mister Pone, I ain't that kind of person. Must be tough to live the life you live."

"I wouldn't recommend it," remarked Pone.

Ella took a puff of smoke followed by a sip of coffee. Pone remembered how the combination smelled when talking to a woman who did the same. He leaned back to avoid the same from Ella.

"Okay…here we are," said Ella.

"You know where Roland is?" asked Pone.

Ella made a face as if it hurt to think. "I ain't no expert on how the criminal mind works. Don't know or care where he is."

"This is important."

"Better be glad I got some God in me."

Here we go with that old time religion, thought Pone.

"Since you say he ain't no-where inside the city…the only place I can think of is a house my grandparents built in Rock Hill. They gave it to his mama." She took a longer sip of coffee. "Ever heard of it?"

Independence boulevard south the fastest route to Rock Hill. If not for the Hummers, White would have lead him to his home, thought Pone.

Pone nodded. Rock Hill was a poor farming community for blacks before the meteor made it obsolete.

"My grandparents and parents lived there all their lives, but wanted us kids to get out of the farming business and here I am waiting on tables."

Pone freshened his cup and leaned back against the wall. He prepared himself for a sad song without the harmony. Thank God it wasn't rap.

Ella slurped a mouthful of coffee. "That land ain't fertile no more since that big rock passed by. Turn that land into a planet rock. Now the name Rock Hill suits it."

Pone watched Ella pour herself another cup of java to help her reminiscence back to an existence far from perfect to a present life no better.

Ella finished her smoke to the delight of Pone. "People like me still go to church to worship God." She shook her head. "Others worship a piece of rock...fools," She looked into Pone's eyes. What beautiful eyes, she thought with a slight smile lasting no longer than a wink. The man killed her son. Ella didn't know Pone put down her cousin Wanda. She figured the poor soul got murdered over drugs.

"I know you ain't come here to hear me ramble, Roland's black ass is hiding out in that raggedy, rotting spider-infested house. Might even have snakes now and Roland's the biggest snake there is living there."

She pursed her lips. "Ain't no more neighborhoods, so it should be easy to find. About a two, three-hour drive. Look for a big dead oak tree, a dead house on dead land." Ella sighed and leaned forward.

Pone took it as his cue to leave.

"Mister Pone."

Pone stopped in his tracks.

"I can forgive...just can't forget. Whatever you do to Roland, I won't hold it against you."

Pone looked over his shoulder tipping his bowler and walked away.

Twenty-Nine

Pone missed taking the elevator down to the basement to play Poker. He even missed his Poker playing buddies. He'd seen Sonny and Stick, and they helped him deal with this gut-wrenching case. As for Ben, he hoped things worked out with Mercury to solve his problem. He smiled thinking about his ladies; Red did her job making the call getting the two bosses together and reliable Birdie giving him use of her establishment without hesitation.

The elevator doors opened and just as he asked Birdie to do with his guest; there they sat across from one another the two kingpins of the Hip-Hoppers and Prohibitions. Pone bade her to seat them at one of the medium sized round poker tables and she delivered.

Macone looked a lot older than the last time he'd seen him; the man lost a daughter. But it didn't stop him from looking like a true mobster: hair slicked back, dyed black, wearing a gray pinstriped suit, crisp white shirt, and black tie. Pone couldn't tell who suffered more from their child's death.

He gave the edge to Macone whose once strong thick body now shriveling into a frail fossil. G. accustomed to death within his family. He'd lost uncles, aunts, cousins, siblings, nieces, and nephews all trying to cash in on blood money with their own blood. Dressed in a black silk shirt, charcoal suit, black bandanna, dark shades, and a gold chain with the initials RG representing his son. A true hip-hopper if Pone ever saw one.

The one thing Pone could relate with the two ancients, his wealth. Like them it came from blood money. Pone stood at the table.

"Gentlemen, glad you both could make it. Drink?"

"Mash," said Macone in a gravel voice.

"T-bird," said G.

Pone nodded. "Whiskey it is."

Pone hated whiskey. Behind the bar, he saw his malt drink Malta Goya, a non-alcoholic beverage. When he wanted to get his drink on he preferred Samuel Adams and Baileys' Irish Cream. Out of respect he'd have a shot of whiskey with the geezers. Pone grabbed three shot glasses and a bottle of Crown Royal. Pone returned to the table. Poured and watched Macone and G down their shots while nursing his.

"Soft," smirked G.

"Anything but," said Pone. "Staying off the sauce keeps my reflexes sharp,"

G toasted Pone.

"All right all ready," growled Macone. "What is this? A tea party?"

"We all can agree that the shoot-out at the club wasn't over territory," said Pone.

"North Graham ain't on the west side," said Macone.

G threw down a shot and poured another. "Either way, y'all silver spoon B-boys are more than welcome to check out black puddin'."

Macone laughed and toasted G. "Back in the day it was brown sugar."

"Things have changed," said G.

"Not all for the better," murmured Macone. "We now share a bond."

Silence took over the room. Pone studied the fossils and saw how the deaths of their children hurt deep. Macone sloped on the credenza holding his glass in both hands rotating it with his fingers. G made a fist bouncing it off the table top.

Helen and Reggie might have built an alliance between the families if they had lived and got married after college, but now what might have been an afterthought.

"What if I can get you both satisfaction and closure," intervened Pone.

G gave a dubious look. "Ain't that what you supposed to do anyway?"

Macone folded his arms and leaned back. "How soon can you deliver?"

Pone turned over his shot glass and reclined observing the two kings. Pone thought of this junction like playing a high stakes poker game. Holding an ace and he planned to play it at the right moment.

"I want a deal," said Pone.

Macone and G. eyed each other.

"What? A piece of the action…what?" questioned Macone.

"He ain't talkin' about no money," said G.

"Immunity," responded Pone.

Macone gulped down his shot. "What're you, a fucking diplomat?"

Pone glared, inhaled and swallowed hard at Macone. "A knight in the royal family and I don't get no respect. If you want things to continue as they are then you better check your boys or take out an ad in the blab sheet."

Macone downed his shot with a purpose. "You got balls Pone. I'll give you that."

"Bodacious," said G.

Macone shrugged. "Your name sends chills. What are you talking about?"

G poured a shot and downed the hatch. He sighed and looked at Pone. "You want a hassle free passage through our territories."

"You think," remarked Pone.

G snorted. "What my boys do is foreign."

Macone chuckled. "Got to give them some freedom."

Pone didn't expect a sensible conversation. Bad feelings between the two ancients and the Brigands. They both got humbled by J. Paul and despite his death, they continued to pay homage to his children.

Linda a bitch. A ruthless, cold hearten miniature female version of her father. They couldn't touch J. Paul's kids, but Pone knew they could get satisfaction if he got clipped.

Pone gave a stern look. "You're both old."

Macone straightened in his chair. "I got eyes. My mirror tells me no lies."

"You trying to make a point by insulting us?" said G.

Pone pursed his lips. "If you don't know what your boys are doing then that's not good." Pone leaned on the table. "Look if you want me to keep putting your guys down then fine, but there comes a time when enough is enough. Revenge is not good or should be a part of what we do." Pone leaned back in his chair. "I could be wrong, but they are people in this world who deserve to die. What happened to Helen and Reggie…it should have been you two." Eyes widened then narrowed to glares at Pone. G threw down his drink. Macone twisted his neck.

"I know I ain't going to heaven and yeah Reggie paid for my sins," said G.

"Not all," remarked Pone.

G gave Pone a look.

"Okay… I take blame my angel is an angel because of me, but that don't mean you can talk shit to us like we're nobody," said Macone.

An uncomfortable chill ran through the room. Damn these old bastard, thought Pone. Set in their ways. Holding a grudge against the late J. Paul and upset being under his offspring's thumb. Pone played his Ace.

"I can drop this in the lap of the police and let this go through the proper channels of the justice system." Pone turned over his glass and poured himself a shot.

He threw the rot-gut down his throat. Frowned and snorted. "You both know the courts don't guarantee justice or satisfaction.

I'm sure old school gangsters such as your-selves would prefer cement shoes and shit."

"What do you propose young blood?" asked G.

"No more trying to get a rep by offing me or I'll rage a private war on the fools that do. What I did for J. Paul was business. You both know it's a credo we live and die by."

"There is no payback because that kind of thinking gets you and others killed. I work for Red and she's nothing like her old man."

Macone rubbed his chin. "That Linda's a bitch."

G snorted. "On a broomstick."

"Macone said bitch." Pone shrugged. "It is what it is…"

"We do this?" questioned Macone.

"I'll deliver the fools who did this to your children, and you can have your gangster style justice," said Pone.

Macone nodded. "I'll talk to my boys."

"Ditto," said G.

Pone rose from the table. He looked at G. "You still got that pig farm in Sumter, South Carolina?"

G glared at Pone wondering how the hell he knew about his swine. "You want a Christmas Ham?"

"Not what you feed those damn hogs." Be wary of a gangster who owns a pig farm, thought Pone.

Thirty

Pone sat alone in Nadine's basement casino nursing a Malta Goya his non-alcoholic malt beverage on a Sunday afternoon. He exhaled looking around the empty room sitting at observing the empty chairs his poker buddies use to occupy. Sonny barking about the good old days, Stick sipping his hard liquor looking serpentine slithering around in his chair, and Ben making fists fighting a craving for a stogie and belching down beer saying shit'd.

"I miss you guys," whispered Pone He toasted the air.

The elevator door opened and out walked Brown with Boysenberry.

"Where are the broads?' asked Boysenberry."

Pone pointed to the square table they sat at their first get together.

"What?" Brown shrugged. "We ain't good enough to sit at this table?"

"Hell no," said Pone.

"You cold man. You cold," said Brown.

"Then warm your ass up over there at that table," said Pone.

The three men made their way to the table where a shot glass s and bottles of Jack Daniels and Olde English 800.

Brown and Boysenberry helped themselves before taking their seats.

"What no shorties and politician?" said Brown sipping his eight-ball.

"If they were here you wouldn't be calling them shorties and broads," said Pone. "The politician is here he doesn't know it."

The two lieutenants gave each other a look.

"What we doing here without the eye-candy?" asked Boysenberry.

Pone and Brown gave each other a look wondering why Boysenberry kept fronting for women knowing he's gay.

Pone looked back and forth at the two men. "How was the sermon?" He knew both men attended Sunday service.

Brown snorted. "Temptation, evil…the good shit."

Boysenberry twisted in his chair. "You don't do the Sunday thing?"

"Got a conscience," remarked Pone.

Brown gave a gruesome sneer. "Demons aren't we all."

"Amen to that," said Boysenberry.

Pone nodded knowing churches didn't guarantee you an entrance inside the pearly gates. Devils in the pulpit. Married preachers with a flock of sexual partners women and men delivering the word of God without shame. This demon will respect the house of the lord, thought Pone.

"What happened to meeting a night?" asked Boysenberry.

"Hard to see," said Pone.

Boysenberry gave a dubious look. Pone studied him after his comment. He knew White didn't order the hits on his life and Boysenberry innocent too. Better safe than sorry, thought Pone.

"Made any progress?" questioned Brown.

Pone wanted to keep the lieutenants in the dark about his hypothesis. If Macone and G didn't tell them what they discussed then he thought it best to keep what he knew to himself.

Pone finished one of his bottles of Malta Goya. "I asked Macone and G for immunity when I solve this case."

Brown frowned. "Man, I done told you ain't nobody thinking about dropping you."

"Relax. Don't worry about getting dusted?" Boysenberry gulped down his hash. "My crew rooting for you to do your job. Not the eternal checkout."

"I don't want the geezers to get Alzheimer," remarked Pone.

"Hey…show respect," said Boysenberry. "Mister M's word is gold."

"G solid. He wouldn't jive you," said Brown.

Pone orchestrated this meeting and not to hear the two men try and outdo each other speaking in their native slang but to see if Brown or Boysenberry worked with Crowe and if they planned their own coup against their bosses. Getting too close to solving the teens murders and he didn't want a fly in the ointment.

"Speaking of safe passage," Pone pressed his lips on his second Malta Goya. "How are you guys on your territory priorities?"

Brown eyeballed Boysenberry. "Two guys got membership revoked."

Boysenberry poured himself a glass of rotgut and toasted Brown. "We made the flatfoot happy."

Bolden alone on his one man crusade against the mafia considered putting two gangsters behind bars a small victory, thought Pone.

"Cop and bow," said Boysenberry.

"What the fuck does that mean?" questioned Brown.

Pone laughed. "Man got to represent."

Boysenberry leaned toward his rival. "Easy come, easy go. You win some, you lose some."

"I understand Spanish better than y'all shit," said Brown.

"Too much lard in those Collard greens." Boysenberry sipped his drink. "That soul food will kill you."

Brown inhaled and straightened in his chair.

Pone rubbed his eye as if something got inside it. "Down boys. We are one. After I take care of business, you can go back to capping each other. No black Halloween."

Pone hit the bulls-eye inflating both men. "We all good on the girl watching thing?"

"Times change," said Brown. "Black pudding for everyone."

"No problem if they want to add cream to their coffee," replied Boysenberry. Pone lean back observing the men with his drink sitting on his lap. Brown hit the nail on the head. Times have change. Interracial dating once in the closet like homosexuality and now both in full view. Marriage and all, thought Pone.

"Life is too short," Boysenberry nursed his drink. "Straight or gay. If you love someone, you should go for it."

Pone and Brown gave each other a glance. Both men aware of exploits about Boysenberry preferring a dick in the rear and mouth over a piece of pie. The man reeked Prohibition, Pone thought he tried too hard referring women as Dames and broads.

"I prefer cutting the cake," said Brown.

"What's that supposed to mean?" asked Boysenberry.

Sensitive and in a reluctant closet, thought Pone. "A lyric from a popular song way back in the day."

Boysenberry glared. "Average White Band. I've heard of it and what's that look you two gave each other?"

"It's a black thang," said Brown.

"What?" Boysenberry shrugged. "Being here with you guys don't make me honorary?"

All three men roared with laughter.

The lieutenants left Pone with his thoughts on White and Krasko and the hip-hopper and prohibition heading off to the hoosegow for the shooting at the club. Crowe want be manipulating those two into doing his bidding. Maxwell will have the honor of prosecuting them. Pone walked over to the mid-size bar and sat on a stool.

Turning his back resting his elbows on the counter top observing the casino. A caucus with the kingpins and their right hand men comfort Pone. He felt relaxed after a good laugh which he shared with Brown and Boysenberry. Like their bosses he knew they wouldn't shed a tear hearing of his demise, but they seemed sincere about him finding Helen and Reggie's killer.

The enemy of his enemies were not his friend. So Macone and G didn't inform Brown and Boysenberry of their conclave and Pone figured the second-in-command would keep their moot to themselves. Pone thought it best to have more info on the two ancients and who better than Google to give him information then the oldest Encyclopedia he knew, Sonny the old timer. Same age as Macone and G, but not an ally to either. Sonny never associated with the two. An over the hill freelance bomber.

Sonny his own man told Pone club memberships weren't for him. Solo the way to go. Sonny shook his head saying no matter how trustworthy, one hater in the group spread a bad word about you and you'd be looking over our shoulder till the bitter end. Trust an issue or what lack thereof. Who better to trust than yourself. Pone couldn't agree more. In his case he had no choice but to be part of the Brigand band with a noose around his neck. A hip-hopper and Prohibition no thank you. Red sexier than both Macone and G. Forget Linda, Sue, Paul J, and mother Mary. Red his boss. He answered to her. Glancing at the table he and his poker buddies sat to play poker. Boysenberry inquired about joining on Pone's poker games. Where would he sit and if he'd keep his hands above the table. You can't play the game distracted and an ill placed hand high above the knee distracting. Macone a racist calling blacks niggers and gay men faggots. Boysenberry a closet homosexual working right under Macone's nose. He played off the look Pone and Brown shared with each other on a comment he made saying let those who love who they want.

Pone noticed Boysenberry trying to keep it a secret, but finding his sexuality hard to control each day hinting with comments while remaining masculine. Pone wondered about Ben showing a lot of love for his missing friend Al McGee. Ben mentioned McGee involved with a woman and a father which never stopped men from being gay. Frolicsome men made gestures towards Pone and in kind told them he didn't swing that way. They smiled, respected him for his honesty, and went about their business.

Pone shook his head thinking fear would cure him of being gay. Getting a death sentence for unprotected sex with another man. The reward for making love with a same sex partner a transmitted disease.

Aids a supernatural curse activated when men engaged each other in sex and how could it not be.

Pone believed since men contained their own sperm then another man's semen not needed to occupy his body and doing so would be blasphemy. Pone admitted giving a handsome man props. Did it make him gay? No.

He summed up his conception; men should not be with men and the same for women.

Biblical laws broken everyday making it a sinful world. Pone exhaled and realized he'd spend enough time alone down below. He got on the elevator heading to the surface.

He got off the elevator and saw two of his favorite ladies, Red and Birdie. Both ladies perched at the bar nursing their signature drinks a Long Island Ice Tea and a Strawberry Daiquiri.

"What do I owe this pleasure?" asked Pone.

"What's the verdict?" asked Birdie. Red gave a dubious look Pone raised an eyebrow. "Mobsters."

Birdie sipped her drink and looked him over like a mother examining her child. "You look no worse for wear."

"We have so little faith…is that why Red's here?" asked Pone.

Birdie pursed her lips. "Wasn't sure if you'd come running up asking us to mediate."

Red frowned. "Will someone tell me what the hell is going on?"

Pone twirled his bowler. "Eye-candy replaced dames and broads."

Red got off her stool. "You had another moot?"

"I'm not full of bullet holes," said Pone.

"We're in this together," said Red. "What game are you playing?"

"I'm sprucing up the yard. Pulling out the weeds," said Pone.

Red turned to Birdie. "And you knew about this?"

Birdie crossed her legs. "You're here aren't you."

Red glared .

"What?" Birdie nursed her drink. "You thought I asked you here to bond?"

Pone sat down at a corner table. He placed his bowler on top and studied the fem fatales. They'd never be friends and he blamed himself. Birdie tolerated Red because of him, but hated their arrangement. Pone didn't like it either and he could end the association in blood. He liked Red and knew things would change if he took out her family. Blood is thicker than water and why Birdie felt the way she did about his situation.

Pone wondered about her concern, sister love or…he wanted her to marry Tony and start a family. He shook his head because he sounded like Wisdom.

At least they weren't arguing. Both ladies too classy to cause a scene. Arms folded. Bodies tight and straight, eye contact not wavering and leaning into each other till Red turned shaking her head making a beeline to his table. She sat down hard crossing her legs looking away from him.

"A get together between the right-hand men?" said Red. "Crossing my T's and dotting the I's."

Red sat facing Pone agreeing with him all bets are off once he solved the teen murders. They sat with both lips winking a smile and eyes looking at each other then back at the table like two school kids too nervous to admit they have feelings for each other. A shame the Prohibitions and Hip-Hoppers becoming an alliance for a brief time, but for a good cause.

Pone cracked his knuckles. "Can't blame Crowe," he murmured.

Red looked up from the table. "His family wasn't the only casualty."

"Everyone handle tragic different." "Brigands expect it."

Pone knew you didn't congenital into a crime or any family. Red came into the world in a successful one. She wore her wealth well, but didn't boast it. Her sisters Linda and Sue rubbed it in your face the way they spoke to you. Linda did it better, Sue found her older twin a hard act to follow; she irritated people just the same.

Paul J and Red handled being jet set different than their older siblings. They didn't make you feel like shit in a toilet. Paul J tried to impress Linda, but a kind heart like baby sister. Must be his feminine side, thought Pone. Red butted heads with Linda on how to represent the family in public. Neither gave in to the others advice.

Pone respected Red for being her own person and knew she'd never trade her family wealth for poverty and he didn't blame her. When you have resources be thankful without regrets no matter how you came by them. She never pulled the trigger or ordered a death.

Pone smiled. "It adopted me and everyone don't handle adoption well."

"Harvey crossed the line."

"You get no argument from me," exhaled Pone.

"If the world became vigilant how could we exist?"

"Everyone don't handle tragedy well," said Pone.

Thirty-One

"Mother fuck!" Roland put the cell in his pocket and punched a hole through the decayed plaster.

"Hey! Don't put this shit on me. You fucked up twice," said Krasko.

Three times, thought White shaking his head and twisting his lip. He didn't want to argue with Krasko about the night Pone tailed him from the club. Calling the man for help. Twice he dropped the ball.

"Where's your big man now?"

Krasko shrugged. "I called and he didn't answer… I'm guessing the long good-bye like your cousins."

Before Krasko could swallow. Roland crossed the room gripping him by the throat. Krasko almost gagged inhaling the breath of death.

"Watch your mouth cracker …" A long icy stare. "You hear!"

Roland threw Krasko on the sofa. Krasko waved a surrender and nodded.

"Remember what you said," choked Krasko whiffing out Roland's breath.

"What you talking about?"

"Split the money and haul ass. See, I spoke a language we both understand."

"That ain't enough money." Ain't no reason this fool need to know about my promise, thought White. "You count it?"

"Don't have to."

"Look, I didn't pay my man a dime, don't know if he's alive or what not. I know you didn't pay your cousins since the money came after they died. Plenty of loot to split between us."

Roland didn't intend to pay his cousins a dime. He hated his family. They always put him down; saying he wasn't shit, even called him a shit-ass and the only time they respected him was because he enlisted in the army. He had to put on a uniform sporting the stars and stripes on the shoulder before they could respect him. So to hell with them.

Little Bucky looked up to him once he got into the Hip-Hoppers click and wanted to follow his footsteps.

It was easy to convince him and his make fast easy money buddies to do his bidding. He knew they had a slim chance to pull it off, but hell sometimes we all get lucky sometimes, but not Bucky and his friends. Then there was poor crack head Wanda. She had respect for him before he went into the military. They were close because they were similar than any other family member; not good in school, destined to have humbling minimum wage jobs, paycheck to paycheck living and never able to get over the hump of leading a productive life.

She caught him in the act of doing blow and wanted to try it, she told him she liked where the drug took her, out of the real world. Wanda became too dependent on it and Roland took advantage of her weakness when he found out she got involved with the wannabe gangster Arnold Pratt. They both ended up dead going up against Pone.

White gave an icy glare. "You don't get it, we in the same boat. We murdered the children of our former bosses. They don't know we are out of the joint. Our memberships revoke and we're snitches because we got out early which means we're dead. This is all I'm good at, and I plan to get set up for life."

Krasko shook his head. "How do you plan to do that?"

"We going to ghost Pone's ass." White's grin gruesome. He remembered what he told the man and Krasko clueless about the promise he made on his mama's grave. White planned to do what

Krasko suggested take the money and run. Not killing Pone, but murdering his roommate. Plenty of money in the bag for him and he wasn't sharing, but Krasko didn't know his agenda. He'd keep fucking with his head till the right time and off him.

"You loose on the brains? I ain't ready for no marble city," said Krasko.

"I done told you about talking probono shit to me."

"Okay, marble city is the cemetery and loose brains means your ass is crazy!"

Roland pointed his finger. "Call me crazy again and I'll kill you. Pone don't know what we look like and he driving that big red ass truck makes him visible." Another lie to keep from Krasko, thought White.

"Got a lot of red trucks," remarked Krasko.

"What I'm saying is I can convince the man to pay us a million apiece for putting Pone to rest. I got to let him know we ain't coming half-assed no more."

Another lie. White hated hearing the man's deep deliberate disguised voice, but wanted to hit him up one last time for more bread. He noticed a twinkle in Krasko's eye. "You know what I'm talking' about."

Krasko licked his lips. "A million bucks?"

"Yeah, man," Whited snorted. "We can't do this half-stepping if the man agrees to do this."

Krasko rubbed his chin. "That's good and all and good luck, but just give me a small portion and you keep the rest and drop me off at the nearest bus station."

What the hell! White flashed a yuck mouth smile. "We in this together mother-fucker. I'm going to make us both rich, and you going to thank me for it. So you just sit back, shut your trap while I call the man, understand?"

White got out the cell. "Got to play this right to convince this fool."

"No problem Roland, I'll wait in the kitchen." Krasko gritted his teeth. He knew he couldn't take White in a fair fight. The guy demented thinking he could take out Pone. Blow up the kids and get the hell out of town was the deal. Instead they stuck around trying to put a hit on a former professional hitman and all three times turned out to be amateur night ending bad for the amateurs. A tough time following the kids around and got the break they needed to plant the bomb with a parking lot of empty cars.

Car blew-up with kids and Krasko thought job done. All they had to do was sit back for the big pay day. Now White wanted to be a millionaire believing he could be the one offing Pone. He'd have better luck getting a million by reviving that game show who wants to be a millionaire. What made matters worse he wanted to involved him again. Being around White made him feel conjoined. Not a good feeling. Krasko leaned on the kitchen counter out of White's view.

A big bag of loot sat in the middle of the living room. Enough to split between the two of them. Krasko wanted a small portion. He came from a poverty stricken family. A drunk out of work father and a mother with a high school education working below minimum wage jobs. His father died a drunk and his mother soon after from depression and heart failure. She gave her son the only advice she could. Finish high school and go into the military. She knew her son was no scholar, but the military could help him to a better life than what they gave him. Krasko had his on ambition and knew he wasn't college bound, but notice the local gangsters driving through his neighborhood and liked what he saw; fancy clothes, women, and fast cars. Took his mother's advice a few years later and joined the military to gain access as the Prohibitions bomb man.

Figured since he came from nothing and looking at the bag, a small portion of the money would be more than he had when he was a kid going to bed hungry. What food they had his drunken father devoured. Staying another day, night, minute, or even a second in a house no better than the house he grew up in…well at least it wasn't smelly and decayed like this dump. His childhood house was a shack, but not a shit-hole. Krasko just wanted enough to make himself comfortable and White could have the rest, but no, dragon breath wanted to be a millionaire and put them both in more danger trying to convince the man they could kill Pone for more money.

Krasko pounded the counter. No more living in a barn of a house not fit for an animal, eating greasy smelly seafood every night in a place that made Sleepy Hollow look like a vacation paradise. Time to separate. Krasko saw the butcher knife on the edge of the sink and grabbed it.

White deep into his conversation with the man. He didn't hear Krasko approaching him from behind holding the knife above his head like the silhouette shadow in the movie Psycho. Before White could utter another word… THUNK!

The phone fell to the mildew floor and White sunk in-slow-motion with a shock expression. He made no sound despite the knife plunging deep into his back. Teeth gritted and a vice grip on the knife handle along with bulging angry eyes gave Krasko the strength to end their alliance. A deep exhale and he released his grip on the knife.

"How you like that you dumb fuck?" said Krasko observing the planted knife in White's spine.

"Should've split the damn money, but no you wanted to bite off more than you could chew. Well, now the money's mine."

Krasko sniffed and frowned. Jesus…the guy smelled worse dead than he did when he was alive. Something must have crawled inside the bastard and died a long time ago. Krasko knew White kept the keys to the truck on him. Finding the keys in the front right side pants pocket. He grabbed the money bag about to walk out of the door when he heard a voice calling out White's name. He stomped the cell cutting off the connection, then he hit the road.

Thirty-Two

"White-White-White!" cried Crowe. He looked at his cell and saw no signal. Crowe slumped down on his sofa. The flood-gates of worry filled his head.

A chill ran up his spine and his stomach felt queasy. He shook his head thinking about previous events such as Red confronting him about changing the time and day to meet, but they haven't met about the tragic since. Pone saw White at a strip club and chased him on the interstate then through the city till he sent in the cavalry and like Custer last stand they got wiped out. He wished they had taken care of Pone. He would've order them to erase White and Krasko too. The black bastard had the nerve to try and squeeze him for cash, he thought. Crowe didn't know what caused their disconnection, but figured it wasn't good. Something happened to White and he considered it a good thing. He lost faith in the convict to finish the job.

Things had gotten sloppy or the Prohibitions and Hip-Hoppers would be at war. They know…they know, and he got an uneasy feeling about his two jailbirds.

Two deep breaths. Don't push the panic button just yet. Putting a tracer inside the bag before dropping it off at the decaying house. White and Krasko's clubhouse gave him chills. Crowe checked his phone…yeah, the money now on the run. He looked at his coffee table. An open family photo album. His parents wedding pictures; together, solo, with both their parents, feeding each other a piece of wedding cake and drinking champagne. Crowe turned the page: his birth photo with each of his parents, all three together, early school years till he was eight. A photo of him holding kid brother when he was a baby till he turned four. An 8 x 10 of the whole family including his mother pregnant with his sister. The album thick, but empty pages.

On the table next to the album a bottle of Scotch. Crowe closed the memento and grabbed the scotch taking a long drink He stamped the bottle on the table leaned back and exhaled. Rubbed his face with both hands stretching his eyes.

A twist to his plan. He hoped one of the two bone-heads would get greedy and his money on Krasko. So plan B worked: White or Krasko would do in the other and haul ass with the money. Plan A issue, Pone alive presented a problem. Kill Pone stopping him from solving the case a job for White and he failed.

Hope he got the ax, thought Crowe making a fist. Krasko too dumb to make a-clean-get-away. Pone dead. Inform the families one of their own killed the teens. They blame each other and go to war. Plan A could still happen.

Crowe pondered his next move. He needed bait. Strong cheese for his mouse trap. Crowe manipulated his cell using his thumb on who would be his cheese.

He smiled.

"Thomas…yeah, listen something just came up about Pone, but I can't tell you over the phone… I know the case haven't been solve, but this is important… I need you to meet me at the Four Tower Motel… we have to be discrete… as soon as possible…good, see you there."

Pone pulled up fifty yards to what he considered something out of a horror movie. The house more like a ruin. He sat back in the Maroon Chevy Astro van loaned to him from Otis. He checked the syringes in the pocket of his jacket. Stick said the juice would make you sleep like a baby. Pone asked Stick if the drug the same stuff a popular serial killer on television used to take out his victims. Stick laughed and said don't believe everything you see on TV. Etorphine if used on humans would cause a thirty-second seizure and the person would die. Something Pone didn't want breaking the deal depriving the two king-pins their revenge. Stick didn't say what he put in the syringes, but guaranteed results. The van wasn't the only change Pone made: a black wool cap on his head, a red pullover shirt hiding under a black bomber leather jacket, wrangler loose-fitting jeans, and black Doc Martens hikers.

Pone observed the landscape; a cartoon back in the day came to mind called Courage the Cowardly Dog. The town Courage lived in; Nowhere and this waste land, badlands or hell out in the heart of nowhere. The Great Meteor did a job on this part of the country.

The government only put money where they thought worth preserving.

Plant life afraid to grow, and Pone didn't blame it. Glad he made the trip during the day. There in front of the house stood a grand hollow decaying tree just like Ella said.

A big mouth asking for a mercy death and the house, well even make-over TV couldn't save it. Pone grabbed Sally, then made his way toward the house on foot. He saw no vehicle of any kind, but figured he'd take a look any-way.

Once inside, Pone wasted no time pulling his shirt over his nose. He saw the crimson trail leading up to an Afro-American male, lying face-down on his stomach.

Roland White was dead with mouth and eyes wide open and a butcher knife in his back like a vampire with a stake in the heart except Roland would not be rising from the dead when the blade got pulled out.

The expression on Roland's face was total shock. Pain from the knife took control of his senses no doubt and his roommate stabbed him in the back. Pone assumed Krasko got tired of the living conditions and who could blame him. How long they were bunked up in this abode, Pone did not know, but living in a place like this could drive anybody mad. Pone noticed the smashed cell near the body. Roland was too busy talking to Crowe to know his life of sorrow about to come to an end. Pone closed White's eyes, but made a beeline back into the frigid air. "Whew!" Pone couldn't believe a human being could smell so awful.

The house excuse for smelling bad; old and moldy. White's odor was hard to figure. Part of the package deal was damage, but two parts left to salvage his promise to the two kings.

Pone inhaled the fresh air until he saw tire tracks heading south. Pone cursed. Krasko got a head start on him. He went back inside the house of death with his shirt over his nose and knelt down over White's body. He wasn't an expert to determine the time of death like they did on TV, but knew after ten minutes a dead body in open air attracts flies to lay thousands of eggs in the mouth, nose, and eyes of the corpse. No sign of insects.

Climate too cold for survival keeping White's body from becoming an incubator and the house would repel them anyway.

Pone needed air on the brain and opened a few windows and propped the door.

The frosty air did the trick. Pone didn't know how long White was dead. He believed all time of deaths not accurate. His hypothesize; since he spoke to Ella, change clothes, switch vehicles, checking the time on his phone… over two hours. White's corpse smelled stronger, so he assumed Krasko got a two hour jump. Before Pone left, he studied White for a moment, looked at his lower body and knew it true by the smell once you die a loss of bladder and bowel contents took place.

In White's case, he had a number three. Pone rushed back outside; he got on his cell.

"What's going on, Pony?" asked Red.

"I need you to shoot me a Photo of James Krasko." He had gotten a glimpse of both men at Red's place, but wanted a picture. "He's on the run. Contact Brown and tell him Roland White is dead. I didn't kill him and this house in Rock Hill needs demolishing. I'll text you the directions so you can give it to him."

"What happened to Roland?"

"A butcher knife wedged in his spine."

"Ouch," said Red.

"Discretion needs…"

"Handle with care."remarked Red.

"Get me that photo pronto."

"Be careful, Pony."

"Always."

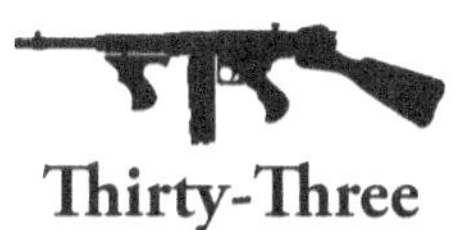

Thirty-Three

Four Tower Inn motel at Sunset Road 30 miles outside of Metro City near I-77 west. It didn't turn into a ruin, but the Great Meteor made it popular with teenagers who needed a place to go after prom night. Prom night wasn't every night so how it stayed in business a mystery; weary travelers used the flophouse for an overnight stay.

A middle-aged woman with a noticeable growth on her nose ran the place. She didn't hang around much leaving an out to lunch sign on the desk, but if desperate for a room then you call her on her cell and wait till she returned. If you caught her there then you might find her asleep with the TV on watching the rerun channel of shows from years past. Her alarm clock a bell on the check-in desk.

Towers shaped like castle rooks gave it a unique appeal. A good place for romantic dinners and a great view of nothing. You enter from the balcony, and if you wanted privacy you put a occupied sign on the door. The entrance and exit both a large arch-way design with a mid-size pool no longer in use; water replaced by moss and mildew. The apocalypse had come and gone without leaving a zombie.

A silver Mercedes pulled up and parked next to a gray Saab near the end of the motel. Car door opened; shiny blackpumps followed by long hose-less legs stepping out.

Red wasn't dolled up, pale complexion, hair in a pony tail, and no lipstick. She didn't need a paint job to look good. She wrapped herself in a black fur coat .

She frowned smelling urine and feces in the air making her feel dirty. Thomas wanted to try something different and now after seeing the lodge she had regrets. A companion when it suited her.

Red agreed to meet Thomas for this discrete encounter because she noticed Pone being somewhat stress free and figured she'd give it a trial. Sex supposed to be a cure for tension. Sure she could have any man, but she respected Thomas enough to go out with him because he approached her like a little shy school boy at a lawyers gala and asked her out to dinner.

She thought so cute and they have gone out together ever since. Thomas Maxwell a casual boyfriend. She wondered if she did this venture out of jealousy.

Her family wouldn't approve of Pone; Red wouldn't kiss and tell. The Brigands made it clear he lived because he worked for her. Red took Pone on as her right hand-man. She kept the former killer-for-hire close to protect her family. Afraid he would get tired of their threats on his life and take them out. She not only protected him from them, but safeguarded them from him. Pone made the mistake of wanting to get out and in their line of work a no-no. In their business, you know too much and will become a rat. Red knew Pone loyal to a fault, but her siblings the twins got paranoid. Linda didn't trust him. Her siblings backed off as long as he worked for her. Paul J. gave her right hand-man a nickname, leave him alone Pone.

Red approached room twenty; Thomas instructed her to just come on in without knocking.

She entered. Red didn't gasp or got moon-eye seeing her little man tied to a chair with a black strap around his head and a cherry sized ping-pong ball in his mouth.

A recognizable voice came from the bathroom.

"Welcome Miss Brigand," said Crowe holding a .38 special. He toweled off his face instructing her to move away from the door.

"Thomas… I know you said you wanted to try something different, but this…" remarked Red.

Crowe pursed his lips. "Laugh now, but you won't later." Maxwell sat with his eyes lowered to the floor avoiding eye contact with Red. A tight fit sitting with his right side against the wall facing the door at the foot of the bed. The bathroom behind him a few feet from the head of the bed. Crowe put him in an uncomfortable position to say the least.

"Are you all right, Thomas?" asked Red.

Crowe smacked him on the back of the head. "Sure he is," Leaned toward Maxwell's left ear, "Tell her…oh crap, I forgot your mouth is full."

Red gave an angry sigh. Crowe flashed a devious smile. "Easy there girly. Your little man all dressed up, but no place to go."

Maxwell gave an angry glance as if to say who are you calling little. Crowe taller by four inches.

"Why Harvey?"

Crowe sat down on the bed holding the gun. Red observed their accommodation looking for a place to sit. A small uncomfortable room. A regular size bed; two chairs, one round wooden table, bathroom, and a window near the door. Red bit the inside of her lower lip pondering what the hell Thomas and Crowe plan on doing.

A threesome…involving Crowe, ewe. Forget about it, thought Red. Her secret fantasy partners didn't include these two if she tested those waters. Red studied both men realizing they planned something and Crowe aborted and instead used Maxwell as bait to lure her out here to the wasteland. Mission accomplished. Red swooned. Got back her balance. She felt light headed needing to sit down.

Crowe pointed the gun at her feeling good and confidant having the big cheese and her mouse in his trap. The Four Tower motel the perfect place for his backup plan to work. He heard about the flophouse from one of his hired guns. Told him about an owner who took extended lunch hours and sometimes didn't come back till the next day. The story proved true and played perfect into Crowes hands using Maxwell as a gudgeon for Red and now Red bait for Pone. He assumed his jailbirds would get greedy and off the other. White or Krasko he did not care, but one of them on the run with the bag. Crowe put his money on Krasko because he believed White would have been smart enough to check the bag for a tracker. Crowe did his homework on both inmates. Eyes and ears at local watering holes in the city where both gangs hung out and did a lot of talking and helped him find his pigeons. Krasko pure white trash coming from nothing and the only way out poverty joining the military or the gangster life.

Krasko like White went the military route and like White stayed in long enough to learn a trade. Crowe so bent on revenge kept tabs on the both of them since they were both part of the Hip-Hoppers and Prohibitions. He set them up for crimes putting them in the pen and got them both out to be his dummies and he their ventriloquist.

"No! You stand. Only I need to sit to tell this story." He nodded toward Maxwell. "Little man here has no choice but to sit."

"Can I at least lean against the wall, you know in case you bore me to sleep?" asked Red.

"You got jokes, good for you." Crowe nodded. "Against the door and arms folded."

Red got comfortable.

"Okay…where do I start…oh yeah the year…that's right ever since that damn rock passed by and sent the world into a future shock; the years aren't quite accurate now is it? The science nerds just gave us an educated guess. Twenty-fifty the year. Let's call this story a few casualties so what, since that's what innocence are when they are victims of mob violence. I was eight years old when I lost my family." Crowe got off the bed and went to the bathroom. He left the door open; urinated, farted then came out with a cup of water. Maxwell squirmed and frowned. Red was relieved the bathroom located at the head of the bed. She knew the odor reached Maxwell by his reaction. The window was down and she hoped the gas died before it got to her. Crowe sipped his water and sat back down.

"My father was a simple lawyer fighting for the little people. Not a lot of money in that kind of law, but he had a good heart. My mother was a school teacher. Anyway, it was a beautiful Autumn day;

every day since then seems like Autumn, but my parents took the family out for sightseeing in Uptown Metro." He took a sip of water and swallowed hard.

"My brother and I, he was only four years old and mother pregnant with my baby sister. A cool breeze, the sun bright, and for a moment hugs, laughter all around good times. Until several cars screeched to a halt on both sides of the street and all hell broke loose." Crowe glared at Red. "On second thought, stand!"

Red stood like a soldier. Crowe smacked Maxwell on the back of his head. "Where was I?" Crowe snapped his fingers. "Oh yeah, all hell broke loose with innocent bystanders wedged in by rapid fire. My dad shoved me to ground and yelled for me to cover my ears and close my eyes. I was in a fetal position. I thought that damn gunfire would never end." Crowe got a distant look in his eyes.

"But it did and when the smoke cleared, the gutless police showed up at the last minute to do their civic duty. I sat up, saw my brother spread out, eyes closed and bloody as was my parents who died with their eyes opened. My baby sister would never get the chance to enter this cruel world…for the best I guess. There were other survivors, they lost loved ones as well." Crowe swallowed hard. "My mother's older sister and her husband raised me with their kids, but they were a substitute family and I should have never needed one."

He pointed the gun at Red.

"But your daddy set things straight between Macone and G. He just did it too damn late."

As a little girl, Red remembered walking into her father's study. It was his sanctuary from the world he built with blood and violence. He had a rule, knock before entering.

Red didn't, but he didn't explode, instead he sensed her presence and asked her to close the door. She did and he swiveled in his chair to face her while nursing a brandy.

Paul J sat his brandy on his desk gesturing Red to come sit on his lap. She did. He inhaled then exhaled. Red smelled the liquor, bur didn't mind. She laid her face on his barrel chest feeling safe. He kissed her on the top of her head. You are going to be better than me.

He said. I can tell you will take the family in a different direction. You will atone for my sins and make Metro a better city. You may have to do it alone or your brother and sisters may follow, but this must never ever happen again. Red knew all the wrongs her father had done. His sins would not disappear by one good deed. But she felt the goodness in her father's heart. He was a man and not a monster.

Red shook her head. "Harvey, I'm sorry, but you murdered two kids."

"Nothing hurts worse than the loss of a child… I'm a monster, but they created me."

"You're a dead man," said Red.

"If they find out the truth," remarked Crowe.

"Kids…why not the old fossils?" questioned Red.

"Taking out G's son was like saying word up homey and Macone's daughter, hey forget about it," Crowe snickered. "Wow, I don't get all that slang shit, but that sounded good if I do say so myself and I do."

Crowe looked at Maxwell. "Nothing hurts worse than your children biting the dust just before graduation. Can you imagine Macone, G. and their clan sitting at home wondering what might have been…believe it or not it even hurts me. Heard both kids were going to college on scholarships, my parents never got to see me graduate, and my brother and sister never made it to school." Crowe smiled. "Life's a bitch."

"Others like you survive that day and manage to put their lives back together," said Red.

"Well sorry toots," Crowe shrugged. "I ain't everybody. People deal with grief their own way and I'm not them. I got into criminal law to erase scum, and I hit those two in the loins where it hurts."

"Crazy," said Red.

Crowe laughed. "I may not know Karate, but I do know crazy."

Red shook her head. "You're a sick man."

"For a long time and in case you're still pondering why Maxwell is here, it's because I told him I would help strengthen his position in the D.A. Office by nailing your boy, but neither of you need to worry about that because you two will be dead."

Maxwell straightened in his chair.

"Got to hand it to you Harvey, you picked the right place to leave our bodies." said Red.

"Yeah well there's a minor glitch, but I'm still on course to start an all-out gang war."

Red smiled.

"What?' asked Crowe."

"You still have to explain how and why Thomas and I died."

"My hired help in the four towers recognized you both and got revenge for what your family have done over the years and you know they are not innocent and Maxwell put some of their friends in the pen…wrong place wrong time."

"What about your man on the run?" said Red realizing after hearing Crowe talk she knew he knew one of his guys was dead and her hypothesis on White.

"I'll send one of my guys to track him down, put a bullet in his head and since he was once prohibition. You see G knows nothing about the other guy who was once pulling out of his crew. As far as he knows his boy is still in the pen and as for Pone, once he gets here my guys will take him out and dispose of his body. I'll make it look like he caught up with my man on the run and got gunned down."

Red shook her head. "You have it all figured out."

"You know something I don't?" asked Crowe.

"Let us go. Turn yourself in. You'll get life, but be alive in a secured holding."

Crowe exhaled. "My plan is better. It doesn't include bars."

"No conscience?" questioned Red.

"Their children made the sacrifice," said Crowe.

"Make one family believe a hit put out on his kid and the other died of friendly fire," said Red.

Crowe smiled, "Couldn't said it better myself."

"It won't work."

"The dead tell no tales."

You got it all figured out. okay, thought Red. He knows which of goons bit the dust.

Crowe shook his head. He pressed the gun against Maxwell's occiput. "Get on your cell and instruct your man to come here. No funny business."

Red took out her phone.

"My plan doesn't work unless Chubby Pone is dead."

Thirty-Four

When you gamble, you take chances and if you're afraid to take chances then you do not gamble. This Krasko thing turned into a needle in a haystack. The more he drove the Astro van, the more of dead land he saw in Rock Hill living up to its name. Pone hoped for a building or something. Maybe one of those last chance gas stations you glance at in those TV commercials to promote gas mileage the latest new car can give you. He spotted a sign that said the nearest town 80 miles. Pone felt like a Twilight Zone episode without that weird music.

There is a God, he thought when he saw a saloon. A sandy stone square adobe building. A billboard sat on top titled The Thirsty Lizard. The lizard a green female with eye-lashes laid out like a model at a photo shoot. Out-side the saloon: two gas pumps, four cars, three Harley Davidson cycles, and wallah, he thought when he spotted a white Chevy S-10 truck like the one he chased down I-77 before two large black Hummers interrupted his pursuit. The needle in a haystack found. Krasko stopped for a drink. Pone observed the authentic watering hole with swinging saloon doors, but a rectangular door for closing time to make the building secured. A post where you tied up your horse gave a look like the old west.

Pone parked next to the pick-up truck and entered through the swinging saloon doors and like a western movie he played the mysterious stranger with all eyes on him. Pone scanned the bar with peripheral vision; eight patrons including the bartender: tall, short, fat, skinny, black, and white. The crowd made Pone feel like he walked into *A Dusk to Dawn* movie. He looked around for Salma Hayek. No such luck. He shook his head thinking once he got settled they would transform into a bunch of vampire serpent creatures. A 1950s jukebox playing Run Through The Jungle inside the bar.

Pone made it to the bar. The barkeep was bald, razor stubble, short, stocky wearing a stained white T-shirt and a heart shaped tattoo with mom written on his right shoulder.

"Beer in a bottle," said Pone knowing the place sold none Malta Goya. "What's a matter? Don't think my glasses aren't clean? "Growled the Barkeep.

"Hell no."

The barkeep smiled. "You ain't from around here, are ya?"

"What gave me away?" Pone hoped nobody was from around here.

The barkeep flashed a gap tooth smile. "You're pretty."

Pone gave a look.

"I ain't gay."

"Just giving credit where it's due." said the barkeep.

Pone took a swallow of beer. "They still looking?"

"Naw. They focused on that other stranger at the end of the bar." Pone saw a man wearing a gray hoodie nursing a bottle of whiskey.

"What's so pretty about him?" asked Pone.

"Not a damn thing. It's his friend on the floor that's interesting. Barkeep shook his head. "Dumb ass."

Pone had to agree. A black athletic bag he figured containing dead presidents. "Get a look at his face?"

"He blends in real well."

Pone took out his cell and pulled up Krasko's picture. Barkeep turned up his lip. "You a bounty hunter?"

Pone paid for the beer, pulled his stocking cap further down over his eyes and made a beeline toward Krasko. Along the way, he saw three muscular, tattoo leather vested men who looked like bikers moving their eyes back and forth at Krasko.

Pone perched himself next to Krasko. "How's it going friend?" asked Pone.

Krasko grabbed the bottle and guzzle himself another drink, then showed Pone the bottle. "This is my friend."

"That friend you got there has put plenty of people in marble city."

"Marble city," choked Krasko.

"Bone yard, bone orchard, plain and simple too much of the sauce can get you killed."

"Fuck off." Krasko took another swallow of booze.

"Tell you what, how about you hear me out and if you don't buy what I'm selling then I'll leave you to your last day on earth."

"What do you mean?"

"You're intoxicated."

"So I got a fucking buzz big deal."

"It is a big deal since you came in here with that big ass bag." Krasko planted his foot on the bag.

"Easy friend. I don't care or want your bag, but every low life in here does." Krasko belched, then took a quick glance.

"They watching you. Watching you get your drink on waiting for the right moment."

"What moment?" asked Krasko.

"They don't know if you a bad ass or a chump. By the looks of things, they waitin' till you've had your fill before making a move and that's why you need my help to keep you from getting your throat cut."

Krasko burped again while scanning the room. Then glared at Pone. "I'll take my chances," said Krasko.

"Say what?"

"I don't know you from Adam and Eve or what the hell ever. You come up to me pretending not to be interested in my bag and besides look how you wearing that cap."

"I have a condition."

"No sale now go fuck yourself."

Pone snorted. Time was a wasting. He reached into his pocket, took out a syringe and inserted it into Krasko's neck. Face down, he went on the bar. Pone observed Krasko's eyes closing, body slumping on the bar and how fast the drug worked. Pone tossed Krasko over his shoulder and grabbed the bag. The three men sitting at the table weren't too happy seeing Krasko and the bag about to leave. A mountain of a man blocked Pone's path. "My friend had too much to drink," said Pone.

"I saw you poke somethin' in his neck," said Mountain. "Diabetic… wife sent me to fetch him."

"Y'all two can go. Bag stays."

Pone looked at the man then around him at his two buddies. They straightened in their chairs sticking out their chest and good size too.

"The bag comes as well. So do you mind stepping aside?" Mountain folded his arms. "If I don't?"

"Ever heard of the Brigand band?"

"They don't run shit out here."

Pone laughed. "From what I've seen, there isn't shit to run. You don't want them coming out here looking for me."

"Drop the damn bag and get yo ass outta here."

Sometimes you can do something long enough that it harden you as a person.

Pone had been in the gangster business long enough not to fear or back down from anybody: young, old, big, small, male, female, black or white. But three mountain sized men would be a task, and he wanted to avoid any kind of violence.

"Ever heard of the combine?"

One of Mountain's buddies jumped up and whispered in his ear. Whatever he said melted Mountain's attitude.

"Look man, at least give us something."

Pone put the bag between him and the bar then set Krasko down on a stool. He frisked him and came up with keys to the S-10. He tossed them to Mountain. Mountain studied the keys then stepped aside. He nodded to Pone. Pone gathered Krasko and the bag. He was glad for the saloon style doors. He made his way through them and got the hell out of dodge.

Thirty-Five

Krasko slept in the back like a baby. Drugs and alcohol were a bad combination. As a precaution, Pone used zip ties to bind Krasko's ankles and wrist.

He parked the van on a hill looking down at the Four Tower Inn. Now paying the price for lack of interest, but still livable. A lot of these type of motels dwelled outside of Metro.

Red sounded cryptic giving directions saying four eyes and tower describing the flophouse. The phone went dead. He hoped nothing bad happened to her, but her speech not articulate, Red's conversation always crystal clear.. A member of a crime family made her battled tested and so he knew she was in trouble.

Pone shook his head; why was she out here in the first place? He didn't have time to ponder that, but from what he saw he was about to walk into a trap. Pone moved the van to the edge of the front entrance. He was glad that he changed his wardrobe and not driving Lucille. Pone walked in the archway entrance. The landscape an eye-sore, the moldy pool would have been a hot-bed for Mosquito if it had water and not for the cool weather. Turned over patio tables and chairs made paradise a dump. Again what the hell was she doing out here?

The door wasn't locked, but he saw an out to lunch sign on the counter near a bell. By the looks of things, why would the desk clerk even return. Pone wasn't big on size or square feet of buildings or whether any patrons were occupying the rooms. He already spotted Red's Mercedes near the other side of the complex, but studied the situation before entering the place.

Pone took the stairs to the balcony to the tower on his left. He assumed the East Tower.

When Pone reached the top, he played the drunken wanderer. Before he could knock on the door, he heard noise. Behind the door an average height man, thin, balding thick beard with gray strands faced him. His body looked military, but the discipline of staying in shape was disappearing as age took over. Pone exhaled relief the man didn't have his gun exposed, instead it was still holstered inside his jacket pocket.

"Get lost pal!"

Pone staggered against the wall head down. "Just need to sleep this off."

"What the fuck? Do I look like I give a shit?"

Pone coughed. "Saw somebody up here and thought you ran the place."

"Well, I ain't and if you don't want your ass handed to you, I suggest you get the fuck outta here. He pulled back his jacket showing Pone his gun."

Pone fell draping himself on thick beard. "What the fuck?" said the bloke.

He tried throwing pone off him. Pone hung on, and the two fell into the tower room. Thick beard got to his feet first. Pone on one knee slipped out his razor, spun and slit the throat of thick beard who had just placed his hand on his gun. He fell like a tree. A voice on the hand radio sounded off.

"Bruce! Bruce! You okay?"

Pone grabbed the radio. "Four," he said in a mufled voice. "Told the asshole to leave, had to put him down."

"Copy that."

"See anybody else?" asked Pone.

"Just the guy you took care of."

"Stay alert."

"Copy that."

Pone pondered if he pulled off the voice imitation.

Radio went silent, and Pone took the short stairs to the patio where he saw a scoped sniper rifle. A SIG SHR 970 with a silencer. Pone used the scope to check on the other would be assassins. West side assassin was all business focused on the outside only; his back turned giving view of a round melon in Pone's cross hairs. Pone checked the rifle, hollow points. Crimson erupted from the melon. Two down and two to go. Pone felt like Race Bannon from the *Johnny Quest* episode where Race sat in a tree taking out the bad guys with a tranquilizer rifle. The difference for Pone was his rifle built for the long goodbye.

Pone aimed diagonal, the other assassin reading a girly magazine with his right shoulder jerking up and down. Where did Crowe find these guys, thought Pone. A bullet through a pair of big boobs on the cover ended the hand job.

Pone hoped he went down happy. Now for the last tower, when Pone looked through the scope he saw a scope looking back at him. Guess I didn't pull off the voice.

Both rifles fired.

Where the hell is that son-of-a-bitch, Pone? thought Crowe.

"You gave your man every way, but he should've been here by now."

"You in that much of a hurry to kill us, Harvey?" asked Red.

Crowe snorted. "I am."

"You sick bastard."

Crowe took out his cell. He wanted his men to communicate with radios, but he and Bruce by cell. When he got Bruce's voice mail, a shade of concern came over Crowe's face.

"Problem?" asked Red.

"Shut up bitch!" Crowe checked the tracer signal on his phone. The signal was getting closer to the room.

"What the hell?" Crowe motioned Red away from the door. He peaked through the Venetian blinds. The Astro van pulled up. Crowe looked dubious.

"What the hell is going on? Who is this guy? He's not one of my men."

Red took advantage of Crowe being confused. Moving with the grace of a ballerina and ferocity of a lioness. A hard thrust to the spine stiffened Crowe like a board. She grasped his gun arm holding it as straight as a pole twisting it. A sharp open hand blow to Crowe's neck followed by a Vulcan style neck pinch grip to the back of his neck forcing his face into a violent encounter with her left knee. A sickening crack and blood came from his nose. Red spun Crowe around flipping him on his back to a ferocious heel stomp to the side of his face and a final twist of his wrist forced the gun from his hand.

"Come on in, Pony," shouted Red.

When Pone entered, he saw Wonder Woman rescuing Steve Trevor. Pone took a syringe from his pocket. He also saw a semi-conscious Crowe on the floor with a bloody nose.

Pone swallowed hard. "Is he…"

"He's useless to you dead," said Red.

Pone knelt down and inserted the needle into Crowe's neck. He went limp. "I'll take it from here."

Red released her grip on Crowe and untied Maxwell.

Pone threw Crowe over his shoulder. "You got to clean up on all four towers and I don't know when who's running this place will be back. "

"I got this, Pony," said Red.

Pone nodded. "A long drive ahead of me."

Thirty-Six

The heavenly shades of night fell forcing the Sun to say good-bye. Pone had a long day and was now preparing for a long night. Thanks to the help of coffee he made it to Sumter with his packages in the peak hours of the morning. The night drive wasn't uneventful though, they both stirred a little; Krasko passed gas most of the trip, but that was the only unpleasant thing that came from him. Crowe seemed to be having a nightmare. when he wakes up, he'd have a big surprise waiting for him.

G's pig farm just up ahead, Sumter the home of Shaw Air Force Base. A country town like Rock Hill, but that's where the comparison ended.

Because of the Air Force, the government made sure not let it become a dust bowl. Big money played a part in keeping Sumter nice and fertile.

Pone felt melancholic about the job he'd done. What gave him the right to deliver two criminals to criminals? He thought of Krasko; a cretin if he ever saw one. He saved him in that bar only to send him to a worse fate. Out of the frying pan into the fire. A classic mob film entered Pone's mind. The main character said it best deciding not to blow up two kids to make a point to another mob family. He ain't killin' no kids and Krasko should have said the same thing.

As for Crowe, Red caught Pone off guard when she walked him out with Crowe draped over his shoulder. He felt like something had change between her and Maxwell.

She supplied him information about the woeful Crowe. If Crowe had hired him to go after the two kings, he might have done it for free, but instead not only did the man hire him through Red, but also tried to kill him and also planned on killing Red. The master plan was to start an all-out gang war between the Prohibitions and Hip-Hoppers.

It would have worked making one believe the other put a hit on their kid even though their own kid bit the dust in the plan. The melancholic feeling Pone had went away. Crowe was a fool to believe he could take out two crime families by eliminating some key players. Like most things in the cycle of life another crime family would just replace the other. Pone felt no remorse, do this job long enough and it will harden you.

Pone followed G's instructions pulling up around the back of a grand weathered gray barn. 8 a.m. sharp. And better than an alarm clock Pone witnessed what few people experience now days except only in the deep south, the sound of a rooster crowing. Welcome to life in the country.

Speaking of welcome, the welcome comity was there as well; Prohibitions and Hip-Hoppers. Pone saw Macone and G united for perhaps the only time in their blood soaked sinful lives standing alongside their lieutenants and four of their most trusted men from each gang. Five green mighty John Deere tractors with chains tied to the back of them and positioned in opposite directions for an unsanctioned tractor pull.

Pone got out of the van to the smell and sound of: clucking, oinks, and moos in the distance.

The smell no worse than a sidewalk of dry urine on a hot day and sewer fumes coming from a city man hole. He saw about twenty pigs oinking and pressing their snouts against the wooden pen begging for feeding.

Pone walked up to Macone and G. "Crowe and Krasko in the van."

The look on Macone's face went from surprise to anger once he heard his former bomb maker's name. G. even gave Macone a look until Pone explained how Crowe plucked a former member of his crew named White to make use of his bomb making skill, but was already dead. The look in G's eyes made Pone realize that White had lucked out.

The goon squad wasted no time retrieving the packages. They were both still feeling the effect of drug being laid out side by side.

"We good?" asked Pone.

Both Macone and G. agreed with a hand-shake. Pone shook their hands knowing damn well that meant nothing.

"You going to wake them?" asked Pone.

"Let 'em enjoy one last good sleep," said G.

Despite the smell of pigs, Pone saw a table with coffee and Krispy Kreme Doughnuts. He motioned to Brown.

"You ain't hungry?" asked Brown.

"Just went on a diet," remarked Pone.

Brown laughed.

Pone opened the side door of the van. "Got something for Ella." He pulled out the bag and gave it to Brown.

Brown gave a dubious look. "What's this for?"

"I'm not apologizing for what I did, but this should help Ella unless her religion is against it,"

Brown snorted ."She is religious, but she ain't no fool," Brown peeked inside the bag.

"How much?"

Pone shrugged. "Didn't care to count it."

"Ain't nothing wrong with Christmas coming early."

"Roland and house?" questioned Pone.

"Ella said he was still family and the house never there."

"I had to tell G about Roland, he gave Macone a look when he identified one of his former employees. He knows Crowe was playing both sides against each other."

"It's all good, man," said Brown.

"Do me a favor? " asked Pone.

"You earned it."

"Make sure I don't get a Christmas ham from this damn farm."

Brown smiled and shook his head. "I know that's right," He rejoined the group.

"Pone!" called Boysenberry.

Can I please get the hell out of here, thought Pone.

"You makin' me jealous giving Brown all the attention," said Boysenberry straightening his tie.

"I have no favorites."

"When you going to let me in on one of your poker games?"

"When there's an open chair."

Both men grinned and parted ways.

Pone stretched and yawned, but wasn't about to sleep. He wanted to make tracks quick as possible. Once he got back on the highway, he looked back at the gathering in the rear view mirror and saw a big stir among the group. Pone shook his head. Always be weary of a gangster who owns a pig farm.

Metro City, back to business as usual. Why Deputy Mayor Crowe was no longer there not discussed and Winslow wasted no time naming possible candidates including Thomas Maxwell. In Crowe's case the media made it a private resignation for unprofessional conduct and not using the proper channels and authorities to handle the murder of two teens. People of the city were not stupid, but were smart enough not to stick their nose into mob business.

Pone smiled cruising around in Lucille again. Before heading home, he made a stop at Nadine. Birdie made it clear that it was very important. Pone walked inside the club and knew that something was wrong when he saw three women of his life together looking bleak, plus Jade was home from college. Red and Birdie sat a table; Jade rushed at him like a linebacker blitzing a quarterback.

It wasn't for an inappropriate kiss this time, but she never did that in front of Birdie. No, this time it was a comfort hug with tears. Pone separated from Jade.

"What's going on?" asked Pone.

Birdie braved a tear stain face getting straight to the point. "Wisdom's dead…he had cancer."

Pone walked out as fast as he entered the club. He stood at the entrance looking toward the gray sky.

"Damn!"

Black Medusa
Mercury Slim Miscelleaneous
Short Story

A cold moonless night with a slight drizzle of rain set the tone for bad things to come. The big black Escalade roared down I-85 North heading toward Sugar Creek road where a neighborhood of a hole-in-the-wall rump-shaking clubs lived. The destination, the Viper Lounge a club where men went to get their drink on and find female companionship. It wasn't a rump-shaking club, but what went on in the private rooms stayed in the private rooms. A little after midnight, they were making good time since the interstate wasn't busy.

Big Ben, not in the mood for drinking or women, focused on finding out what happened to his friend, Al McGee. Riding shotgun was the man Pone recommended to help him with his problem a man named Mercury Slim. For three month's Mercury played the gracious host to Ben while working on his friend's disappearance. During their time together, Mercury remained a mystery to Ben.

Mercury had joked he worked as an under the radar P.I. His name was not listed in a phone book or on the Internet. There was nothing commercial about him, he did however, charge a fee ranging from one to ten thousand dollars to get the job done depending on the client and type of job.

Ben assumed when Mercury had hinted about it depending on the client and the job he had meant how dangerous the job was and a missing person could be dangerous since his friend was a hired killer and got into something he couldn't get out of. Therefore his disappearance could mean the six o'clock news reporting about a body found in a ditch or wooded area fitting his friend's attributes. Mercury could tell whether a client had money to spend, and Ben did. Ben paid ten thousand and waited for the results of his investment. With a good feeling in his breadbasket Ben hoped Mercury would prove to be as good as advertised.

In the month's Ben spent with Mercury, he knew Mercury owned the biggest house on the block, but overall a modest house. If he did make a lot of money, the house didn't give off any impression of wealth. He put his money into his late model Mercury Cougar in mint condition and to keep it in good shape. Ben considered Mercury a unique man.

A chef, and domestic around the house he had said he had inherited these traits from his grandmother. Her photos decorated the walls and mantel, and he liked walking around the house in his Buck Naked Brand Boxers. Ben didn't care to see Mercury in his underwear, but since he was staying as a guest, he couldn't complain.

Mercury Slim his birth name, and not because he drove a Mercury and had a slender build.

However, he gave Ben plenty of information on what they were up against. Mercury made most of the trips to the night-club in which he got close and personal with a young woman named Unique.

There are times when a woman of pleasure forgets her code of being a professional. She fancies a man and gives him more attention than he pays for. Mercury became Unique's fan and vice versa.

She liked him enough to tell him whatever he wanted to know about the establishment and the woman called Black Medusa.

Mercury also used his contacts to dig deeper into the club owner's past. He informed Ben about Medusa's background; she had a talent for taxidermy and the more he heard about the strange woman, the tale of Medusa got darker and more disturbing. Her mother had died when she had been very young. Medusa took up the womanly duties of the house including pleasing the men, her father and older brother.

"You sure that's true?" asked Ben.

"My sources don't lie," said Mercury.

"Shit'd," Ben snorted. "That's enough to make anybody lose it."

Mercury was glad for the conversation no matter how disturbing; it made a long ride shorter.

"Don't make it right if she's done what I think she's done."

"You saying she killed Al?"

"From what Unique told me, she has it in for men who mistreat women," said Mercury. "Al didn't believe in playing husband and father… Shit'd, I just hope he ain't dead. What else this girl told you?"

Mercury sighed. "She heard some of the other girls talking about how Medusa has a son, but didn't raise him. Some relative who lives up north raised the boy and set up a trust fund for him."

"You figure she sent him away because she despised men?" asked Ben.

Mercury nodded. "Pretty much. She wouldn't be a good influence on a girl either."

"Don't tell me the daddy or the brother is the father?"

"I hope neither, but if she spared the kid sending him to live with a relative then she must have a heart," said Mercury.

Ben grunted. "If that girl told you all that then she must got your dick."

"She sounded scared and wanted out, and I said I would help her."

"Just quit and leave."

"Come on, Ben. You know when you're around somebody that's corrupt it ain't that simple."

"Yeah, hate that shit when they say you know too much."

"That's when I got suspicious."

"Hold up! How you know this girl wasn't pumping you for information and told Medusa about you?"

"How do you know your friend Al went to the Viper Lounge?"

Ben took out his cell and showed the text message. "Wanted me to join him, but I declined. Now I wish I had."

Mercury nodded. "Okay."

"That girl going to be there tonight?"

"I told her to stay home."

Ben snorted. "We going to kill these people?"

Mercury let out a short laugh. "About that, that's you and Chubby's thing. I don't go around putting people six feet under."

"What? You better than us?"

"I'm not a cold-blooded killer."

"But you have killed?"

Mercury swallowed hard. "Only when I had to."

Ben studied Mercury. "Shit'd."

Mercury kept quiet. He didn't want his response to upset Ben. Anger makes a man do foolish things and for what they were about to do, Mercury needed Ben with a cool head. He changed the subject.

"So Ben, the probonos talk the way they do?"

"What do you mean?"

"You know, do they say 'Youse guys going to do things my way', see." Ben roared with laughter.

"Probonos and hip-hoppers, some of them fools try to keep it real, but they might as well talk like you and me."

"Trying to belong, huh?"

"If you already in then you should already know," said Ben. "Glad I live a suburban life."

"You ain't never met one of them in your neighborhood?" asked Ben. "Have you met my nosy neighbor across the street Mrs. Crabtree?" Ben frowned. "She worse than a watchdog"

"Barbecue and backyard cook outs and I'm fine with that."

"Hey I ain't mad you," said Ben.

Their conversation faded as they arrived at the Viper Lounge. In the past couple of months, every time Mercury had seen it at night, it looked more like a house of horrors. A grand square black stone box with one door the same color.

A tomb, thought Mercury.

It was two a.m., closing time, the time Mercury came each time he visited the lounge. The Escalade came to a stop.

"What's the plan?" asked Ben.

Mercury scoped out the area. A few cars parked in front of the building, and he hoped it belonged to the employees. He also hoped Unique took his advice to stay home.

"Got to improvise this. That means…"

"You going get our asses killed making this shit up as we go along," growled Ben.

"Anyway, I'll go up pretending I forgot my wallet." Mercury reached into his back pocket and placed his wallet in one of the cup holders.

Ben shook his head. "No weapons, right?"

"Nope."

"Again, you going to get our asses killed."

Mercury acted as if Ben hadn't said a word. "She has a muscular bartender with a shotgun under the bar, and four goons that I know of are packing."

"And we going in empty handed?"

"What? You don't like my plan?"

"Shit'd. You claim to be an amateur detective, look…a plan on the fly don't sound good to me."

"I brought you this far big man."

The two men stared at each other for a moment. Mercury blinked.

"Okay, it's show time. Just wait until I get the guy at the door inside, make your move and let your instincts tell you what to do."

Mercury made his way to the entrance. Sure enough, he pretended he had left his wallet, and the bouncer did his part to keep him out of the club. The goon was a tall, thick man, but Mercury fended him off making it inside the lounge.

Ben shook his head. He saw the chiseled six-two, one-seventy-five Mercury in his boxers, handling the goon with ease. Ben knew there was more to the man than he had led on.

With Mercury now inside, Ben had the cue to do his thing.

Ben stood at the entrance checking out the area. Mercury had cleared him a safe passage to get in position. He saw four thick goons in black suits and a thick broad-shouldered bartender matching them in size. He heard Mercury at the bar arguing about getting a drink.

"Look man, I'm thirsty…saw y'all lights on and decided to come in." Mercury scanned the club: the bartender in front of him behind the bar, a man behind him, one at the door, and two flanking him "No wonder this place is empty the way you treat your customers."

"You told me you forgot your wallet," said Goon One. "What? I can't look for my wallet and get a drink?"

"How you going pay for that drink if you ain't got no money?" asked the bartender.

"I got money if I find my wallet," Mercury snorted. "You can give me a tab or how about a drink on the house. Act nice and I'll tell people about this place." He smiled. "How about y'all help me look for it. Got to be around here some place. We find it and I can buy a drink."

Goon One grunted. "If it had credit cards and cash then it's long gone."

Mercury slapped the counter. "Damn! What's wrong with people now-days? Would it hurt for somebody to be honest?"

Goon One inhaled. "Look man…"

"And I carry cash no credit cards because you just borrowing money when you use cards. So help me find my wallet and then I can pay for a drink."

The bartender folded his arms. "We're closed, so get the fuck out of here or get fucked up."

Mercury slapped the top of the bar again. "That's why I want a drink so I can get fucked up."

The Bartender chuckled. "We got us a comedian fellas. Show mister funny man what we mean about fucked up."

Ben was tired of waiting. The goon at the door stood with his back turned. At about six-five, Ben had no problem apprehending the six-foot-five goon. He grabbed the man by the neck. A sickening crack followed as he went down like a puppet with loose strings.

"What the fuck?" said the bartender getting moon-eyed when he saw what had happened. He reached under the bar grabbing a sawed-off shotgun.

Ben dropped to a knee using the dead man as a shield. Everything from that point went on in slow motion. Ben got to see Mercury go to work and from what he saw he knew the man possessed special skills.

Mercury gave a side-kick to Goon One's shin scraping down with his heel to a foot stamp causing Goon One great pain. The bartender turned his attention to Mercury, but didn't fire trying to avoid shooting his own man. Mercury took advantage and figuring they all carried firearms, reached inside the man's coat, and pulled out a Glock.

He grabbed Goon One whirling him around, and the man took the full blast of the buck-shot to the chest. Before the bartender could reload he ended up with his back against the wall leaving blood and brain matter on it. Mercury placed a bullet between his eyes. With two more goons at large, and Ben used the time Mercury gave him to find his own Glock on the body of Goon Two.

Mercury turned over a table and hid behind it while Ben used Goon Two as a shield to a barrage of bullets. Once the storm cleared, Ben put three bullets in the chest of Goon Three. Goon Four concentrated on Mercury putting holes through the table he hid behind. When goon four ran out of bullets, Mercury took his turn, but the Glock jammed a common occurrence with Glocks.

Mercury tossed it away with cat quickness he rushed to Goon Four getting hip to hip while he grabbed his gun hand. He locked his extended arm and twisted the goon's wrist disarming him.

Ben wanted to put an end to the action, but also wanted to watch Mercury work. Goon Four acted big and clumsy, while Mercury seemed confident and comfortable with hand-to-hand combat.

Goon Four gave a hay-maker swing trying to end it all, but Mercury blocked it with his right hand. In the same motion he connected to Goon Four's jaw followed with a back-hand with the same fist, then a left hook of his own that made the goon spit up blood dropping him to a knee.

Mercury was disciplined, smooth, fast, and direct with bad intentions. Ordinary man my ass, thought Ben. Mercury had trained as a fighter, maybe military by the looks of things. Goon Four knew something didn't feel right and like a raging bull he charged grabbing Mercury around the waist forcing him back hard against the bar.

Mercury grimaced, but regained his composure. He trapped Goon Four with a front headlock putting leverage on his opponent's neck. Mercury applied enough pressure forcing Goon Four to arch his back like a camel. A precise knee sent to the man's groin followed by a sharp elbow to the spine made Goon Four's legs tremble as if he had lost feeling in them. He released Mercury from his waist high bear hug.

With the man stunned, Mercury placed his chin on the edge of the bar. He lifted his leg like a Rockette bringing down the heel on the back of his neck crushing the man's throat. Goon Four crumpled to the floor.

"So much not for not killing," said Ben. Mercury glared. "Let's finish this shit."

"Music to my ears."

Unique had told Mercury about a hallway door near the back exit that said "Employees only," She had said it was where Medusa and her goon squad entered.

She and the other girls never went inside the room. Mercury stood in front of the door with Ben behind him. He tried the knob…locked.

Ben nudged Mercury aside and kicked it in. "It's opened now."

Just as the two men were about to enter, single shots were fired and they jumped to opposite sides of the door. Mercury saw a camera over on the far wall. He pointed it out to Ben. Ben shot the camera. Mercury took a quick look inside the room and from what he could tell by glancing in, the door led to a basement. Mercury saw a stairwell thanks to the hall light.

"Unless you got a box full of ammo, that revolver won't help you hold us off," said Mercury.

"Give up, Bitch!" roared Ben.

More shots fired towards them.

"Way to go you sweet talker you. Who's going to get us killed now?"

"So I ain't a damn diplomat." Ben glowered. "How you know she holding a revolver?"

"The woman is old and frail. She can't handle the kick a Glock gives you. With that being said, I want you to count the shots." Ben frowned. "How many she fired already?"

Mercury shrugged. "I lost count talking to you."

"I see why Pone likes you." grinned Ben. "What are you going to do?"

"I got a plan."

Ben rolled his eyes. "Now you got a plan."

"Be the snake sticking its head out of the grass."

"Say what?"

"Just be ready to count."

Ben shook his head. "Ready when you are smart ass."

Mercury ducked his head in the doorway and backed out. Shots fired. He did it again, and more shots fired.

"Four…five?"

Mercury shook his head. "Charles Bronson told an adversary he could count all the way up to three."

"Six if I have to," said Ben. "Once Upon A Time In The West."

"Mercury gave him a look. "It's nice to know you can count."

"Fuck you."

"Shh…"

Mercury looked in again, but this time he darted like a big cat down the basement stairs. Ben lumbered behind searching the walls for the switch. When the lights came on it left the big man with his eyes wide and mouth open.

Mercury got the drop on Medusa. A sound like clanking on the floor made him make his move. He saw shells and Medusa trying to reload. Mercury grabbed her by the wrist.

"Put the gun down. It's over."

The frail charcoal woman did as instructed. Mercury let her go grabbing the gun and bullets.

"You see this shit?" asked Ben.

Greek mythology, Medusa was a hideous witch-faced creature with scales for skin, serpentine eyes, a snake body, and hair of lively serpents. Once men saw her face they turned to stone. Mercury shook his head. What he saw wasn't men of stone, they didn't even look like mannequins.

They were dead and wore the same clothes they had on when they had entered the club now her personal trophies. Vivian Grooms this modern day Medusa lived up to her name and used her taxidermy talents in the sickest way. Mercury counted at least twenty men dressed in the clothes of their demise standing on boxed mantles with their names intact. They all wore the same expression on all their faces as they had died of suffocation. The room was creepier than a wax museum.

Mercury focused on the relic woman. A true Medusa. "Fuck!" Ben came charging like a raging bull.

"Hold up, big man. Hold up," said Mercury.

"That bitch got to die…she got to die!" said Ben.

Mercury stood in front of Ben. He looked over his shoulder at Medusa. If she feared the giant, she didn't show it. Mercury assumed that Ben found his friend Al McGee. He turned to Medusa. Her amber eyes looked like they wanted to pop out of their sockets.

"Why?"

"They didn't know how to treat women. They were rough with my girls," she said.

Mercury shook his head. "If they were rough, you had four big ass men that could handle telling them not to come back. I'm sure they would have listened."

Mercury spun around pointing at the victims. He recognized some of the poor souls from news reports about men missing and he knew they had families.

"This is just wrong."

"Fuck that shit! Al didn't deserve this," said Ben.

"Perhaps you didn't know your friend," said Medusa.

Ben shove Mercury aside and wrapped his hands around Medusa's throat. Her neck looked like a broom handle between his fingers.

Mercury grabbed Ben's arm. Dammit Ben, no more killing."

"She deserves to die."

Mercury looked at Medusa. Her eyes started bulging. "I promise she will pay, but not this way. Let her go… Ben!"

"Not until her last breath."

Mercury didn't know whether he could take Ben in a fair fight nor did he want to know.

He thought words could reach a mind if it opened to reason and Mercury hoped Ben contained a reasonable mind.

"Ben, I don't know how it works in your world, but if you kill this frail old woman, it makes you look like a punk. I give my word she will pay."

Ben released his grip and Medusa dropped to the floor. Mercury helped her to a chair.

"What are you going to do?" asked Ben.

Mercury saw a black relic phone on the desk. "Call the police."

"Police? Shit'd."

Mercury looked around the room. "Al ain't the only victim."

Ben nodded. "Yeah."

"Get your friend and clear out of here."

"How are you getting home?"

"I'll ride back with the police."

"You sure?"

"I've worked with them before, and me and the captain are pretty tight. This is one of those missing person cases. Now get your friend and go."

Ben nodded. He glared at Medusa, grabbed Al McGee, and left. Before Ben left, Mercury observed the way Ben handled his friend carrying him in his arms. Intimate more than close friends, or brotherly love. Al was a father, but a lot of men go both ways. Mercury then understood Ben's rage over his friend's death.

Mercury got on the phone, called the police and gave details about what took place. He hung up and stared at the witch.

"May I ask a favor?" asked Medusa in a raspy voice.

Mercury shrugged. "Not that you deserve one, but what the hell?"

Medusa pointed to the far corner at two men who like the others were standing on their mantle. Mercury walked over knowing Medusa wasn't going any-where. Before he got any closer, he saw the resemblance. She and her brother inherited their father's features.

"I want you to burn them," she said.

About the Author

2017 International Writers Inspiring Change MOST INSPIRING AUTHOR AWARD.